Chords and Discords

Roz Southey

Praise for *Broken Harmony*, Roz Southey's inventive debut historical mystery:

... points for originality... different, absorbing, and with an unhackneyed setting...
- Alan Fisk, Historical Novels Review

paints a wonderful background... a complex plot which intrigues, teases and cajoles the reader into a complete suspension of disbelief, and the quality of the writing hurtles one along until the end.
- Amazon

Southey's sure-handed use of period detail...
- Publishers Weekly, USA

what really makes the novel come alive is its setting... she seamlessly incorporates the historical information into the novel... The dialogue, too, rings true: just ornamented enough to feel right for its time... A charming novel...
- Booklist, USA

A fascinating read, and certainly different.
- Jean Currie, Round the Campfire

... it is good to see a publisher investing in fresh work that... falls four-square within the genre's traditions.
- Martin Edwards, author of the highly acclaimed Harry Devlin Mysteries

Creme de la Crime... so far have not put a foot wrong.
- Reviewing the Evidence

First published in 2008
by Crème de la Crime
P O Box 523, Chesterfield, S40 9AT

Typesetting by Yvette Warren
Cover design by Yvette Warren
Front cover image by Peter Roman

ISBN 978-0-9557078-2-7
A CIP catalogue reference for this book is available from the British Library

Printed and bound in Germany by Bercker.

www.cremedelacrime.com

About the author:
Roz Southey is a musicologist and historian, and lives in the North East of England.

www.rozsouthey.co.uk

My thanks ...
... to Lynne Patrick at Crème de la Crime for her unfailing patience and generous help, and to Lesley Horton for her expert editorial guidance.

... to my sisters, Jennifer and Wendy, and to my brother-in-law John, who have given me endless moral support throughout the years, and to my husband, Chris, who never stopped believing I really could write a publishable novel.

... and especially to my parents, Charles and Edna Williams. Many years of sitting in village church choirs listening to my father playing pipe organs taught me to appreciate the largest of musical instruments and the way its music seemed to be born out of the air; my mother's wide-ranging reading habits amazed librarians everywhere. Although it's fair to say she would have preferred me to have written a good saga ...

For my mum
Edna May Williams
1918-2008
'the loveliest person in the world'

The present high winds have done much damage in the town…
[Newcastle Courant, 28 February 1736]

It was cold, it was wet, and it was windy. Freezing rain splattered against my face and spotted the cobbles at my feet. Wind swirled, tugging at the skirts of my coat and threatening to bowl my tricorne all the way down Silver Street into the Tyne below. In short, it was March, and no one dawdles on streets in March unless there is a very good reason. So why were those fellows fidgeting at the entrance to an alley near All Hallows Church?

I am as curious as the next man, even when shivering and damp. Besides, what better had I to do? I'd just come from the first cancelled lesson of the day. The family had evidently removed from the town for Lent. With no public amusements – no theatre, no dancing or card assemblies, no concerts – one might as well withdraw to the yawning boredom of a country house. And if a few bills have been forgotten, belonging to say, the odd musician, well, these things can't be helped. Never mind if the musician in question (your obedient servant, Chas Patterson) is down to the last guinea in his pocket.

I accosted a fellow with a grubby bagwig and asked what had happened. He squinted at me. "Someone's dead."

And I had been hoping for something to cheer me up.

"Murdered," he said, with relish. "Blood everywhere."

I should have turned my back and walked away. Just before Christmas I'd got myself involved in murder, and I didn't much like the consequences. But I had nothing to do and one way of passing the time seemed as good as any other. I peered through a gap in the crowd and glimpsed a yard at the other end of the alley. A middle-aged woman was glowering at a weeping girl; Bedwalters, the parish constable, was staring down at something I could not see. This was the alley leading to the organ manufactory – perhaps the dead body belonged to William Bairstowe, the organ builder. Someone must have taken violent exception to his rudeness at last.

"All this fuss!" said a voice behind me, scornfully. I glanced round. The voice came from a door on the other side of the street; when I looked closely, I saw the gleam of a spirit lodged on a stone bunch of grapes carved into the door lintel. The spirit slid round the carvings towards me; the living man must have died on the doorstep and his spirit, like all spirits, could not leave the place of his dying.

The spirit sniffed. "No one made a fuss like this when *I* died."

"But this is murder."

"No such thing!"

"No?"

"I have the true tale."

"Oh yes?"

"From Mrs Forbes's spirit, who lives opposite, who had it from Mr Ross's spirit on the churchyard wall, who had it from the girl's spirit in the alley."

Spirits can pass a tale from one end of the town to another in the time it takes a living man to cross the street. I wondered why the girl's spirit had no name.

"So who's died?"

"Bairstowe the organ builder. Hit on the head by one of his own pipes."

I thought of the largest diapason pipes in the organs of my acquaintance. One such would have given him a nasty bump, I supposed, but could it have killed him?

"Blown over by the wind." As if to corroborate the spirit's evidence, the wind bowled an empty basket along the street.

"The wind was very strong last night," I mused. It had blown against my window and the rattling had kept me awake several hours. "An accident, then?"

"Of sorts."

I sighed. The spirit wanted to be encouraged. It's always wise to keep on the good side of spirits – when spiteful, they don't mind too much what they say. I hope that when I am finally lodged in some place for the inevitable eighty or a hundred years after my death, I do not turn sour and vicious. "You don't think so?"

"Well, have you seen the state that yard is in? Asking for trouble. Have you seen it?"

"No."

A note of doubt crept into the spirit's voice. "You are Patterson? Charles Patterson, the musical fellow."

I stared uneasily at the gleam on the damp lintel. "I had no idea I was so well known."

A chortle. "You are notorious, sir, after your exploits before Christmas!"

My heart sank. "I do know William Bairstowe," I said, hoping to distract the spirit. "But I haven't been in his yard since my childhood." I hunted for a way out of the conversation. Was I really that anxious to know how Bairstowe came by his death? Anxious enough to brave the wind and the splattering rain, and the lonely, garrulous spirit?

"Never seen such a mess," the spirit said. "Wood everywhere, stone, lead. Pipes all over the place. Piles of rubbish. Don't know how he works there." It paused. "Well, he doesn't work much, does he? Or he didn't. Anyhow, he's paid the price now. Wind took the lead and hit him on the head with it and now he's dead."

Thankfully, as the spirit threatened to burst into verse, I saw the man with a grubby bagwig beckon from the crowd. I went back to him. "Bringing him out," he said. "He's one of the lads in the leather merchant's shop."

"A lad?" I echoed, startled.

"Courting the maid," the fellow said, with a wink. "Weeping fit to float a ship, she is."

And out they came in procession: Bedwalters first, standing respectfully aside to let two labourers carry out a hurdle with a body on it, covered by a sheet. The crowd strained for a sight of blood but there was none. Then came a girl, burying her face in her apron, then the middle-aged woman – that was Mrs Bairstowe no doubt. A second wife, if I remembered my gossip correctly. And behind her, bracing himself in the narrow entrance to the alley, was William Bairstowe the organ builder, heavy and red-faced.

We doffed our hats, and stood getting windblown and wet as the procession turned out of the alley and made its way down the street. The crowd began to disperse and the spirit slid away to call to someone else. I pushed my tricorne back on to my head and turned to go, then caught William Bairstowe's gaze as he stared across the street. For a moment I thought he was about to call to me, but his mouth twisted into a grimace instead and he swore at a child that bumped into him. The next moment he had swung back into the alley.

Not the sort of man I like to keep me company. Still, I thought, no need to worry myself over a fellow I'm likely to meet twice a year at most.

No one can predict the future.

1

The GENTLEMEN DIRECTORS of the SUBSCRIPTION CONCERTS are desired to meet at the Assembly Rooms, Westgate Road, on Friday the 5th Inst. March at 11 o'clock in the Morning, to consider the next season's concerts.
[Newcastle Courant, 20 February 1736]

The rain had blown up into a full-scale squall by the time I reached the Assembly Rooms on Westgate Road an hour or so later. I was wet and angry over yet another cancelled lesson. This one had been on Butcher Bank, a place I always hate visiting. Rain had washed most of the blood and discarded offal down the gutters, but the street still stank. And all to hear the servant telling me the family had left and wouldn't be back until after Easter.

When would anyone pay me? At the end of the March quarter they would all be in the country; they might come back to town after Easter, but by the end of the June quarter they would be sweating out the summer heat in their country houses again. September quarter? Perhaps, but is it worth coming up to town before the amusements start at the beginning of October? December quarter? Well, of course bills are always paid in full at the end of the year. If one remembers. After all, it's only the tradesman.

I'd be starving by December. I had hardly enough in my pockets to get to the end of the month. Damn it, what was I going to do?

I came to the street that led into that most genteel of areas, Caroline Square, and paused to glance in. Tall elegant terraces of townhouses surrounded a central garden where trees reached bare branches to the sky. The events before Christmas had been intimately tied up with one of the houses in that square – the house in the far corner – and I had not been back there since.

It was not only the memory of murder that haunted my sleep, but the recollection of a greater mystery. In Caroline Square I had caught a glimpse of another world, lying next to our own, a world very like ours, yet in some particulars unlike. There were no spirits in that world, for instance, but there were our own counterparts, sometimes identical, sometimes subtly different; I had met my own self there. Someone had likened these worlds to the pages of a book, lying next to each other but entirely separate. Yet it is possible, for those who know how, to step directly from one world to another.

It seemed I had this entirely unwanted ability. And I had nearly died as a result.

I took one last look and moved on. The memories unnerved me still.

The stuffy warmth of the Assembly Rooms settled round me as soon as I closed the door on the wind and the rain. God knew how many fires must have been burning in the building. The gentlemen who were meeting here today were all men of substance who could afford the expense: gentlemen with coal on their estates, ships in the river, stocks and shares in their banks. Men who knew themselves to be much better than me, without knowing very much about me.

The Steward of the Rooms greeted me with a face down which rivulets of sweat ran. "They're upstairs, Mr Patterson," he said. "In the small room."

Rain stained the windows and cast patterns on the stairs as I climbed. At the top of the first flight, a door stood open on to the narrow gallery where the band played for dances; beyond and below stretched the elegant assembly room itself with its marbled columns and sparkling chandeliers.

I paused to glance down; the chandeliers were devoid of candles and looked stunted and forlorn. Barely a week since the last concert and the last dancing assembly, and the floor was already dusty. Not until June would it be polished up again, and new candles put in the chandeliers and the doors opened for the dancing assemblies in Race Week. Half a guinea every night of the week for the lucky few musicians hired – no more than eight and sometimes less. There are eleven professional musicians in the town so we are always squabbling over the places. I shall argue as much as the rest of them, with as little dignity; lack of money changes a man's character.

Up another flight of stairs. The door to a second room stood open. A polished table gleamed like water in the light of dozens of candles augmenting the poor daylight; red wine glinted in crystal glasses. The gentlemen at the table had not noticed me yet so I had leisure to stare at them. The twelve Gentlemen Directors of the concerts. Well-bred gentry who had never had to do more work than to scan a page of accounts now and then, or wealthy tradesmen who could employ others to do their work. Twelve gentlemen who knew their worth, from Mr Jenison, at the head of the table and of an ancient lineage, to Mr Sanderson, the clockmaker, and Mr Griffiths, the brewer, at the foot of the table.

Oh, and Claudius Heron, another of the wealthy gentry, who was leaning back in his seat with one hand outstretched to finger the stem of his wineglass. Heron had shared that unsettling experience with me before Christmas though we never mentioned it. He was the only one to notice my arrival and turned his head to regard me with a perfectly neutral expression. No pleasure or dismay in it, just the slightest quirk of an eyebrow. That's when I knew there was trouble brewing.

"Ah, Patterson," Jenison said, deigning to notice me. "This is Patterson, our harpsichordist," he explained to the gentleman on his left, a newcomer to the group. I tasted the bitter tang of resentment. I was a harpsichordist, true, but in the last season of concerts I had been their musical director too, which was musically and financially more rewarding. Why did Jenison not use that term?

"As you know, Patterson," Jenison said, "we have met today to peruse the accounts of the last year's winter subscription concerts, and to consider the matter of the Race Week's entertainments, and indeed next year's concerts too."

Nobody around the table was meeting my gaze. My feeling of alarm intensified. What the devil had they decided?

"I was under the impression, sir," I said carefully, "that the concerts would run in much the same manner as this last year."

"Indeed. With – um – one or two minor alterations." Good God, was the man embarrassed? No one was coming to his aid; the other gentlemen appeared greatly interested in the antique table at which they sat. Claudius Heron regarded Jenison steadfastly.

"Twenty-one concerts, of course. At weekly intervals."

I maintained a grim silence. The gentlemen were full of fine plans and would never listen to reason. It's all very well to put on a concert every week, but you won't get the audience to turn out every week, particularly in cold weather. In any case, for two weeks out of four, the moon will be new and only a fool travels in the country at night without a full moon – you might as well send out an invitation to robbers.

"One guinea subscription for the entire series," Jenison said. "Or, for those who prefer to buy on the night – three shillings a ticket."

I couldn't help it; my voice rose incredulously: "Three shillings!"

Jenison looked up sharply. "You have an objection, Patterson?"

"Not at all, sir." All I could do was practise a little guile and hope to persuade them to reconsider their plans. "I know," I said with care, "that your intention – and that of the gentlemen here present – is to make the concerts as good as any in the country." I nodded respectfully round the table. "Better even than in London."

Jenison was plainly pleased at my understanding. "Exactly."

"And that is bound to cost money."

A tiny smile played around Heron's lips. The expenditure of money must be Jenison's least favourite occupation.

"And therefore," I continued, "it will obviously be necessary to raise ticket prices." I paused. "I'm sure no one will object to paying a little more than last year."

Since we had had a considerable discussion (some say argument) over the price of the tickets last year when they were raised to the previous level of two shillings and sixpence, my assertion was doubtful.

"The matter has been decided," Jenison said sharply, then added more mildly: "We have also been forced to think most carefully about the matter of a vocal soloist."

Lord, here it came. Poor Tom Mountier. My old friend had almost certainly sung his last at our concerts. To roll into the concert room, enquiring loudly the way to the necessary-house, and to sing a song that is not fit for the ears of gentlemen, let alone ladies, is beyond the pale. Drink had for a long time been getting the better of Mountier; now it had finally triumphed.

"We have come to the conclusion," Jenison said, "that it would be a pleasant change to have a female singer."

A young and attractive lady, no doubt, I thought.

"Signora Ciara Mazzanti," Jenison clarified.

La Mazzanti! In heaven's name, I thought, did Jenison know what the lady charged? I chose a bland tone. "I hear she's very good," I said. "She costs thirty guineas a concert."

Griffiths, the brewer, spluttered over his wine. "Thirty guineas! Devil take it – "

"One pays for quality," Heron said, speaking for the first time.

His tone was so savage that the gentlemen all looked at him in puzzlement. He was in a rage about something, I knew him well enough to be sure of that, although no hint of it appeared in his cool face. I had been right; some disaster was about to befall me.

"The lady," Jenison said, with the air of being determined to quash all opposition, "is willing to accept a single sum for the Race Week concerts and for the winter series. Providing, of course, that she is granted a benefit on both occasions."

Nothing rankled with me more than the question of a benefit. It is usual to grant the musical director of the band a benefit at the end of a concert series; the profits would have kept me in comfort over the summer. But Jenison had wanted to stage a concert that had been cancelled for snow in January and that took up the last available week before Lent began. So I had had no benefit, and now had no money.

"In fact," Jenison said, "the lady will sing for as little as one hundred guineas."

A hundred guineas! How did the gentlemen think the concerts could bear the cost? There were also the other professional players to be paid, the hire of the hall, the cost of coals and candles, and the remuneration of the Steward for opening up the rooms – at a very quick and rough estimate, something like a hundred and fifty subscribers would be necessary to pay the costs alone. And how many subscribed last year? One hundred and two.

"Well worth the money," Jenison was saying with satisfaction. Other gentlemen nodded, and Jenison cleared his throat. "And the lady has a husband who is, I am told, an excellent violinist."

My heart skipped a beat. I risked a quick glance at Claudius Heron but he was as still-faced as ever. Here it came – the blow.

"We have agreed," Jenison said, avoiding my gaze, "that he will have direction of the concerts next year. And in Race Week."

I was speechless with rage. Last year I rescued their concert series from disaster and near dissolution and now I was to be thrown over in favour of some Italian who had the good fortune to be married to a singer Jenison lusted after!

"But in recognition of your sterling service to the concerts last season," Jenison said, clearing his throat, "we would like to express our gratitude. We have therefore decided that you should be paid more than the common run of musician. Instead of the two shillings and sixpence per concert enjoyed by the general players, we are pleased to offer you three shillings."

Enjoyed? I thought savagely. Can anyone enjoy himself on three shillings for a day's work? Would gentlemen consider such a wage enjoyable? And as musical director, I had had ten shillings and sixpence per concert.

I glanced at Heron; he responded with an almost imperceptible shake of his head. I swallowed my rage. It would not go away but I would not show it or give them the satisfaction of knowing how keenly I felt the insult. "I am most grateful, sir," I said, stonily.

If I could have afforded to resign from their concerts, I would have.

2

We hear that conditions for travel are good at this season, despite the inclement weather. The London coach yesterday arrived several hours early.
[Newcastle Courant, 2 March 1736]

I was at the door to the street when I heard Heron call my name. He never needs to raise his voice; somehow there's a note in it that stops you in your tracks. But at that moment a carter in the street dropped some barrels with a clatter; I stepped out and strode off up Westgate, pretending I had not heard. I could not bear to speak to anyone just now. I could not have been civil.

I stalked up the street. Women were walking home with empty baskets and pockets jingling with coins; children were shrieking at their games. I ignored them all. I turned into the alley beside the clockmakers, into a door, up a narrow flight of stairs. Past the dancing-school door, up again past the widow's lodging, where I heard her speaking sharply to her children, and up to the attic where lives my good friend and dancing master (beloved of all the young ladies), Hugh Demsey. I banged on the door. It was ajar and I fell in.

"And they expect me to be grateful!" I roared. "For three shillings!"

Hugh had his back to me, he turned, gave me a measured look. A shirt lay folded in his arms. Even in my rage, I noticed how tired he looked.

"The managers of the concerts?"

"We are most grateful for your sterling service," I said, in savage mimicry. "But thank you and farewell."

Hugh was staring. "They haven't sacked you!"

"As near as."

"Good God!"

"And who saved their precious concerts last year?"

"Yes, yes," Hugh said soothingly. "Calm down, Charles. Tell me all about it."

For the first time I registered that the attic room was strewn with clothes – street clothes, evening clothes, dancing pumps. "My God, Hugh! You're not still thinking of going to Paris?"

He was pouring ale from a jug into the only two tankards he had. Anyone would think him a pauper, instead of the owner of this building (left to him by his late master) and the receiver of rents from both clockmaker and widow. But then Hugh was never fond of possessions, except clothes. "Yes," he said, and I fancy the word came out with more defiance than he intended. "You know I always go to Paris in the spring, Charles, to learn all the latest dances."

"You'll never survive the trip."

"Yes, I will."

"You'll collapse before you get to York."

He gave me the tankard of ale with a mutinous expression on his face. In that matter before Christmas Hugh was shot while trying to help me apprehend the murderer, and he only survived because of the quick wits of a lady. Of course he had insisted on being out of his bed and teaching long before he ought, with the inevitable result that the ill-effects of the wound still lingered.

"Save your breath, Charles," he said. "I'm going."

"You're a fool," I snapped.

"I'm going!"

We stared at each other. Outside, the carter yelled at a recalcitrant horse.

"What did the gentlemen say?" Hugh asked.

I told him. I got carried away and did a fine sarcastical imitation of Jenison and even sniped at Claudius Heron, who did not deserve it. The rest of them had plainly been set on the idea and one man could not overrule them.

"Signora Mazzanti," Hugh said doubtfully. He pronounced it the Italian way, which is to say properly, as Mat-zan-ti. Hugh is a damnably quick hand at picking up foreign tongues. "Do you know her?"

"I've heard of her."

"Good, is she?"

"I'm told."

"And the husband."

"Never heard of him."

"She'll have insisted on them employing him. Probably wouldn't come unless they did."

"That's no consolation, Hugh."

"Well, at least they haven't fired you altogether."

"Three shillings!" I said savagely.

"Don't let's start that again," he said hurriedly. He hesitated. "Charles – tell me to go to the devil if you like but – how much money *do* you have?"

I pulled out my pockets dramatically. Two halfpennies fell out. Hugh bent to pick them up, and gasped in pain.

"You'll not get to Darlington, let alone York!" I pushed him back on to the bed.

He had gone pale but rallied. "Let me fund you."

"No."

I sat down again and stared at him with obstinacy equal to his own. After a moment he sighed. "At least it's only three weeks till the end of the quarter. You'll get paid then, surely."

"Some of 'em haven't paid me for last quarter!"

Hugh considered this carefully. He was still sickly pale and a trickle of sweat ran down his right cheek.

"What about Heron? He's appointed himself your patron."

"I can't dun Heron! Fastest way I know to lose a patron."

My whole mind revolted at the idea of asking Heron for money. He'd look at me with that expressionless face of his and say nothing. He already had a poor opinion of the generality of mankind – my asking for money would make him think I was as mercenary as the rest. Patrons buy tickets for concerts, they subscribe to compositions, they recommend you to their friends and talk publicly of your virtues. They do not lend you a few guineas now and again when you're hard up – not unless there are special circumstances, like illness. And I've always been as healthy as an ox.

Hugh pushed himself up from the bed, swayed, bent to pick up a pile of clothes. "Of course, there is one other possibility."

"What's that?"

He took a deep breath. "You could marry a rich woman."

"No," I said forcibly. "No!"

We both knew which lady he meant. As I went down Westgate again, still simmering with rage, I passed once more the road that led up to Caroline Square where I had had my disquieting glimpses into that world lying next to our own. In the house where the lady in question lives.

I have long since ceased to question the vagaries of fate and taste that lead us to form attachments to another person. In my own case I had had the folly to form a liking for a lady a dozen years my senior, of a much higher social standing than myself, and of considerable wealth. There is not much greater folly than that.

I had hardly seen the lady, Esther Jerdoun, since Christmas; she had been here and there about the country – up north to Berwick, down south to Norfolk – engaged with land agents and lawyers from morning to night, over estates she inherited from her cousin. There could be nothing between us; the best I could hope for was that she would patronise my concerts and my publications and be polite to me when we met. I thought I could count on that. But I could no more ask her for money than I could ask Claudius Heron.

March is a damnable month. Wind funnels down the narrow streets and makes you stagger and weave against its force. The river down in its valley is turgid; smoke and coal dust blow into your eyes, and burrow into your throat. I struggled down to the Sandhill, trying to get those late November days out of my head. Ridiculous to brood over it – it was all past and done with. On the Sandhill, the fish market was in full spate. Seagulls screeched overhead; fisher girls shrieked with laughter; their menfolk shouted. Housewives haggled over fish for dinner. Over all their heads loomed the ugly hulk of the Guildhall, with gentlemen lounging on the balconies, surveying the bustling scene of commerce below.

I spent some of my few remaining coins on a bowl of buttered barley at one of the sellers outside Nellie's coffee house and ate it with my back to the wind. The smoke had somehow got into the barley as had the taste of fish, and the bitter taste of resentment. I left it unfinished. An hour yet until my next lesson and I'd probably find that family out of town too. I was reminded of my stay in London, three or four years ago, of tramping from house to house trying to sell concert tickets to Lord this and Lady that, gentlemen and ladies who had only to look at me to see that I was not glamorously Italian. A mere Englishman. Only a tradesman. Damn them, damn them all. How did they expect me to live?

Someone was watching me. I felt the gaze, like a prickling in my back. It was probably Heron again; if he was in town he usually ate at Nellie's. Was I going to have to swallow my pride after all and apply to him for money? I saw no alternative. I hunched my shoulders, steeled myself and turned.

Not Heron, but the organ-builder William Bairstowe stared

at me from the middle of the road.

Carters shouted for him to get out of the way; he did not seem to hear them. The wind threatened to lift the wig from his head, and whipped the skirts of his coat about his thighs.

He strode towards me.

3

WILLIAM BAIRSTOWE, ORGAN-BUILDER,
SILVER-STREET, NEWCASTLE
MOST respectfully begs Leave to inform the Nobility, Gentry, &c. that he makes and repairs all Sorts of Church and Chamber Organs, on the most reasonable Terms.
[Newcastle Courant, 2 March 1736]

As Bairstowe came up to me, he dug his fingers into the pocket of his waistcoat and brought out a guinea. He held it up in front of me with a contemptuous look. "You'd like this, eh, sir?"

The 'sir' sounded like a slap in the face. I said: "You have the wrong man."

"Patterson." He waggled the coin in the air. A woman looked at him curiously as she stepped round him. "Notebasher and caterwauler, eh?"

"I don't need insults, sir," I said, loading the last word with sarcasm. "Forgive me but I have an appointment with a *gentleman*."

He tossed the guinea into the air. "Ten of 'em."

Ten guineas was half a year's wages for an organist. I stared. "What the devil for?"

"Finding a scoundrel and a knave."

"I know too many already," I said dryly.

"Twenty," he said.

My God, was that a trace of desperation in his voice? Twenty guineas – I'd have to play a hundred concerts to earn that much. Despite my annoyance, I hesitated. Bairstowe must want something very badly.

His hand, I saw, was shaking as he slid the guinea back into his pocket. A couple of children jostled him as they ran past, manhandling a fish twice as big as they were. "Well," he demanded, "do you want the money or no?"

Of course I wanted it. I braced myself against the wind and the stink of fish.

"Why not go to the constable?"

"He's a fool," he said contemptuously. "I want someone who'll do a proper job."

"I'm just a musician – "

He sneered at me. "We all know what happened afore Christmas. Despite it was so well-hidden."

Dear God, was the affair halfway round the town? I had thought it well hushed up. Bairstowe surely could not know the whole of it, only that I had found a murderer.

'You sorted it." He snorted. "That's what I want. Someone sorted, good and proper. A fellow causing me grief."

He chinked the guinea against another in his pocket. I hesitated. Just for a moment but he saw it. "Can't talk here," he said and strode off.

My pride hurt to be ordered around in so peremptory a fashion but I followed. Across the Sandhill, up Butcher Bank and on to Silver Street in the shadow of All Hallows' squat tower. Jenison was churchwarden of All Hallows, I remembered. He and his cronies had hurt my pride too. Damn them all.

Maybe I was about to get a chance to prove I wasn't dependent on their goodwill.

Bairstowe turned into the narrow alley that led to the organ manufactory. The wind funnelled down the alley and bore me with it, over dog turds and apple cores. For a moment I could see nothing but darkness at the far end of the alley; like a night sky. I heard the wind moaning and a woman singing. An old song, murmured very softly, somewhere close, ebbing and flowing on the wind.

We came out into a large yard, gloomy but by no means the black pit I thought I'd seen. As the spirit had said, it was 'in a state'. Debris was piled in almost every corner; heaps of half-rotten timber, scraps of lead, flattened organ pipes, fragments of leather. Two large seasoned timbers were propped against a wall; the yard was sheltered, but even so the wind shifted the smaller of the timbers along the wall.

To the left, the door to a house stood closed; the solid bulk of the church loomed over the house and cast a shadow across the yard. On the far side of the yard was another building. long and low, with many windows. My attention was caught by a black stain on the cobbles outside it. Dried blood. I looked again at the shifting timber and wondered precisely what had happened to the poor shoplad.

Bairstowe seemed to hesitate, cocking his head as if he thought he'd heard something. He muttered and pushed open the workshop door. The smell of old wood enveloped me. In a dim musty interior, I saw saws and other tools hung in racks about the walls. Organ pipes stood everywhere: square wooden pipes, round pewter-dark tin-and-lead pipes. In one cleared space lay a soundboard with a small rank of flute pipes stood upright on it. The size of the work made me think it was for a small house organ, something the gentry like to install in their libraries to impress visitors. But it looked dusty, as if Bairstowe had not worked on it for an age.

I was half-distracted by all the paraphernalia. I have an ambition to be an organist myself, partly, it is true, because such posts afford a yearly salary, but also because I like the sublime sound mere wood, and metal, and air can produce. A world away from the puny voices of the harpsichords I generally play.

Bairstowe turned to me with that contemptuous smile of his. He had his hands in his waistcoat pockets; I saw that they were still trembling.

"You find this fellow for me," he said. "Discreetly, mind – and I'll slip you twenty guineas."

I regarded him sourly, making guesses at his problem. Perhaps this 'fellow' owed him money – a great deal of money, if he was willing to part with twenty guineas. But anyone who owed Bairstowe a large sum of money must be gentry or even, God forbid, nobility. How the devil was I supposed to bring someone like that to book? I'm the son of a fiddler, and a musician by profession; no nobleman is going to grant me an interview, let alone pay his debts on my request.

But there were those twenty guineas and God knows I needed them.

"A debt?" I said.

"You fellows are all the same," he said scornfully. "Think of nothing but money. That's all musicians are good for. Like that fellow at the church."

He meant the organist at All Hallows, Solomon Strolger. Bairstowe's contempt for Strolger was boundless – if there was anyone in the town who didn't know of it, he must be deaf and blind. What I suspect galled Bairstowe most was that Strolger was magnificently indifferent to Bairstowe's emnity.

"A thief then?"

"Like the sound of your own voice, don't you?" he said brutally. "If you keep quiet, I'll tell you."

Twenty guineas, I reminded myself, and bit back the urge to walk out into the street. I folded my arms instead and tapped a foot meaningfully. But now he had leisure to speak, he was curiously reluctant. His mouth worked as if he was trying to summon up the courage to talk; his fingers toyed with the coin in his waistcoat pocket.

"Threats," he said at last, spitting the word out as if it was poison.

"To do what?"

He said nothing.

"Damage the workshop? Run you out of business?"

"Kill me," he said in a low voice. "That lad." He jerked his head towards the stain outside the door. "He got what was meant for me."

"I understood it was an accident."

"Understood," he mimicked in a prissy voice. "You *understood* wrong. God, have you no sense?"

"If you want me to find this fellow for you," I said, levelly, "you could at least attempt to be polite."

He sneered. "Twenty guineas says I can do what I like. I'm the one with the power here and don't you forget it."

He really was remarkably unpleasant; he laughed at the sight of my reddening cheeks. But he was also right.

"Notes," he said. "Six of 'em, pushed under my door, threatening to kill me."

I held out my hand.

"Burnt 'em," he said.

"All of them?"

"The lot. They were rubbish. A child could have written better."

"What did they say?"

"Rubbish," he said again. "*I'll kill you* and *Look behind you* and *Be afraid*."

"No signature?"

He crowed with laughter. I gritted my teeth. "If you want me to find this man, you have to let me go about it in my own way."

"No signature," he said. "No mark neither."

"And that's all there was – just notes?"

He hesitated just long enough for me to know he was about to lie to me. He jerked his head at the windows. "Just broken glass. And a dead cat nailed to the door. That's all. Except for the lad killed in my place."

There was no proof of what Bairstowe said; he might be inventing the whole matter. My instinct was telling me to let the matter be. My empty pockets were telling me I couldn't afford to.

"Who do you think sent the notes?" I asked finally.

"That's what I'm paying you to find out."

I swallowed anger. "Suggest someone."

He chewed on the idea, said finally: "Heron."

I echoed incredulously: "Claudius Heron?"

"Or that Jenison fellow." He kicked fragments of wood under a workbench. "Neither of 'em will pay me."

This was preposterous. "I doubt they'd kill you to avoid paying a debt."

Another laugh. "These gentry fellows like to pretend they've got fortunes as big as the Tyne Bridge. Probably not got a penny."

I knew this to be untrue of both Heron and Jenison. Bairstowe was merely trying to pay back a few enmities. If he wasn't going to tell me the truth, I might as well go home now. I nearly did. I nearly walked out of that musty workshop, out of the debris-strewn yard and the filthy alley.

But those twenty guineas...

I persevered. "Anyone else?"

"That London fellow."

"You've mentioned Strolger before." I couldn't believe Strolger capable of something like this. Though he would have had the opportunity to leave the notes; no one would have been surprised to see him near the church or the organ manufactory.

"If you didn't keep the notes," I said levelly, "what evidence is there to go on?"

"Told my wife."

"You showed her the notes?"

"One on 'em, aye."

"Can I speak to her?"

"You can," he said. "But it'll do you no good. Haven't had a bit of sense out of her since I married her. Not a day's work either."

"Nevertheless – "

"She ain't here. She's off gadding about. Come back tomorrow."

I wanted to say no. I didn't care for Bairstowe's company in the least – God help me, I even had a certain amount of sympathy with the fellow trying to kill him. There was not the slightest chance of finding out anything with so little information. But those guineas – those twenty guineas...

"I'll come back tomorrow afternoon to talk to her," I said.

He nodded. His hand came out of his pocket and something shiny twisted through the dust-laden air towards me. The guinea. "On account," he said.

I longed to toss it back to him.

I did not.

It was still early evening but in the alley leading to the manufactory it was already dusk. I called softly: "Hello?" The singing I had heard while I was talking to Bairstowe, that old song sung in the alley by a young voice, could only come from a spirit.

"I heard you," I said. "I know you're here. I want to talk."

Another long moment. Then the spirit came, a faint shine on an old stone, like the sheen rain leaves behind. She darted off, up high on the blank wall, so that I lost her in the gloom. Then her breathy voice came behind me.

"Hello – "

God help us, she was, or had been, a coquette. There was no mistaking that teasing murmur, like one of Demsey's more bashful pupils. How old had she been when she died? Eighteen perhaps?

"I want to talk," I repeated.

"Oh." A breathless sigh. "It's been such a long time since anyone took any notice of little me."

"I can't imagine why."

She was off again, darting from her perch on an old nail, to a stone that jutted out from the wall. "I've so many stories to tell."

My heart sank. "Really?"

"But first – " like a maiden bartering a kiss. "Tell me, what year is it?"

"1736."

I heard the murmur of laborious arithmetic, then what might have been a sob. "Maybe I'm wrong," she said. "I died in the siege. Tell me, how long ago was that?"

She was old, very old. In 1642, the King's party and the parliament had clashed in this part of the country, and in the siege of this town of that year, she must have died. Her spirit had been here nearly a hundred years, which was almost as long as any spirit could linger. And as in life, the older the spirit, the less reliable the memory.

"Do you know William Bairstowe?" I asked.

"Oh yes." The faint shimmer darted along the rough wall. "Who?"

"The organ-builder."

"No," she said firmly. "He's a carpenter." She almost cooed. "And *so* handsome."

I would not remotely have called William Bairstowe handsome. And her confusion over his profession did not bode well for the accuracy of any other information I might get out of her. "How old is he?"

"Oh." Now she was uncertain. "Twenty, thirty? Well, maybe a bit older than that. What do you think?"

I reminded myself of the twenty guineas. "Does he have any brothers and sisters?"

"Only Thomas," she said dreamily. "No, Edward." She giggled.

"Sometimes I get confused."

"Was Edward older or younger than William?" I persevered.

"Oh, older – but he died years ago."

"Here?"

"On the bridge." She started humming again. "Just dropped down dead." She added, scrupulously. "I'm told."

The news would have come back to the house from one spirit to another almost as soon as Edward was dead, passed on by an invisible network of dead voices. I stared at her dull sheen on the dark wall, wanting to be out of this place; it is unwise to linger in unlit alleys after dark. And this spirit was making me feel oddly uneasy. It is easy to blame all confusion on the age of the spirit, yet I sensed something more. But what?

"I didn't like Edward," the spirit said. "William is much nicer."

"Really? Do you know anyone who doesn't like William?"

"No. Of course not."

"No one has come down here to put notes under the door?"

"No," she corrected. "No people. Just voices. So many voices in the dark." Her voice was fading, coming and going like the ebb and flow of the river tides. The spirit was on the edge of dissolution; it would not be long now until the breeze took her, and then the alley would be silent, unspirited.

"So much arguing," she said with a sigh. "I hate arguments, don't you?"

"Who argued?"

"Oh, all of them," she said dreamily. And then she was gone, sliding along the wall and rising, rising out of my sight until all I could hear was the faintest of songs.

4

It is common knowledge that the youth of this town care for nothing but their own pleasure – family, friends, and piety, all are subservient to their desires and delights.
[Revd A. E., Letter to Newcastle Courant, 9 January 1736]

The house belonging to Bedwalters, the constable, was like all the others on Westgate – tall and thin, shabby but trying to keep up appearances. The front door was open to a room filled with low tables and chairs; books were scattered across shelves running the length of the far wall. On one table, a primer lay open at a picture of a sleek cat; the picture had been hand-drawn and -coloured, and labelled in large letters: C-A-T.

"Mr Patterson, sir." Bedwalters, the constable and writing-master, stood in a doorway to the inner part of the house, his arms full of slates, a middle-aged man, stocky and drably dressed. A man of habitual calm. We had become acquainted the previous year and I liked him greatly.

"I hope I am not keeping you from your pupils," I said. With Bedwalters, you always feel that you should apologise for inconveniencing him.

"No, Mr Patterson," he said, levelly. "My pupils will not be here for another few minutes. How can I help you?"

"The lad who was found dead in Bairstowe's yard this morning. I was wondering if you might explain what happened?"

He began to gather up apple cores scattered across the nearest table.

"May I ask why you are interested, Mr Patterson?"

"William Bairstowe suspects that he is under threat."

Bedwalters pursed his lips. "Perhaps you would be so kind as to sit down and explain all to me."

I perched on one of the small chairs and stated William Bairstowe's case as best I could. Explaining it to Bedwalters' calm and sceptical face made me acutely aware how unconvincing it was, but he listened without comment until the end.

"Notes in a childish scrawl?" he repeated. "Which he burnt."

"Indeed."

"A dead cat nailed to his workshop door?"

"And broken windows."

"And from this he deduces that he is under threat of death?"

"He believes the shoplad died in his place."

Bedwalters straightened a chair or two. "Tom Eade died when the wind blew a piece of seasoned timber down on his head."

"One of the pieces stacked against the wall?"

Bedwalters nodded. "You've seen the place? Mr Patterson, there were, and still are, many accidents waiting to happen in that yard. Sharp pieces of metal on which a child might cut himself, rubble to fall over in the dark, timber to come crashing down – "

I shifted on the uncomfortable chair. "Do you know what the lad – Eade – was doing there?"

"Courting the maid." Bedwalters looked briefly disapproving. "He crept into the yard after dark to persuade the maid to let him into the house. She says she was watching out but didn't hear him."

"A strong wind rattles windows and doors," I said thoughtfully. "No doubt it swirls around that enclosed yard with a howl that could drown out all other noises."

He nodded and bent to pick up a dead leaf from the floor. "It brought down the timber on his head. Or in the darkness, he brought it down himself. He didn't have a candle or a lantern so he'd be feeling his way about."

"No light at all? In a strange place?"

A thin smile. "Not a strange place at all, Mr Patterson, if the maid is to be believed."

"Ah," I said. "A well-established liaison. When did this accident happen?"

"Late last night. She was expecting him at midnight."

"And he was found – "

"This morning, when the maid went out to get rid of the night soil. She was hysterical, I understand."

"It is not possible that someone attacked him and then arranged it to look like an accident?"

"I believe not," he said. "And Gale the barber surgeon concurs. We'll talk to the spirit when it disembodies, but I have no doubt of what it'll say."

"And you know of no one who might wish to kill William Bairstowe?"

"That, sir, is not a matter for me to comment upon. It is out of my remit as constable."

I heard the sound of children's voices outside and hurried on. "But speaking in your private capacity?"

He held my gaze steadily as four or five boys and two girls came rushing in, giggling and trying to be prim.

"In my private capacity, Mr Patterson? I follow the tenets of the Christian church, sir – speak evil of no man."

Without looking away, he told the children to be seated.

Speak no evil implies that there is evil to be spoken.

At the door, Bedwalters gave me the place of Tom Eade's employment – a leather merchant's shop on the Side – and the direction of his mother. The mother lived on the Castle Stair so I turned across town. The wind was gusting rain into my face, lifting the skirts of my greatcoat, and trying to snatch the tricorne from my head. It put itself behind me and hurried me into the maze of poor tenements that clustered around the castle.

Hens scurried around my feet, children scratched themselves on doorsteps. An elderly man sucked at a clay pipe in a sheltered doorway, grunting to a garrulous spirit lodged on a grimy windowsill like a stray patch of sunlight. I turned through the looming Black Gate into the castle, passed the grimy Keep and crossed wet cobbles to the postern gate leading through the ruins of the curtain wall. Beyond were steps, worn with centuries of use; alleys came off to left and right, filled with tumbledown houses. Holes gaped in rotting roofs, sacking flapped over broken windows.

Halfway down the Stair, I found a shabby door and knocked. After a long moment, the door was opened by a woman. Perhaps forty years old, grey-haired and tired, she looked at me with dulled eyes, dragging a ragged shawl about her against the rain. "Ain't got no money."

I stood bare-headed, wondering what on earth I could say. "I've come about your son. Tom."

"Oh," she said, with sudden fire. "Him. Sure, no one worried about him when he was live. Now he's dead, everyone's sorry. 'He must have been a fine lad,' they say." She thrust her face into mine; she smelt of sweat and gin. "Well, he never thought of me so I'll not think of him. Be off!"

"Don't you want to know how he died?"

"Ask his spirit." She laughed, a dry mirthless sound. "Maybe he'll tell you the truth for once. And ask him where he hid his money. Because he never spent a penny on me, that's for sure."

"He had money saved?"

"Ask the girl," she said bitterly.

"The maid?"

"What maid?"

"William Bairstowe's maid, at the organ manufactory."

"What are you talking about?"

"The girl he was going to marry."

"Her?" She pulled her shawl tight. "She's no maid. One of the stinking fisher girls on the Key. All red hair and green eyes, and wild ideas. Going to make her fortune, she is, going to wear fine gowns." She laughed again, bitterly. "She'll learn."

No mother ever seemed less grieving; I walked off into the rain with a great deal of sympathy for Tom Eade. Filial respect is to be praised, but a mother so sour tests duty to the limit. And it must be hard to know your hard-earned money will turn into gin.

I went on down Castle Stairs towards the Key and the river. William Bairstowe was probably imagining threats where there were none, but those twenty guineas still called. While there was a chance I could earn them, I must continue. There was still the leather merchant – Tom Eade's employer – to investigate. If nothing came of a visit there, then I would resign myself to losing the money. I did not know what made me more bitter, the prospect of losing the money, or earning it and having to take it from a man like Bairstowe.

From the Stair, I walked across the Sandhill into the Side, the narrow street that leads from the lower town up to the more genteel regions. I had seen the leather merchant's shop here a dozen times but had never had cause to enter. It was a timbered building, all angles and corners. I ducked through the low door.

The smell inside was abominable; I have never much liked the stench of new leather. Dozens of small goods were on display: purses, leather-bound notebooks, walking canes, a scabbard with a wooden dummy sword thrust in. An open door to the back of the house showed skins slung over tables and a young man in shirt sleeves and aprons poring over them. I could hear whispering too, a constant background murmur. Was that a living man or spirits?

A lanky lad materialised in front of me, bowing obsequiously.

His face was pocked with scars, his coat dusted with flakes of skin. Under his fashionably small wig, his scalp must be scabrous. I cut off his extolling of the shop's goods.

"I'm enquiring about Tom Eade."

The lad stopped in mid-sentence; the man in the back of the shop turned to stare at me.

"He's dead," said the lanky lad.

I was irritated at not knowing his name and said carelessly, "You must be Ned."

"Richard, sir. Richard Softly." His voice copied his name, a *sotto-voce* respectfulness that set my teeth on edge.

"His mother was hoping to obtain his effects."

The lad looked blank.

"His clothes, books – "

That provoked an explosion of laughter from the back room. The aproned man strolled through into the shop, a man of twenty, open-faced and smiling. "Forgive me, sir, but if you were a friend of Tom, you'd know reading wasn't his favourite occupation. Except accounts – he was very fond of money!"

"Damned miser," Richard Softly said, sourly. He turned away and made a great play of tidying up the walking canes. The aproned man winked and mouthed at me, "Argued. About a girl."

The shop door opened; the man retreated to the back of the shop before I had time to turn round. Richard Softly said, very respectfully, "This gentleman was enquiring for Tom, sir."

The newcomer, hesitating in the shop doorway, was a slight man, in his mid-forties perhaps, though his face, beneath a ridiculously small wig, was creased with lines, his eyes rimmed by dark circles. He was dressed up to and beyond the fashion, in a coat that that could only have come straight from London. He was, I deduced from Softly's respectful manner, the owner of this shop, John Holloway.

He smiled at me benignly. "And you are, sir?"

He was not musically inclined or he would have recognised me from concerts. "Charles Patterson, sir. At your service."

I bowed. He bowed back. And, as I straightened, I saw that the smile on his face had disappeared. He might not know my face, but he certainly recognised my name.

5

Where youth can be brought to apply itself to business, some very good results have been known to ensue...
[Revd A. E., Letter to Newcastle Courant, 9 January 1736]

The stairs up to the second floor were not level, leaning into the wall and throwing me off balance as I climbed behind John Holloway's well-dressed figure. Each step creaked. It was a very old house, not particularly well cared-for; plaster was crumbling from the walls, holes in the floorboards carried the voices of the men below up to me. And all around, other voices were murmuring, a disconcerting flow of barely audible sound; light flickered on window panes, on polished wood, on ceiling beams. The place was infested by spirits.

Upstairs, Holloway's private room was small and dark, lit only by a small window whose frame was irritatingly askew. There was a great deal of old-fashioned furniture in it – big heavy side-boards and chairs; and too many ornaments – a vase with dead flowers, a bowl stamped with patriotic slogans to commemorate the King's Coronation, eight years ago. An engraving of the Queen propped against the wall was curling with damp.

"Wine?" Holloway asked. He smiled beneficently at me. "Not often I get a visitor, Mr Patterson. No, pray go away."

Bewildered, I stared at him as he poured wine into glasses that did not look clean.

"No, no, not now," he said, without looking at me. I heard a low murmur; and realised that Holloway was talking to a spirit, a very reticent one. "Your wine, Mr Patterson. Leave us alone if you don't mind."

I assumed his last irritable comment was meant for the spirit and settled into the chair he offered me. Its tapestry upholstery was fraying and dusty, and even as I sat down I saw something crawl upon the arm. The room was airless, and I was afraid to move for fear of knocking over one of the ornaments. Damn Bairstowe for getting me into this!

"Poor Tom," Holloway said, with a big sigh. "Such a tragedy."

"A good worker, was he?"

"Oh, the best." Holloway sipped at his wine and I followed suit, just preventing myself wincing at its sourness. "Excellent, excellent," Holloway said, then, in an aside to a gleam of light on the window glass, "No, we will discuss the matter later." He smiled at me again. "Good wine always ages well, don't you agree, Mr Patterson?"

His habit of chatting to spirits while conducting a conversation with me was beginning to grate; I restrained my irritation, said, "You never had any trouble with the lad?"

"Far from it," he said with obvious sincerity. "For one so young, he had an excellent head for business. Very good with figures." He sighed. "I shall be hard pressed to replace him."

"Your other lad, Richard Softly – "

He made a contemptuous noise. "Poor stuff." He waved away a near-inaudible spirit. "He has done very well to cast off his low origins. But he is not the same quality as poor Tom."

I forced myself to sip the vinegar he called wine. "You have a great number of spirits here."

"A very old house," he said with some pride. "Used to be a lodging house, you know, till fifty years back."

Which explained the multiplicity of spirits. Lodging houses provide a floorboard or two for the poorest sort to lie on, and the poorest sort sicken and die with appalling ease.

"You haven't asked me why I'm so interested in Tom Eade," I said. I felt a twinge of pain in my arm and resisted the urge to scratch. Devil take Holloway if he had given me fleas.

"My dear sir, I know! You are looking into the matter for William."

"You know Bairstowe?"

He threw back his head and laughed to the ceiling. It was not a natural gesture. "My dear sir, William Bairstowe is my brother-in-law!"

Mrs Bairstowe, it transpired, was Holloway's elder sister. "A second mother," he said. "No, no, you are quite right," he added in response to the very quiet spirit, "my *only* mother." Another huge sigh. "And William is of course a customer too," he added. "Buys only the best quality leather for his organ-building."

"They have no children?"

"Alas, no."

"And there are no brothers and sisters in the house?"

"There was Edward, William's elder brother. But he died five years ago." He gave me a wink. "And the least said about him the better! Gambling and women, you know."

That at least made sense of what the spirit in the alley had told me. "Has Bairstowe told you about the notes he has received?"

Holloway snorted with derision. "Which notes? My dear sir." He leant forward, wine dregs slopping in his glass. "My dear sir, William is a good man but a sad one. Weary with life."

I had started the interview in an irritable state; any more of Holloway's sanctimonious sentiments would drive me to fury. I said: "What is this to the purpose?"

"He has, shall we say, permitted matters to overwhelm him." Holloway gestured widely. "Have you seen that yard? The piles of rubbish allowed to accumulate in every corner, instead of being carted away?" I thought he had audacity to complain of William's rubbish, given the clutter around us. I had already knocked over an engraving of Westminster Abbey. "He says as excuse that he hates the place, that the spirits there drive him mad." He lowered his voice. "But William knows that if he had kept the yard in better order, there would have been nothing for the wind to seize hold of and poor Tom Eade would not have died."

"You think he feels responsible for the lad's death and is seeking to remove the blame on to someone else?"

"Exactly!" Holloway sat back triumphantly. "Therefore he fabricates the story of the notes, tells everyone poor Tom was killed in his place." He assumed a doleful expression. "And the saddest thing of all, I do think he believes it all himself."

I certainly agreed with that last statement. But could I credit Holloway's theory? "Do you know what Eade was doing there?"

He winked at me, a great contorting of his face, from one man of the world to another. "Courting the maid."

"At that time of night?"

He spread his hands. "They were betrothed, and not enough money to be married on. The young are so impatient."

He allowed his voice to trail away meaningfully. I wondered if Holloway had ever felt that kind of impatience for a woman. He seemed too ordered in his person to become heated or overwrought.

"Let me refill your glass," he murmured, and did so before I could protest. "I don't in the least seek to interfere, sir. But I do not wish to see you waste your time. These threats are a figment of William's imagination! In any case, he doesn't have the money to pay you." He straightened suddenly, swatting at the glass in his hand. "Go away, sir, go away!" I caught a glimpse of brightness on the curve of the bowl before the spirit slid down the stem, across Holloway's hand, up his elegant sleeve and on to the chair back. Involuntarily, I shuddered. The touch of a spirit is like the slipperiness of a snail, yet ice cold.

"Who inherits your brother-in-law's property should he die?" Holloway looked taken aback.

"The person who has most reason to kill is the person who is most likely to profit from the death," I pointed out. "Bairstowe has no children and his brother is dead. There is no other male relative?"

"What are you saying, sir?"

"His property would descend to his wife?" I paused for effect. "Your sister."

"Are you suggesting that my sister is threatening her husband?" He looked genuinely outraged. "She is a fine woman, a fine woman. Preposterous!"

His admiration seemed real.

"William has no property to leave," he added, curtly.

"Oh, come!"

"He is well nigh bankrupt." Holloway drained his glass. "He has done no work for months now. He drags himself about the yard all day, complaining he is being persecuted, then disappears all night into the brothels on the Key. He has nothing!"

"He exhibits a chamber organ in the Cordwainers' Hall next week," I pointed out. "According to an advertisement in this week's *Courant*, he hopes to obtain one hundred guineas for it. He may pay me out of that. Leaving himself and his wife eighty guineas."

He snorted. "A paltry amount."

"Many a family survives on a quarter of that a year. Or less," I added, thinking of the widow Eade.

"In London," he said, "you couldn't live a month on it." There was an odd note in his voice, a kind of longing. I remembered how I had once felt like that, travelling south wide-eyed, anticipating the streets of tall houses, the street traders, the glittering shops, longing to hear the cries of the picturesque sellers, the rattling of elegant carriages, the squealing of sleek horses. And instead it had been all foul smells in the wide streets, and sour looks from handsome gentlemen, and amused contempt from fair ladies, empty seats at my concerts, and tedious hours waiting for pupils who never came. And empty pockets.

But, to be fair, I have only a few pence in my pockets now, and Bairstowe's guinea hidden under my mattress.

There was plainly nothing else to be gained and I had begun to hate this stuffy, cluttered room with its incessantly murmuring spirits. I pushed aside the sour wine and stood. One spirit was gleaming at Holloway's shoulder. And another, a sharp-voiced woman, spoke suddenly from the door: "Mind how you go on the stairs," she said. She glittered on the hinge of the door and it whipped open. "So easy to fall."

Holloway smiled at me from his chair.

6

Work, sir, is the chief element of a contented and virtuous life.
[AMOR PACIS, Letter to his Son, printed for the author, Newcastle, 1735]

I was half-asleep. "Damn it, why does the coach have to go so early?"

And why did the rest of the world have to make such a noise? I had hardly slept and the clatter of horses' hooves drummed into my aching head; the shouts of the ostlers made me wince. Passengers hurried hither and thither. The only person who seemed calm was the driver, who stood on the Golden Fleece's doorstep and contentedly worked his way through an enormous tankard of ale.

This was no time to dwell on my affairs. There were more important matters to deal with. I took Demsey's arm and ushered him to one side. There was a green tinge to his skin that I didn't like in the least.

"Hugh, for God's sake, call this madness off."

"No," he said obstinately.

"You'll never get to Paris. You'll kill yourself first."

"I'm doing it in easy stages, remember." He rubbed at his shoulder – the one that had taken the shot four months back. Even after all this time it apparently still ached. "I'll stop at Darlington tonight then go on on Monday. You know me, Charles, too respectable for Sunday travelling."

"It'll still be too much for you."

He seemed to grit his teeth, started to say something, then stopped. He said, with careful moderation, "My bags are already on the coach."

"Then we'll take them off again." I shivered; a chill early-morning mist lay across the river, blurring the view of Gateshead.

"Charles, I must go. My reputation will be ruined if I don't get the latest dances."

"Rubbish. How will they ever know?"

I took his arm firmly. Hugh and I have been friends since we occupied the same bench in All Hallows' Charity School. It was my fault he had been injured and his welfare was more important to me than anyone else's in the world. Bar one.

"Let me take you back home."

"Charles," he said calmly. "If you say something of that sort once more, I'll throw you in the river!" He glanced round, then eased forward in a conspiratorial fashion. "There is one thing – "

"Yes?"

He nudged me. Glancing down, I saw a pile of coins in his palm. "Pay me back when I return," he said.

I was embarrassed. "As a matter of fact – "

He tried to press the money on me. Reluctantly, I told him about Bairstowe and the guinea he'd paid me, hurrying because the driver was climbing up on to the box of the coach and passengers were making a scurry for the interior.

"Bairstowe?" Hugh echoed.

"You'll miss the coach."

"You're working for that scoundrel!"

"He's paying me well."

"How well?"

"Twenty guineas."

He whistled. "There's something shady going on."

"That's the point."

A late arrival was throwing bags up on to the roof. "Hugh, you'll miss the coach!"

"Tell Bairstowe to go to the devil, Charles. You know what happened last time you got involved in something like this.

I nearly died!"

"You're not going to be here this time, Hugh. You'll be in Paris, remember."

"Then you'll get yourself killed."

"Not a chance of it," I said soothingly. "You'll miss the coach."

"You've got to promise you won't do it."

"I need the money."

"Bairstowe of all people! The rudest man I ever met. Don't do it, Charles."

"Too late. I've already agreed to help. Hugh, get in that coach."

"But – "

I took him by the elbow and pushed him into the coach. An ostler tossed up the steps behind him and the horses lurched forward. And it was only then that I remembered I'd been trying to prevent him going.

I walked out on to the Key after the departing coach, watching it rattle across the bridge. I still thought I'd get a note from Darlington, pleading for help.

I had four lessons that morning. The first was at the house of Thomas Saint, the printer, who publishes the *Courant* every Saturday. I can rely on his daughter to practise assiduously; she has a musical gentleman in view as a prospective husband. My second lesson, however, was with the Revd Brown's youngest daughter, who requires all my tact and diplomacy. She adores her papa and wants to emulate him in playing the cello; it is the very devil to persuade her that it is not an instrument fit for ladies.

I was early for the first lesson; I bought gruel at the Cale Cross and idled along the Key towards the Printing House. My anger of the previous day had dissipated although I still longed to follow Hugh's advice and tell Bairstowe to go to the devil. But I needed the money so I might as well grit my teeth and get on with the matter.

I had lost sleep from mulling it over. There was no proof the threatening notes had existed or that poor Tom Eade's death was anything but an accident, though I firmly believed that William Bairstowe thought he was in danger. But one small thing gave me pause – I had been told conflicting stories about Eade. Bedwalters had said he was courting the Bairstowes' maid, but the mother had referred to a fisher girl. It might be nothing – the mother might have been mistaken – yet it nagged at me.

Thomas Saint's daughter was as attentive as ever, Mr Brown's as rebellious; I bit back irritation and looked forward to the afternoon which promised much better, in the shape of the Heron family.

The Heron house is an old one, standing in one of the most genteel parts of town, upon Northumberland Street. Outside, it bears the imprint of previous centuries, with stone lintels like raised eyebrows over the windows; inside, it is as modern as Heron's considerable fortune can make it. The son, Master Thomas, is a reluctant harpsichordist with clumsy hands, but his father, whom I instruct on the violin, is more purposeful and more talented; if he were not a member of the gentry I would say that he could make a good musician. As it is, he does as I suggest, listens to criticism without taking offence and practises between lessons; I cannot ask for more than that. Moreover, he has taken to giving me a glass of wine before I leave and lingering in conversation with me. I fancy he prefers a little rest before returning to business; he is not a man who takes much pleasure in life.

So, after the lesson, we repaired to the library which was warmed by a good fire. Heron poured wine, and went straight into the attack, just as I was being soothed by the warmth of the room and the comfort of his chair.

"Debts, Patterson?"

My heart sank but there was no avoiding the question. "Always," I temporised.

He nodded. "Three weeks until the end of the quarter. A difficult time."

He certainly does not speak from experience. Claudius Heron has never known a moment's poverty in his life. I sat back in my comfortable chair, and tried for a good-humoured tone. "Especially," I said. "When half the town is *out* of town."

"So that is why you are contemplating this business of Bairstowe's?"

I laughed, reluctantly. "Do you know everything, sir?"

"I was talking with Bedwalters this morning." Heron settled in the chair opposite me and contemplated the ruby luminescence of his wine. "He is not a pleasant man – Bairstowe, that is."

"Not one that knows the meaning of tact, certainly." Sunshine was seeping in through tall windows, gleaming on the polished wood floor, and glistened on Heron's pale hair. (He wears his own, gathered in a bow at the nape of his neck, in defiance of fashion.)

"He has a vicious temper," Heron said. Heron himself is irrevocably cool; I have only once seen him angry and it is not an experience I wish to repeat. "His father was the same and he suffered the inevitable fate."

I raised an eyebrow.

"He died of an apoplexy. I am told he clutched his head, fell down in the street and died on the instant. He was barely fifty years old. The men die young in that family."

My own father was forty-two when he died; I smiled uneasily.

"So," he said. "Do you continue?" He looked at me over the rim of his glass. "I would have thought that matter before Christmas would have been sufficient excitement."

It was the first time he had referred to the affair; there was no hint in his voice of the fear that had seized us both on the occasion itself.

"Needs must," I said lightly. "In any case, this matter can hardly be of the same kind. And Tom Eade deserves the truth. Whatever it is."

"Eade?"

"The lad who died."

"Bedwalters says it was an accident."

I sighed. "I'm inclined to believe him."

Heron was silent for a moment, no doubt turning over what both I and Bedwalters had told him. I looked at him at my leisure. A slight, reserved man of forty years or so, with no liking for anyone at all in the world and no friends that I could discover. I would not exchange Heron's wealth for my friendship with Hugh, irritating though Demsey could be, but a guinea or two of Heron's fortune would be welcome.

"Does Bairstowe name any particular person as his attacker?" he asked at last.

"No." I sipped the wine. "Though he mentioned several persons as his enemies." I laughed to show I did not take Bairstowe seriously. "Including yourself, sir."

He stared at me for a moment, then pushed himself to his feet. "Bring your wine."

He led me through a succession of rooms I had never seen before, all exquisitely and expensively furnished. Plaster work ceilings displayed astonishing craftsmanship; huge mirrors hung between long windows – both kinds of glass would have cost several times my annual income. Brocaded chairs stood on Turkish carpets; curtains framed tall vases. All the rooms were impeccably kept but I doubted they were often used; Heron was a widower, and he and his son lived frugally. These public rooms were probably used twice a year for receptions or dinner parties.

We came into a dark wood-panelled gallery, hung with pictures of Herons from centuries past. A wooden floor was polished to perfection; square panels of coloured glass in the windows depicted coats of arms. "Yes," Heron said. "It is archaic, I know, and in the most extravagantly bad taste. All this wood was the height of fashion fifty years ago – it was used throughout the whole house when I inherited the property."

"It must have been horribly dark."

He nodded. "I thought I had found a use for the gallery at last." We walked down the echoing room, towards a huge shrouded something that stood against the far wall. "I decided to convert it into a concert room."

I thought of trying to make a harpsichord heard in that vast empty space. Heron was looking faintly amused. "Clearly, something with considerable carrying power was needed, and, like a fool, I thought Bairstowe was the man to provide it."

He bent to a covered pile on the floor beneath the windows, tugged at the concealing sheet and whisked it away. Beneath was a pile of organ pipes – and a long gouge in the glossy wooden floor. Glancing up, I saw a gaping hole where something had been poked through the stained glass panel in the nearest window.

"His organs do have an excellent reputation," I said reluctantly.

"So I have been told by several fine judges," Heron said. "But Bridges of London is equally good. And I am tolerably sure that he would not have irretrievably damaged centuries-old floors and windows."

He pulled down the covering from the shape on the wall and revealed the framework for the proposed organ. Heron had thought large – not a full-size organ as one might find in a church but something bigger than a chamber organ. I peered closer; the woodwork looked dusty.

"How long is it since he did any work on it?"

"Several months. First he was called in to tune the organ in the Song School in Durham, then it was Mrs Jenison's harpsichord that needed repair. Then it was illness, then he was waiting for a new supply of wood. And, finally, I read the paper last week and discovered he is to exhibit a new organ at the Cordwainer's Hall next week."

"He has lost interest in this project," I concluded.

"He has still been taking my money for supplies," Heron said dryly.

"I had heard he was apathetic about his trade now. I wonder why?"

"Despair?" Heron suggested.

I glanced at him but he was as urbane as ever. "There is, after all," he said, "very little of worth in this world. A fine wine." He gestured with his glass. "Pleasant conversation with a friend. Nothing more."

I was embarrassed, as always, by Heron's cynicism, and by his implied compliment to myself. We stood, silent for a moment, in the echoing gallery, with the wind whistling in through the hole in the window and disturbed spiders scurrying from the pile of organ pipes.

"I had meant to apologise," Heron said, astounding me. "For the decision of the Gentlemen Directors of the Concerts."

I did not know what to say. A gentleman apologising to a musician? Unheard of.

"I tried to persuade them to give you a benefit," he said.

"I'd rather not speak – "

"And as for this business of the Italian woman," he said, instantly changing the direction of the conversation. "The matter will be simply ruinous. They cannot recoup their costs."

"So I judge."

"Well," he said. "So be it. They will learn. I –"

A discreet cough behind us; we turned to see a servant, in dark-blue livery, standing in the middle of the polished floor. "A message for Mr Patterson, sir," he said deferentially. "From Mr Bairstowe."

The message had been brought by the maid, Tom Eade's bereaved lover. She was a slip of a girl maybe seventeen years old, timid and wary, with eyes permanently cast down, and answered all our questions in a soft Scotch accent. Jennie, she said her name was, Jennie McIntosh, and Mr Bairstowe wanted me urgently to 'see what has been done now'.

Heron insisted upon coming with me and we walked down to Silver Street together. We must have made a strange group: the demure maid, the self-possessed gentleman in his brocaded coat, and the tradesman (myself) in drab brown with green cuffs. A crowd of eager beggar children gathered around us as we walked down Pilgrim Street into Silver Street but I had nothing to give them and Heron merely looked on with distaste.

The alley to Bairstowe's manufactory looked worse in daylight than it had at night; the light displayed the dog turds and discarded apple cores all too clearly. Distantly, I heard the sound of singing.

William Bairstowe came striding out of the house into the chill, cluttered yard, and sent the maid back inside. He baulked when he saw Heron. "What the devil are you here for?"

Heron was unperturbed by the rudeness. "I came to see how the work on my organ goes on."

Bairstowe sneered at him. "You want to see how the work goes? Well, come look." He gestured melodramatically at the workshop.

The door was jammed half-open; we sidled in through a narrow gap to behold a scene of chaos. Pipes and lengths of wood were scattered everywhere, tools cast down from their places and trampled underfoot. An adze had been smashed into the half-made soundboard along the grain, splitting a great portion of it away. Leather had been tossed in a corner and liquid poured over it; the pungent reek of piss was unmistakeable.

I thought I heard a new voice, but when I glanced around I saw only Heron, examining the lock on the door.

"Aye," Bairstowe said. "That's the way he came in. Broke down the door."

I kicked at the soundboard. There was plainly no salvaging it.

Bairstowe swore at me. "Stop gawping, damn you, and get down to earning your ten guineas!"

Ten guineas? He had offered me twenty. In fury, I started to speak but Claudius Heron interrupted. "I believe the sum was thirty guineas," he said lazily.

We both looked at him. He stood nonchalantly just inside the door, his hand on the lock he had been examining. His tone was bored. Bairstowe started to speak but Heron said again, "Thirty guineas."

"I offered – " Bairstowe stopped under Heron's steady gaze. "Yes, yes," he said hurriedly. "Thirty guineas. Of course. Get going, man. Get going!"

"When I've had a good look around," I said, determined to assert myself.

I trampled over the smashed pipes and the crushed lead, deriving a great deal of satisfaction from the crunching and crackling of the debris under my feet. I examined the windows and the door, and looked for footprints in the dust and the sawdust. Bairstowe stood in the middle of the floor and glared at me; Claudius Heron hardly moved. I didn't have the slightest idea what I was looking for, and I found nothing. Or rather – only the one thing Claudius Heron had already noted.

We went out in the street again, Heron and I. I took deep breaths of the cold March air and tried to calm my temper. The faint sun that had gleamed through the windows of Heron's house came out from behind the clouds again and mitigated the worst effects of the chill wind. Below, we caught a grey glimpse of the Tyne, and of the bank of Gateshead on the other side.

"You saw the lock," I said to Heron, when I trusted myself to speak.

He nodded.

"The door was forced from the inside," I said.

"A remarkably foolish mistake to make."

"He vandalised the workshop himself."

A moment or two's silence; Heron stirred and said, "I advise you to withdraw from this matter."

"I cannot, sir," I said, as neutrally as I could. "The money he offers will see me through the rest of the year, whatever transpires with the Italians. And if you think I should withdraw, sir, why did you take the trouble to beat Bairstowe up to thirty guineas? – for which," I added, mindful of my manners, "I thank you."

"Carefulness with money is admirable," he said. "Meanness is abominable." I was reminded of Tom Eade – he had been a miser, according to his mother. "And," Heron added, "William Bairstowe is truly abominable." He turned to look directly at me. "I know you like a challenge, Patterson, but there is something dangerous about this matter. I say again, pull back."

7

Man is born to worship the Divine; it is a duty upon us and nothing can excuse us from it.
[Revd A. E., Letter to Newcastle Courant, 24 October 1735]

On the Key; the breeze snapped at the rigging of seagoing ships, gulls wheeled overhead, diving for scraps of food. The keelmen with their yellow waistcoats sauntered insolently along with dogs barking at their heels; boys ran shrieking, drunk with the prospect of their first voyage. Heron had left me to undertake some business; I had wandered off alone. I was in need of solitude, time to think and order my thoughts.

This was plainly not the place to find it. I walked towards the Tyne Bridge, passing great heaps of coal and wood and the ruins of the city wall. On my right, narrow entrances gave on to chares of the most unsavoury reputation; further along was the magnificence of the Guildhall. And beyond that were the arches over the river, sturdy and high, scattered with houses and shops.

I climbed the slope up to the first shops. It is never completely quiet here, but in the early evening only a few people ride home after a long day's journey. I passed the tower that is used as a prison, passed Fleming's stationer's shop. The last of the sun gleamed through clouds, showing cracks in the stones, rot in the wooden timbering of the houses.

A spirit gleamed on a shop window and called to me in a smug, self-satisfied way; I ignored her and walked on, towards the blue stones that mark the centre of the bridge – the boundary between the boroughs of Newcastle and Gateshead. The road on the Gateshead side is markedly better kept. I leant on the parapet and stared down at the grey water.

It did not pay to dismiss Claudius Heron's advice lightly. He was a cautious man and always inclined to believe the worst of everyone. But he was right to think that Bairstowe was playing with me – the man had clearly wrecked the workshop himself. If the threatening notes had indeed existed, I'd wager Bairstowe had written them. Yet those twenty – no, thirty – guineas: how could I turn them down? And more importantly than that, a man had died. If his death was not an accident, Tom Eade deserved justice.

I was roused from my reverie by the sharp clip-clop of horse's hooves, loud on the cobbles. I glanced round – and caught my breath.

The lady that sat astride the chestnut horse walking wearily towards me was flagrantly wearing breeches, albeit under a long concealing coat with ample skirts. Dear God, I had forgotten how beautiful she was: pale hair gleaming under a tricorne hat, slim figure so tempting in that outrageous outfit. And blue eyes settling on me with cool composure.

"Mr Patterson," the lady said, nodding.

"Mrs Jerdoun," I said, flushing.

It was two months or more since I had seen Esther Jerdoun, and she affected me not one whit less powerfully than she had before. At first consideration, there is nothing odd in this – what is more natural than that a single lady (the title *Mrs* is of course honorary) and a single man should be attracted to each other? But she is a lady of ample means and I a mere musician of none. She is a woman of thirty-eight and I a man of twenty-six. There is a vast gulf between us in social standing, in wealth and in age, and between us there can be nothing.

I looked up, trying to conceal my pleasure at seeing her.

"I trust you had a good journey, madam."

"A weary one," she said wryly. "And I return a good month

later than I had hoped. Take my advice, Mr Patterson, and keep out of the clutches of lawyers. They are never content with anything less than complete thoroughness. Every detail must be scrutinised at extraordinary length, every phrase debated with exquisite care."

"But your inheritance is secured, I hope, madam?"

She sighed, controlled the shifting horse. "In part. But there is still much wrangling over some of the land. It drives me to distraction!" Her gaze searched my face. "You are well, Mr Patterson?"

I was hungry, to tell the truth, very hungry.

"Very well, madam."

"I was sorry to miss your benefit concert," she said, then added sharply: "Have I said anything amiss?"

I must have given something away by my look, I supposed. "I did not have a benefit concert, madam. The gentlemen did not think – "

I could not think of any polite way of describing the gentlemen's conduct. The sentence hung unfinished between us.

"No benefit?" she said, at last.

"There was not time before Lent began and the entertainments ceased."

"Then no doubt they will give you a benefit in Race Week?"

Awkwardly, I explained about Signora and Signor Mazzanti. Mrs Jerdoun sat above me on the tall horse, looking down, the wind blowing tendrils of her pale hair about her neck. Her face set into a hard, unreadable mask.

"Indeed?" she said. "So the town will enjoy extracts from Mr Handel's Italian operas? The audience will no doubt hang on every word."

I winced. I doubt if more than half a dozen ladies and gentlemen of the town have enough Italian to say *yes, no* and *thank you*; Jenison is proud of knowing nothing but English and so are all his fellow merchants. I had a vision of the concert: Signora Mazzanti, statuesque and well-bosomed no doubt, letting the liquid syllables dance about the concert room, half the audience looking on disapprovingly, the other half whispering desperately for translations. And Demsey, with his knack at foreign languages, sitting at the back of the room, guffawing over some joke only he can understand.

"Well," Mrs Jerdoun said. "We shall see. Good day, sir."

And she urged the weary horse into motion again.

I had a drink at Mrs Hill's in the Fleshmarket but had too little money to get drunk and sat in increasing sobriety while everyone else around me grew steadily more inebriated. I kept seeing Tom Eade in my mind's eye, that covered body being carried out of the alley. What had I to complain about in comparison to that?

The lodging house was dark when I let myself in and wearily climbed the stairs to my rooms. Esther Jerdoun would be wallowing in a hot perfumed bath by now, ministered to by her attentive maid, slipping from water to scented nightgown and thence to solicitously warmed sheets in an antique bed. All I had was a single room, a table piled with music books, two chairs, one bed with a lumpy mattress –

I paused outside the door, key in my hand. I could hear snoring.

I pushed open the door and there he was, sprawled face down on my bed, with his greatcoat wrapped around him and his bags scattered about the floor. Snoring like a thunderstorm.

Hugh Demsey.

I didn't wake him. I tried but I could not. I gave up and flung myself into a chair to look at him. His colour was healthier than it had been in the morning but that might be owing to the fact he had brought in a jug of ale from the nearest tavern and drunk the lot. Crumbs from a meat pie were scattered over the music books on the table.

I sighed, dragged a blanket from under Hugh's legs and curled myself in the chair. It was damned uncomfortable.

Church bells woke me next morning. I was stiff and aching, with a crick in my neck. I crawled across Hugh – still asleep – to peer out of the window. A faint sun stained the cobbles of the street and picked out the widow ladies, four or five of them in all-enveloping black, stalking off to the early services. Sunday always brings out the widows, eager for consolation – or a sight of the handsome unmarried curates.

I was stiff but I had slept surprisingly well and my mind was refreshed, my purpose certain. If I could get to the truth about poor Tom Eade and do myself a good turn financially, then why not? And I knew where I could start in the matter: by questioning those men who might have had a grudge against William Bairstowe. As always when I see a course of action in front of me, and a puzzle to get my teeth into, I felt a great deal happier.

I splashed my face with cold water and dressed hurriedly. Fortunately, I had had a shave yesterday, wishing to appear my best before the Managers of the Concerts. Hugh woke as I peered into my scrap of mirror to arrange my cravat; he struggled on to one elbow. "Charles –"

I regarded him in the mirror. "Why aren't you halfway to Paris, Hugh?"

He frowned as if he wasn't sure himself. "Got off the coach at Durham," he said at last.

Sick as a dog, no doubt. "I said you were not yet recovered."

"Not ill." To judge by the way he ran his hand through his tousled hair, he certainly had a hangover. "All because of you."

"Me? I'm not taking the blame for your folly, Hugh." I shrugged myself into my coat.

"*My* folly! Damn it, I came back because of *your* folly. Working for Bairstowe! Remember what happened last time you got yourself involved in someone else's business, Charles. Damn near got me killed."

He groaned and lowered his head to the bed again. "Can't desert a friend," he said thickly, and I thought he added something about ingratitude, but as he mumbled into the blankets I couldn't be certain. It was a good excuse but I saw what must have happened. Demsey had known by the time he reached Durham that he wasn't fit enough to continue and he had used my doings as a convenient excuse for turning back.

I regarded him with some amusement. "You'd better stay here until you've slept off that ale. Though I'd be grateful if you don't put pie crumbs in my bed!"

He raised his head and peered at me. "You're in the devil of a good mood. And dressed well. Where are you off to?"

"Church."

"Church!" he shrieked, pushing himself up again. "Charles, are you mad?"

I assumed a pious look. "I am a good Christian."

"So am I," he retorted. "That is why I avoid all that nonsense. Charles," he added pleadingly, "Think of the psalm-singing!"

I shuddered. "Some things must be endured." I snatched up my prayer book. "I'll come to your rooms tonight, Hugh! Tell you all about Bairstowe."

"Charles!" he called after me but I dashed off. It doesn't do to be late for church.

Bairstowe's enemies were no doubt legion. I was starting with the most obvious.

Solomon Strolger, organist of All Hallows Church.

8

Every Organ in our churches is an encouragement to Piety and an incentive to Devotion.
[C. A., Letter on the present State of Church Music, Newcastle Courant, 14 February 1736]

All Hallows is not the most attractive of the town's churches. Its age is against it; the walls are zigzagged by disturbingly large cracks and the window glass bellies out as if the weight of the roof is too much for it. Inside, there is the chill that all churches possess, and a dimness that strains the eye.

The best-placed pews are of course all rented; I found myself a place near the back of the church where a pillar obscured my view of the altar and the pulpit; consequently, I hoped, I would not be able to see the chaplain. He is a young callow man who has only been here a year or two; he still trembles at the sound of his own voice and is visibly conscious he is laying down the law to merchants and seamen three times his own age.

The organ was playing when I went in – quite a decent organ, though clearly not well maintained; I heard at least two ciphers, caused by the mechanism sticking and allowing the air to resonate in the pipes when it should have been cut off. The effect is a drone, rather like that of the bagpipes, though even less pleasant. My pew was directly under the gallery at the west end of the church where the organ was placed, so I could see nothing of the organist.

During the horrors of the voluntary, I knelt and pretended to pray. Strolger is well-known for his fanciful productions. His music is too quick and cheerful, modulates from one key to another with bewildering rapidity, and is much too secular to call devout men and women to worship; I could have sworn I heard hints of the Scotch song *The Highland Laddie.*

The psalms too were as bad as I feared. All Hallows follows the old-fashioned practice of lining out the psalms, that is, the parish clerk sings each line in turn and is then copied by the congregation. The method destroys all the poetry of the text by breaking up the sense in ridiculous places, and there is the tedium, intolerable to a musician, of inferior tunes sung at so slow a pace that one must breathe after every note. I was almost tempted to copy Strolger and add a few ornamental flourishes to enliven the boredom.

Meanwhile, I looked about to see if I could spot the Bairstowes. Perhaps some member of the congregation would make life easy for me by staring at William with more than usual animosity. Bairstowe was nowhere to be seen, but his brother-in-law John Holloway was in a pew near the front, as smart as a man with three times his wealth and six times his ancestry, bending solicitously over the prayer book of a woman ten years his senior. A plain woman, with a country air – the sour-faced woman I had glimpsed staring down at Tom Eade's body. Mrs Bairstowe, I assumed.

On the other side of the woman was the Bairstowes' maid, head demurely bowed. As if she sensed my gaze on her, the girl glanced round, caught my eye, glanced away again. A timid, scared look, I thought. Well, that was hardly surprising. Anyone living with William Bairstowe would be cowed.

I got through the service. The curate's voice trembled in the prayers, Strolger played another voluntary, based on an air from the latest opera at the theatre, and the parish clerk took the rest of the psalms even more slowly than I had imagined possible. The sermon lasted an hour and a half.

As the congregation began to file from the church, I contrived to edge against the flow and work my way up towards the choir and high altar. It is the peculiarity of the church that the organ is over the west door but the stairs to the organ loft are in the middle of the church; one must climb narrow steps, work one's way along the ornately painted Sailors' Gallery and thus come to the west end. The last of the charity school children were eagerly slipping from their special pews in the loft, and Solomon Strolger played on, and on, and on, flourishing fugal entries here, teasing the listener with hints of familiar tunes then dashing off into wild improvisation again. It was all very cleverly done, I had to admit, but not devout.

At last, the organ ceased; there was a murmur of voices and out came the bellows blower, a burly fellow with huge red hands. Now Strolger climbed down from his stool like a hesitant stork, all legs and no body. He started when he saw me and peered short-sightedly. He is a young man, or youngish, being in his mid-thirties. "Oh, it's you, Patterson. Want a lesson, do you?" He has an engaging grin that allows you – almost – to forgive him his pretentious playing.

"I wanted to talk to you, if I may."

"Gossip, Patterson?" He chuckled. "Nothing better!"

"About Mr William Bairstowe."

Now he stared at me. "You're not a friend of his, are you?"

"Not until he mends his language," I said dryly.

He grinned again. "Good," he said, then, "Heard that cipher?"

"On the flute stop?"

"Bairstowe put that right."

"But it's still there."

"That's what I said. But no, Mr Bairstowe says it's entirely my imagination." Strolger grinned impishly.

"You don't like him?" I said, stating the obvious.

"Nothing to worry about," he said cheerfully. "He doesn't like me."

He darted to one side to pick his coat off a hook driven into the organ case. Down in the body of the church below, I heard the last of the congregation leaving.

"Why doesn't he like you?"

Strolger grinned. "He didn't like my comments on one of his organs."

"And you said?"

He wriggled into the coat. "I said it squealed like a new-born piglet and sounded as devout as a hedgehog."

"I can see why he might be annoyed."

Strolger was a picture of innocence as he smoothed down his sleeves. "But it was true!" He cocked his head to consider me. "What's your business with him, Patterson?"

"He's employing me."

He chortled. "Wants you to play his organs, does he? Show 'em off to their best advantage? Take it from me, Patterson, they don't have a best advantage. Rubbishy things. There's one exhibited at the Cordwainers' Hall next week."

"I know. But it's nothing of that sort. He's being threatened and wants me to find the fellow doing it."

"Good heavens!" he exclaimed, melodramatically. "Someone's putting the fear of God into him? Patterson, find the fellow and send him to me so I may congratulate him!"

He was outrageously offensive yet an oddly likeable fellow. There were no hidden depths to him; he was all on the surface and you would never be deceived by him, unless you deceived yourself. "I wondered, sir, since you are so often about the church and the street, whether you had seen something – or someone – "

He crowed with laughter. "Confess it – he has accused me!"

"He has named you as one of his enemies," I admitted.

He chuckled, bent across the organ stool to gather his music together. I heard the chaplain below calling a nervous farewell to a parishioner.

"A lad died," I said quietly.

Strolger paused, glanced round at me. "I was told that was an accident."

"Possibly," I said. "But what if he was merely in the wrong place at the wrong time?"

"Mistaken for Bairstowe, you mean?" He was quick, no doubt of that. He stared at the decorative organ pipes at the front of the case, as if for inspiration. "Come, come, Patterson, the lad was scarcely twenty, slightly-built – no one would mistake him for good friend William."

"You knew the lad then?"

"I've seen him." He sorted the music on to a shelf set to the right of the organ. "He couldn't find the manufactory the first time he came and asked my oldest boy. Got a civil reply and the information he wanted, and couldn't give the boy a farthing for his help."

"Ungenerous," I commented, remembering that both Eade's mother and Richard Softly had called him a miser. "But the maid liked him well enough."

Strolger grinned. "Only after he'd worked hard on her! Many's the time I've seen her creeping into a doorway to escape him. Still, persistence pays – he seems to have won her in the end. Though much good it did either of them."

Below us, the church was almost empty. The curate, head bowed, hands gripped together, came out under the gallery and hurried up the nave to the vestry door. Strolger was chortling. "Wrote her odes!"

I brought my attention back to him, startled. "The lad?"

"Reams of the stuff – verse after verse on Holloway's best notepaper." He leant forward conspiratorially. "Stolen, of course."

"The paper or the verse?"

"Both!"

"The maid showed you the verses?"

"No, no – she dropped one in the porch." He added scrupulously, "I gave it back to her, of course."

"But not before reading it."

"I read the first line. That was enough to tell me the rest wasn't worth noticing."

I was thinking of the notes Bairstowe had received. "And the hand? Was the writing ill-formed? Childish?"

He was surprised but answered readily enough. "Not at all. Very neat. I'd wager he was one of Bedwalters' pupils." He glanced around, was apparently satisfied that everything was in order. "Care for ale, Patterson?"

He went to the left side of the organ – the side nearest the charity pews – and lifted a curtain that hung over that side of the organ case. I ducked under it, and saw a very cosy sight.

The curtain enclosed an area of the organ loft from which the pews had been removed. On the right, the side of the organ case had also been taken away, exposing the inner workings – ranks of dusty metal pipes on wooden soundboards, hung with cobwebs and scattered with mouse droppings. A chair had been placed for the bellows blower by the handle he had to pump, and an ancient armchair, clearly for Strolger, stood by the side of a shelf screwed on to the wall. On the shelf was a large jug of ale, nearly empty, and two tankards, one close by the bellow blower's chair, the other by the armchair. London newspapers were piled on the floor.

"Have to have something to occupy us during the sermons," Strolger murmured impishly. Now I was close to him, I could smell the ale on his breath. "The chaplain's a good fellow, but so earnest."

I could not argue with that. Strolger took up the bellows blower's tankard, wiped the top of it with the flat of his palm and poured ale into it for me. The floor was thick with dust except in a narrow band well trampled by Strolger and the bellows blower to and from their respective chairs.

I went across to look more closely at the innards of the organ. It was in a worse condition than I had anticipated. Some of the pipes stood drunkenly askew and part of one rank – six or seven large flue pipes – had been taken from its soundboard and stacked against the wall. Judging by the dust, the pipes had been there some years. The soundboard on which they had stood was warped and cracked.

Strolger was watching me from his armchair. "Quite right, Patterson. Whole thing needs replacing. If it was just a case of dusting the sliders or something of the sort, I'd do it myself. But I can't put right something as serious as that."

"How long since you asked Bairstowe to deal with it?"

"Five years or more."

"Call in Bridges," I said, ducking out of the interior. "Or some other London organbuilder."

He threw up his hands in mock horror. "And pay all that expense when we have a perfectly good local builder? I quote the gentlemen of the vestry of course."

"But if Bairstowe doesn't do the work – "

Strolger grinned. "My dear Patterson, you know perfectly well that all the gentlemen and ladies want is a loud noise. Who cares whether it is in tune or not?"

I considered him for a moment. "You haven't said yet, sir, whether you are to blame for the threats."

He chuckled. "No putting you off, Patterson! Very well, a straight answer. No. I wouldn't give William so much of my attention. Try that wife of his. She's distinctly odd. I'd not want to take her to bed."

Strolger's own wife is a pretty young thing, and remarkably so because she has borne nine children in six years. And the fellow is known for his uxorious temperament, indulging her with gifts and treats almost every week.

"Apart from Mrs Bairstowe," I said doggedly, "did you see anyone else?"

"Plenty of fellows." He shook his head at me. "You're on a fool's errand, Patterson. Half the town hates William Bairstowe – he never does his work, he never pays his bills and he's the rudest man in the county! Try finding someone without a grudge against him."

I thought of Claudius Heron. "That kind of dislike rarely leads to threats."

"Perhaps someone merely wants to frighten him?"

"Whoever it was, they killed a boy."

"An accident," he said firmly. "The wind took the wood. Stick to music, Patterson. Much less fuss." He lifted his head at a call from below and hurried out to hang alarmingly over the gallery rail. I followed him. A boy of not more than five years old stood below and shrieked up that dinner was ready. Strolger abandoned the ale and scampered down the stairs; I saw him scoop up the boy and carry him laughing down the length of the nave to the door where an older boy waited solemnly to take his father's hand.

There is nothing so insidious as envy.

9

We hear that last Sunday the Revd Mr Ellison, afternoon lecturer at St Nicholas's Church, preached a sermon on the sanctity of the matrimonial bond. Nothing is so pleasing to God, he remarked, than the care taken by a good husband for his wife, and nothing more beautiful the duty and obedience shown by a good wife to her husband.
[Newcastle Courant, 23 August 1735]

I hesitated outside the church, surprised by bright sunshine. The churchyard was deserted, except for a single figure sitting on one of the benches by the gate. I put my tricorne on my head then whipped it off again as the figure rose up and turned to face me. Esther Jerdoun.

We looked at each other for a moment then I was brought back to my senses by some noise in the street. I bowed; she inclined her head and smiled. My heart turned over.

"I like to see a devout man, Mr Patterson," she said – a mischievous comment for she knows my views on church-going.

"I thought you attended St Nicholas's church, madam."

"Indeed I do. I have just come from there. The spirit in the church porch asked after you for me, and said you were here."

It seemed she had sought me out; I was both pleased and humbled.

"You are walking up into town, are you not?" she said. "I would be glad of your company." That faint smile again. "A woman is never quite safe alone."

I would like to see anyone tackle Esther Jerdoun. I fancy they would have a shock.

I bowed my assent and opened the gate for her. As befitted a

Sunday, the street was quiet. The chaplain hurried towards his rooms; a well-dressed couple in middle-age, a tradesman and his wife, strolled arm in arm up the street in pleasurable and comfortable conversation.

We hesitated at the gate. I was acutely conscious of the difference between us; I was dressed in drab brown with buff facings; the lady was delicate in pale blue embroidered with flowers of white, with a fall of lace at neck and sleeves. Her cloak was of velvet and she pulled it more closely about her.

"I have, as you know, sir, been much from home of late."

"You have had a great deal to occupy you."

"This wretched legal business." She sighed. "Still, I have reason to believe the worst of it is over, at least for the time being. I am determined to stay at home the next several months at least."

"You will be glad to be settled," I said, somewhat at random, distracted by her closeness. We took a step or two up the street; the warmth of the sun was unexpectedly strong.

"I have decided to take up the harpsichord again," she said.

I looked sharply at her. Mrs Jerdoun's interest in music is, by her own admission, tepid; she sees it, she says, as a pleasant way to pass an hour chatting with her friends.

"I have after all inherited a fine example of the instrument."

"Indeed."

"But I find myself dreadfully out of practice."

There was no doubt now where this conversation was heading; I was at a loss to know whether to help it along, or merely to let the whole pleasure and fear of it break over my head unaided. We strolled along in sunshine for another moment or two in silence.

"I feel I should take the whole matter more seriously." She cast me a sideways glance.

I said: "Indeed, madam."

"So I intend to take lessons," she said, with a touch of exasperation.

Now the moment had come, I hardly knew whether to leap for joy or run away. Ridiculous. I took a firm grip on myself. "A wise move, madam." Did she expect me to present her with my terms: *half a guinea entrance, madam, and half a guinea tuition per quarter*?

"Shall we say tomorrow?" she said bluntly.

I took fright. A single gentleman teaching a single lady with only a maid for chaperone? A lady moreover whose interest in music is known to be slight? And at her house? I hated that house.

She must have read my thoughts in my face; she added quickly, "I thought we might use the harpsichord in the Assembly Rooms. The Steward frequently says he wishes it was played more over the summer months."

"Indeed it should be." I breathed more easily. The Assembly Rooms were a public place; the Steward would pop in and out, we could hardly be accused to being alone.

"Very well," I began – but then my name was bellowed along the street.

William Bairstowe strode towards us. He had clearly not been to church; he was dressed in crumpled clothes that looked as if he had worn them for days, slept in them even.

"What the devil are you about, Patterson?"

"Good day, Mr Bairstowe," Esther Jerdoun said.

He ignored her. He was so forceful, I thought he might even seize hold of my coat to drag me into the alley. "I want results, man. I want this fellow's name!" He sneered. "I see what kind of fellow you are. You want the money but not the work, eh?" In the light of what Strolger had just told me, I considered that an unwise comment. "Well, question the folks that matter. Like my wife. She'll tell you all about the notes. I've told her often enough."

If all Mrs Bairstowe knew was what her husband told her, I did not consider that of much value. But Bairstowe was seizing me by the arm and propelling me back down the street towards the alley. "Get in there, man! I've business to do so you have a clear run at it. Go on, man!" And he strode off down Silver Street.

"So it is true," Mrs Jerdoun said. "You are investigating this matter? Claudius Heron told me something of the sort but I could not believe it. I would have thought you would steer well clear of such things after your experiences before Christmas."

"Needs must, madam," I said dryly.

"Money?"

"Indeed."

"Debts?"

"A few." I did not wish to discuss the matter but she persisted.

"Unpaid bills, sir? I mean, your bills are not paid by your pupils?"

"A natural hazard in my profession."

She studied my face. A few lines showed around her own eyes and mouth – she was after all a woman in middle life.

"I am not accustomed to letting problems defeat me, Mr Patterson," she said at last. "Though I confess they often send me into a frenzy of frustration. I cannot abide to stand back and do nothing!"

"Madam – "

She gathered her cloak around her more tightly. "Tell me frankly – is it essential that you obtain this money from William Bairstowe?"

"If I am to escape a debtor's prison." I spoke lightly but it was the stuff of my nightmares.

"Very well." She took my arm, steered me into the alley. "Then we had better question the lady."

We?

In the shadowed yard, overhung by the church tower, I felt an ineradicable chill, almost like the deep cold that had always struck me just before that other world had opened up during the Caroline Square business a few months ago. I shivered violently, walked across the yard to the workshop; there was a new lock on the door, fresh wood and gleaming metal. Cupping my hand against the window, I peered through fly-speckled glass. At first, I saw only the deepest of darknesses, the speckles on the glass giving the illusion of a starlit sky. Then the inside of the building came into focus; it had been tidied after a fashion; ruined pipes had been thrown into one corner, wood piled in untidy heaps.

"Who the devil are you?"

I started, turned. A woman stood at the door of the house, a bowl in her arms. "Get out," she said. "We don't give to beggars."

As Mrs Jerdoun was dressed in a gown of expensive quality, this was patently a calculated insult.

"Mrs Bairstowe?" It was the woman from the church, the woman Holloway had been so solicitous over. She made a contemptuous noise and flung the contents of the basin past me. The stink of it, and the colour, told me it was the pot from under their bed; some of the contents splashed on to my stockings and on to the hem of Mrs Jerdoun's skirt. The woman smiled grimly.

"Take yourselves off and bother other folk," she said.

"My name's Patterson," I said sharply. "Your husband has asked me to find out who is threatening him."

She stood with the basin loose in her hands, regarding me with calculating hardness. "Has he now? And the lady?" She gave Mrs Jerdoun no chance to reply, said contemptuously: "Fashionable ladies have nothing better to do, I suppose, than see how their inferiors live."

"If I'm to help your husband, I need information – "

"And you reckon I know something?"

"Do you?"

"Nay," she said. "I'm just a stupid woman. All brawn, no sense."

She did indeed have brawny arms; her sleeves were rolled up past the elbow and I saw muscles cording her forearms. She was a big woman – perhaps an inch taller than myself, and I am above the middle height. Her face was weathered, and her dull brown hair pulled back into a loose knot. She looked like a farmer's wife, not the wife of a prosperous tradesman. Next to Mrs Jerdoun, she appeared battered by life, worn down.

"Can we talk?"

"Aye," she said. "We can. I don't know that we will."

She screwed up her face in a kind of grim triumph but stood back to allow us into the house. I found myself in a kitchen so clean it might never have been used. Bowls stood in regiments upon a dresser, strictly in order of size; on a table, knives were ranked from largest to smallest. The fire was not lit and a deep-seated chill pervaded the house.

She was still standing in the doorway behind us.

"Well? Are you going to ask or not? I don't have all day to idle."

I curbed my annoyance. Mrs Bairstowe was plainly a match for her husband when it came to rudeness. "I understand your husband has been receiving threatening notes."

"He says." Her incredulity was palpable.

"You've not seen any of them?"

"What good would it do to show me?" She was bullish with me, but Mrs Jerdoun's calm silence seemed to unsettle her – she kept glancing at her, although Mrs Jerdoun did nothing but stand in the middle of the room, showing polite attention.

"He didn't mention them to you?"

A pause. "He might have," she said at last.

"Is that yes or no?" Mrs Jerdoun asked.

The woman reddened but rallied. "He's paying you to look into the matter too, is he, my lady?"

"Did he tell you about the notes?" I said, sharply.

"Aye. He told me."

"He showed them to you?"

"Nay," she said scornfully. "Never shows me anything. Anyhow, what would I have done if he had?"

"You cannot read?"

"What do I want with reading? A stupid lump like me?"

"So you think he invented the notes?"

She laughed contemptuously.

"Why should he fabricate threats against himself?"

"Ask him," she said.

The maid came into the kitchen from the house. She walked to the table, laid down a pile of sewing, took up another pile from a chair and walked out. She cast Mrs Jerdoun one quick, wary glance and did not look at me at all.

"And the ransacking of the workshop the night before last," I persisted. "You saw no one in the yard?"

"Nay."

A noise outside. A stray dog barked, a man called to it to get down. Then Holloway appeared in the doorway, stopping in mid-greeting as he saw us. His gaze lingered on Mrs Jerdoun – I saw such pleasure in his eyes that I wanted to kick him.

"Mr Holloway," Esther said.

"Mrs Jerdoun, madam." Yes, definitely a note of over-familiarity there. He turned his gaze on me. "Are you still investigating William's affairs, Mr Patterson?"

"I am, sir."

That didn't please him. "I think I made the situation clear at our last conversation."

"You were most clear," I said. A quirk of a smile touched Mrs Jerdoun's lips.

"Very well," he said impatiently. "Let's deal this matter straight away." He glanced at Mrs Bairstowe and I saw the oddest look pass between them – I could have sworn the sternness of her face relaxed and his expression briefly hinted at a smile. "Have they spoken with the maid?" he asked.

Mrs Bairstowe said sharply: "I'll not have the girl waste her time."

"But she knows – " He looked significantly at her.

She seemed almost to snarl. "Five minutes," she said. "Nothing more."

The maid was summoned back. She stood before us, head bowed, hands wrapped in her apron, speaking in a child's voice, all breathy and humble. The evening before last she couldn't sleep, she admitted in a whisper: too upset over Tom Eade. She had heard a noise in the yard and peered out of her attic window to see Mr Bairstowe going into the workshop. Then there had been a great banging, and when he came out he was covered in dirt. Then she saw him take a hammer to the door.

Not once during the tale did she look at any of us; we let her go when it was obvious that she had nothing more to say.

Both Holloway and Mrs Bairstowe were looking smug; I said, "And you heard nothing of this, madam?"

"Slept through it," she said. "Nought disturbs a lump like me."

"How old is the girl?" Mrs Jerdoun said, moving from her station in the middle of the room.

Holloway seemed surprised by the enquiry. "Seventeen, I believe."

"She looks older. Where does she come from?"

Holloway glanced at Mrs Bairstowe. "A local girl, from the Sandhill. Her father's a keelman." Another glance. "I am right,

I believe."

"Aye."

Holloway laid a hand on my arm. I looked down at it, at him. He was plainly trying to be conciliatory, but his touch made me squirm – I could not help but remember how the spirits had crawled about his neck. "Mr Patterson. You must trust me in this. William is a deeply unhappy man who feels he is not appreciated – this is perhaps his way of getting attention." He leant closer. "I would not go so far as to say he is mad, but instability runs in the family. His brother killed himself."

"Jumped from the bridge," Mrs Bairstowe said loudly. "Swept out to sea."

"Alas," Holloway said punctiliously. But I saw the quick glance pass between them; Mrs Bairstowe was far from pleased that Holloway had mentioned the brother.

"And Tom Eade?" I asked.

"What of him?"

"He died," I pointed out. "Do you believe he walked into a trap set for your husband?"

"Nay," she said scornfully. "I know who the trap was set for. That stupid girl. I'd have turned her off if she'd got herself with child. You can be sure of that."

I was. As I ushered Mrs Jerdoun out of the yard, I found myself, to my surprise, a little sorry for William Bairstowe.

10

The habit of thrift should be greatly encouraged amongst all sections of society, but particularly amongst the lower orders, where temptations such as gin and gaming are all too often indulged in.
[Revd A. E., Sermon preached at St Nicholas Church, 7 March 1736]

Mrs Jerdoun and I walked up the street together. A chill breeze blew up from the river. "That woman is lying," Mrs Jerdoun said. "Though I cannot imagine why. She is not even doing it cleverly. She should have said she heard the noise. She could have made some excuse for not getting up to look – she did not feel well, she thought he was drunk, something of that sort."

"I swear the maid's not lying," I said. "Bairstowe did wreck his own workshop."

"But why?"

We turned out of Silver Street into Pilgrim Street, crossing to the side of the street where the sun lay. "Perhaps the notes and threats are real," I suggested, "but Bairstowe thought I did not believe him. He staged this attack in an attempt to convince me. He is very afraid."

By unspoken agreement, we were walking across town in the direction of Mrs Jerdoun's house. My annoyance at the Bairstowes still lingered but I would not let it spoil my enjoyment of Mrs Jerdoun's company. She gathered her cloak around her and glanced in the window of a mantua-maker's. She said in a conversational tone: "I dined with Mr Jenison last night."

"Indeed?"

"The company was extremely thin. A number of families have

already left town for Easter."

"It's very late this year," I agreed.

She nodded. "They will not think of returning until the beginning of May and some may decide not to return until Race Week at the end of June."

"Indeed."

"Which will delay their payment of your bills."

I was taken aback by her directness and half-afraid she intended to offer me financial assistance. "I beg you not to consider the matter, madam. It is merely a temporary affair and will rectify itself."

"Therefore," she said, not heeding me, "Mr Bairstowe's offer is most opportune. But can you be sure he will pay you? Indeed, that he can? I have heard rumours – "

"He has advertised a chamber organ for sale at the Cordwainers' Hall next week. He may pay me from that."

She glanced at me, but said merely, "I trust he will."

We had come up to St Nicholas's church; it is large and well-appointed, in much better condition than All Hallows, and has an organ of high quality. There was a time I cast envious eyes on the position of organist there but I have long since concluded that some things are not meant to be. The tower and spires cast long shadows over the street.

"I did not find the dinner congenial," Mrs Jerdoun said. "I was disappointed in the company."

I took a moment to remember that she was referring to Jenison's entertainment the previous night. I glanced at her. There was a trace of implacability in those blue eyes.

"I broached the subject of your benefit," she said.

Dear God, her wish to champion my cause was both gratifying and frightening. If she should give the gentlemen cause for gossip –

"There was nothing but 'oh, this was not possible' and 'oh,

that was not desirable', and 'the expenses of these matters must be carefully considered'. And not a trace of consideration of *your* position or the services you rendered them over the winter." She was in full flow of indignation now. "Or there was mere indifference and silence. Heron, for one."

"Mr Heron has been very generous to me."

She said with some scepticism, "Indeed?"

We parted the other side of St Nicholas's church with some reserve. I fancied she was not pleased I had spoken in Claudius Heron's favour and I in turn was distressed that she seemed to dislike the man. I would have preferred my benefactors to be on good terms with each other.

The day was well advanced by this time, and I was feeling extraordinarily hungry; I looked about for a tavern so far removed from decent morals as to serve drink on a Sunday. Something was nagging at me, some inconsistency in what I had been told but I couldn't quite place what it was. Then I recalled Mrs Bairstowe saying that her brother-in-law, Edward Bairstowe, had jumped from the bridge. Had not the spirit in the alley said he was killed *on* the bridge?

It was a small point but would make a large difference, at least to Edward Bairstowe's spirit. If he had jumped from the bridge, his spirit would be lost in the pull of the tides, washed here and there in a truly dreadful fate. If he had died on the bridge itself, however, his spirit would still be there. But the alley spirit was hardly reliable; Mrs Bairstowe was surely far more likely to know what had happened to her husband's brother.

What struck me particularly was the way Mrs Bairstowe had leapt in so quickly to explain the matter, the way her glance had suggested Holloway had said too much. Was there something odd about the death of Bairstowe's brother that she did not wish me to know? And could that something throw any light on the threats against William?

I was in the Iron Market by this time, looking for one of the taverns that butchers frequent. As I passed a narrow chare, a girl burst from it into my path.

I smelt her before I saw her for she stank of fish. A girl of perhaps twenty, in a raging fury. She gripped an old shawl around a dress that was ragged at the hem; the hands that held the shawl were reddened and swollen. She glared at me from behind heavy brows and dark tangled hair.

"You're Patterson." She was a local girl, clearly, from her accent, born and bred along the Tyne.

I knew at once who she must be. "You're Tom Eade's girl."

"We were betrothed," she said fiercely.

I took care to think over my reply. I had no wish to get scratched for my pains, and she looked capable of it. A couple of colliers, drunk already despite the early hour and the holy day, sneered at us as they reeled past. We stood in the chill shade and I was shivering but she seemed too angry to care.

"Some say he was courting the Bairstowes' maid."

"They're fools," she spat.

"Then what was Tom doing in the Bairstowes's yard?"

She hesitated. There was clearly something she didn't want to tell me. That piqued my curiosity and suggested a solution of the mystery to me. Strolger had described Eade's writing as neat but well-formed. Well, there is nothing so easy for a good writer to imitate a childish scrawl; Eade could have written the threatening notes to William Bairstowe, left them under his door and courted the maid on the sly to gain access to the house. But why?

"Tom didn't like William Bairstowe?"

The girl laughed harshly. "Who does?" She flung her tangled hair back from her face. "To the devil with William Bairstowe! I want the ones who killed Tom."

"The wind killed him."

She looked me up and down contemptuously. "You're no better than the rest of them!"

"I need facts," I said irritably. "Why should anyone want to kill Eade?"

She stared at me for a long time, biting her lip. But she had already taken the decision to trust me or she would not have approached me.

"We were going to be married," she said. "We were going to set up a stall selling gruel. We were saving for it. And once we'd got that, we'd have saved every penny for a coffee house. We were going to make our mark in the world." She was as tightly coiled as a jack-in-the-box, as tight and as powerless.

I was reminded of Tom's alleged miserliness; had it merely been prudence after all? Saving for his own future, and for his lover's? But why should that cause his death?

"Find them," she said, fiercely.

And she whisked herself back into the chare and was gone.

I went on, mulling over the small amount of information the fisher girl had given me and cursing her for not being more informative. The Bairstowes' maid had believed Tom Eade was courting her, but the fisher girl had denied that. So what had Eade been doing? Had he merely been philandering? Perhaps. The fisher girl seemed to imply that money had been involved. How? One thing was for certain; I was becoming increasingly sure Eade had not died accidentally.

I had reached the end of the Iron Market when a spirit stopped me. It clung, a dim sheen, on a lantern above a house door. There was a rough edge to the spirit's voice that suggested the living man had been from Devon or those parts. A seaman, undoubtedly.

"You Charlie Patterson?" he said.

"*Charles* Patterson."

"Aye, that's the one. Yer wanted."

"How flattering," I said.

"The gent in the shop."

"John Holloway?"

"The gent that sells leather."

Where the devil was the spirit? He had gone from the lamp. He startled me by laughing close by, in a deep shadow cast by an outjutting stone. I was forced to remind myself of the advisability of keeping on the good side of spirits; they can spread a discreditable rumour from one end of the town to the other in the time it takes a living man to walk two or three steps.

"Tell Mr Holloway," I said with extreme politeness, "that I will wait on him tonight."

"It'll be too late. He says it'll happen this afternoon, during Evensong."

I was unsure the exact time they said the late service began at All Hallows but it could not be far off. An hour perhaps – it was generally in mid-afternoon.

"What will happen?"

"Just a messenger," the spirit said, with pleasurable malice. "That's me. No one tells me anything worth knowing, no more than they did in life. He said to get there at once, sir. To the shop. On the Side." And the spirit was off, leaving only a blank wall patched with sunshine.

The Side was not far from the Iron Market; if I cut through two or three alleys, I could reach Holloway's shop relatively quickly. Why in heaven's name did he want to see me? Had there been another threat? I turned into the first alley, a long narrow passage between grimy walls. No sun here – just a chill damp. Into a second alley at right angles to the first.

I became aware of a great silence.

I stopped.

I was deep in the maze of alleys, all of them the same: grimy, befouled, narrow. Doors were closed firmly against the world. Windows were broken; some were patched with paper, others open blankly to pitch-dark rooms. Empty rooms, uninhabited.

Silence.

I could hear my own breathing, uneven, too quick.

The alleys were unspirited. That was all. Nothing to be afraid of. Merely an absence of both life and death. Nothing and no one but me.

My footfalls echoed. I was walking slowly now, trailing my hand against the filthy wall. I felt slime on my fingers, snatched them back. I quickened my pace.

An unspirited street? How could a whole street be unspirited? Particularly a street like this where the poor had lived for generations? No spirits at all? My heart was beating more quickly; I forced myself to keep calm. What danger could there be in an unspirited street?

A whisper. Somewhere above me. High on a wall, under the eaves. A spirit. A spirit after all.

So why was I so scared that I suddenly started to run? The words, the words I had heard whispered. That was it. Words.

"That's him!"

And then the blow.

11

For I tell you that the end of all evil is Death.
[Revd Righteous Graham, Sermon preached on the Sandgate, Newcastle, May 1642]

The force of the blow knocked me to hands and knees. Hard cobbles came up to hit me. Pain jarred my elbows and shoulders. I tried to twist, to come to my feet. My right knee buckled.

Another blow. In the small of my back, pushing me down again. I scrabbled to crawl out of the way. A punch to the side of my head. The world exploded in pain. I gasped, tried to yell. No breath. More blows. To my back, my shoulders, my neck, my skull. I curled up, found myself against a hard wall.

And still the blows kept coming.

I had shut my eyes in protective reflex. I squeezed them open, trying to look at my assailant.

All I saw was a sparkle, a great shimmer of light.

A punch landed in my stomach, winding me. A woman's voice shrieked in excitement. And all the time, the light, the brightness of it hurting my eyes...

In God's name!

And suddenly...

Nothing.

I lay against the wall, eyes closed again, gasping for breath, aching, trying to hold my breath against pain that stabbed through my ribs. My right knee was on fire.

No footsteps. I had heard no retreating footsteps. They must all still be there, looking down at me, grinning at me, waiting for me to get my breath back, to be fit for another pummelling. I was shaking with fear and rage. All that was left to me was pride;

I lifted my head, opened my eyes and saw…

No one.

No living man, at least.

I set my head back and stared at the wall an arm's breadth away, across the alley. It gleamed and shimmered and sparkled like a country river on a summer's day. Diamond-bright points of light quivered and shook; paler gleams were like visible echoes. Across the bricks of the wall, the crumbling lime mortar, the rotten window frames, the fragmented glass. Across the cobbles to within an inch of my feet.

Spirits.

Spirits had beaten me?

"He's scared," said a female spirit mockingly.

"Afraid of a few dead men," said a man, in malicious pleasure.

"Anyone would think we could hurt him."

They all laughed, laughed and shimmered and taunted, and skimmed up and down the wall like a river on fire. I took a breath – a stinking charnel breath. My voice shook as I tried to speak; I caught and steadied it. "Having fun?"

There was a silence. A man said: "Dinna tempt us." He had been a ruffian in life by the sound of him. "We might have a second try at ye."

A howl of laughter.

"If you'd told me you didn't like strangers," I said, with savage fear and anger, "I'd have gone the long way round." I was damned if I'd humour this rabble. Spirits attacking the living? Mothers keep naughty children in bed at night with frightening stories (*there's an old old spirit that eats children*) but no one past the age of breeching believes such tales. In God's name, how had they done it!

"Tell us you're sorry, dear," the woman said. "We might spare ye yet."

I swore at them. "Why did you attack me?"

They roared, a cackling of laughter like the burning of dry hay. It made my head ache. And there was that dreadful stench, like hair singed by fire.

"Why not?" said a man.

I remembered the whisper I'd heard, just before the first blow. "That's him." They'd been waiting for me. For *me*. Why? And how the devil could they know I was coming that way?

The spirit in the Iron Market had been involved, I realised, the one who told me John Holloway waited to see me. I'd wager Holloway had sent no such message. It had been a trap. From the Iron Market, I was almost certain to come this way to get to the Side. And if I didn't? Well, nothing was lost. They could try again later. But why?

"Why attack me?" I demanded.

"Why not?" said the woman again. "Got to have our fun, ain't we? What else is to do when you're dead?"

Their laughter folded around me, ringing in my ears, aching in my knee. They were yelling at each other in strange triumph; I heard rough voices, a Scotchman or three, even an Irish voice. I gritted my teeth – I must conquer this fear.

"I know who you are," I said, interrupting them. "You were killed in the press gang riots in Queen Anne's time."

"You're clever," said one of the Scotchmen. He made the words sound like an insult. "Know how many o' us got killed that day?"

"Thirty-one, dear," said the woman. "And they blamed *us* for it." A mutter of anger from the other spirits. "If we hadn't tried to hide the menfolk from the pressmen, they said, there'd not have been a stampede and no one'd got trampled."

"Nah," said a new male voice. "We'd all have gone to sea in Her Majesty's navy instead and got ourselves killed the proper way, fighting the Frenchies or the Dutch. Much more respectable way to die."

"So, dear," said the woman. "What are we going to do with you?"

The great shine on the wall shifted. Every part of it was a single spirit, darting here and there, drifting from top to bottom of the wall and back again, the brightness of them all piercing my aching head.

"You could just go away," I said, then started to laugh. There was an edge of hysteria in the laughter but it made me feel better. They were dead, confined to this one small street; I could get up and walk away. "No," I said. "*I'll* go away."

I took hold of a rotting window frame just above my head and pulled myself to my feet. The wood splintered under my fingers and came free with a scurry of wood lice, and centipedes and cockroaches. I couldn't get myself quite upright; the pain in my ribs bent me over, my right knee barely held when I put my weight on it. Would they let me go, or would they attack me again?

"Go safely, dear," the woman said, and the laughter of the spirits followed me all the way as I limped down to the safety of the Side. I felt sore to the bones. Shaking and bruised. Still afraid. And angry, angry beyond all reason.

I must have looked drunk, reeling along the Sunday-quiet streets, muttering and cursing, holding my ribs as if I felt sick, limping like the most melodramatic of beggars. I knew I could not get all the way to my own lodging – Hugh's rooms on Westgate were much closer. I would go there.

It was a struggle; at times I could hardly breathe for the pain in my chest. The worst part of it was the last part – climbing the stairs up to Hugh's attic room. I got up the first flight, to the door of Hugh's dancing-school, then felt I could go not a step further. I yelled and it came out a croak. I yelled again. Pray God Hugh was at home.

There was movement upstairs; a woman's voice called sharply,

"Go and be drunk elsewhere. It's Sunday – do you have no shame?" The widow on the first floor. I yelled again.

This time Hugh came clattering down the stairs, swearing when he saw me. Somehow we staggered up to the attic and I collapsed on Hugh's bed under the attic eaves. He dithered here and there, threatening to call out the apothecary and listening in mounting incredulity as I told him what had happened.

"Spirits!"

"Dozens of them."

"How can spirits hurt a living man?"

I closed my eyes, trying to remember. The buffeting, the rushes of air, the loud noises close to my ears. "Some disturbance of the air, perhaps? Some vibration? I caused some of the damage myself. My knee cracked against the cobbles when I fell, for instance. Hugh, never mind *how* they did it! *Why* did they do it?"

He perched on the edge of his table. He was only half-dressed, shirt loose and open, stockinged feet, hair awry. I guessed I had surprised him dozing.

"Bairstowe," he said. "He set them on you."

"Why?"

He frowned. "He is trying to make you think the matter more dangerous than it is." He warmed to his theme, started to pace about the room. "He sees you think he did the damage to the workshop himself so he persuades the spirits to attack you. You will think you are attacked because you know something you shouldn't and will therefore insist on continuing to investigate the matter."

"It's more likely to frighten me off," I said tartly, pushing myself up against the wall. "I've never heard anything more preposterous."

"Very well," Hugh said, glowering at me. "Then it was Mrs Bairstowe – *she* was trying to frighten you off."

"Why?"

"She sent the notes."

"I don't believe there were any notes."

"Then she doesn't want you to investigate because she knows there is nothing to investigate. She doesn't want her husband to make a fool of himself." He added, conscientiously: "Any more of a fool that he already is."

"She could just have told me that. She could have taken me aside politely and said, 'Mr Patterson, my husband is a little disturbed at the moment.'" No, on second thoughts, I couldn't imagine Mrs Bairstowe being polite. God in heaven, my knee hurt.

"Then it was Holloway," Hugh said, beginning to scrape the barrel.

"Why?" I asked wearily.

"Because Bairstowe hasn't paid his bills."

"That's reason to attack Bairstowe, not me! Really, Hugh, you'll be accusing the maid next!"

"She's no better than she should be," he said darkly.

"You've never seen her!"

"I know the type."

"No, I don't believe it. Hugh, she's a timid thing. I warrant you Bairstowe abuses her. He'll have had her in bed the first day she came into the house." I rubbed my aching knee, tried to get comfortable. "You don't have to convince me that half the town has a grudge against Bairstowe. Probably he owes them all money. But the attack was on me, not him."

"To stop you finding something out." Hugh started walking about again, along the middle of the room where he could stand upright under the ridge of the roof. I set my head back against the wall and longed for sleep.

"In that case," I said, "they have succeeded. I know nothing at all." And suddenly, the terror of it all nearly overwhelmed me. I was so tired – I heard my voice shake. "Hugh, I'm giving the matter up."

"Charles!" he said, horrified. "You can't! Are you going to let whoever's behind this get away with it?"

"The spirits were behind it," I said. "What am I going to do? Ask Bedwalters to clap them in prison to await the next Assizes?"

I could still hear that whisper: *That's him.* "Hugh," I said. "My mind's made up. I am going to go to sleep on your bed and when I wake up tomorrow, I am going to tell Bairstowe he can sort out his own problems."

"Coward," Hugh said scornfully.

I felt better already, for having made the decision. "Swords at dawn," I said sleepily, stretching out on the mattress. "Call out your seconds. I let no man call me – "

I woke in the early hours of the morning, when twilight was filtering through the thin curtains across Hugh's window. Hugh, beside me, was snoring. For a moment, I could not remember what had happened, then it all came flooding back. The spirits, the great shimmering wall, the buffeting, as of a strong wind, that had felt like blows on my body. I tried to turn over and my bruised knee screamed at me.

That's him.

They had known me. They were targeting me. No one else. No casual unfortunate passer-by, no chance victim; the whole affair had been arranged to frighten *me.*

Arranged by whom?

Damn it, I would not be scared off by a gang of spirits tied to one alley of ancient, disintegrating houses. I was a living man, and as free as any man to decide his own actions. And I chose not to be intimidated by thugs and bullies, alive or dead.

I crawled out of bed, washed my face in Hugh's cold water, pissed in his chamberpot. Then I went out to find out who was behind this affair.

12

We hear that there have been disturbances latterly in the area of the Key, with low elements setting upon innocent passersby. We trust that the perpetrators of these outrages will be dealt with severely.

[AMOR PACIS, Letter to Newcastle Courant, 30 January 1736]

I limped down the Side towards John Holloway's shop in a drizzle that failed to wet my clothes and hair. The first task was clearly to check whether Holloway had indeed sent a message for me – if he had, it would suggest that the spirits had merely taken advantage of a chance encounter. But I could not believe that. "That's him," they had said. They had been expecting me.

Near the foot of the Side, I came face to face with Claudius Heron, climbing purposefully in the opposite direction. For a fashionable man, he was up early. He halted, stared at me. "What the devil have you been doing?"

I was startled by his unusually intemperate language, all the more because I knew from Hugh's mirror that I had not even one bruise to show for yesterday's encounter.

"I slipped," I said. "Injured my knee."

He said, brusquely, "Come with me."

"I have an appointment – "

But he was already striding away, his coat skirts slapping against his thighs.

I was in two minds as to whether to defy him. I had come all this way to see John Holloway and it would be a wasted journey if I did not; moreover, I had soon to struggle back up Westgate to the Assembly Rooms for the lesson I had promised Esther Jerdoun. But it would be the height of folly to offend a patron.

And it soon became apparent that Heron was heading for Nellie's coffee house; a chance to sit down appealed to me enormously. Walking had tired me more than I cared to admit.

In the coffee house, we sat in a corner, Heron with his back to the wall and me stretching out my leg to ease the pain in my knee. I sipped at coffee and discovered a headache I didn't know I had; the coffee eased it. The house was unusually quiet; occupied only by a few gentlemen lounging in comfortable chairs, rustling their newspapers or turning the pages of the latest pamphlet.

I told Heron everything that had happened since I had last seen him; he sat very still, his fair hair ruffled slightly by the back of his chair. Telling the story calmed me, although I was only too well aware how incredible it sounded. Something of my anger came through in my voice, I fancy, for he looked very closely at me.

"You are not leaving the matter there, I take it?"

"Not in the least. There is no one else to deal with it. I can hardly ask the constable to raise the hue and cry against spirits!"

He permitted himself a grim smile. "I agree. It is difficult – one so rarely hears of such things."

I was startled. "It has happened before?"

"Once, to my knowledge. Four or five years ago."

"I don't recall it – I must have been in London at the time."

He stretched. "There was an incident in one of the chares down by the Key. Colvin's Chare, I believe. A band of spirits set on an elderly woman. One of them had a grudge against her – he thought she had cheated him of something in life. I forget the details." He looked at me soberly. "The woman died, Patterson. You were lucky."

"Unpleasant though the attack on me was," I mused, "they left no injuries – my knee was hurt when I fell. How can spirits kill?"

"The woman died of fright." Heron frowned. "Lawyer Armstrong was coroner – he would be better able to tell you than I. She was frail, and in these cases the body can simply give out. There were witnesses. They said she gasped, clutched at her chest and fell over." His lip curled. "They did not seem to feel it incumbent upon them to help her. Some evidently even joined in the attack."

I took little notice of these last comments. Heron's sour view of mankind leads him to believe the worst of everyone.

"What was the verdict of the jury?"

"Murder," Heron said. "What else?"

It must have been a unique verdict, I reflected: murder by the dead. But, in effect, the woman's age had killed her; a robust man in the prime of life would not have been in danger.

"The spirits who attacked me merely wanted to frighten," I said with conviction. "Not to kill. It might simply have been for mischief's sake but I think not. I think it is something to do with this affair of Bairstowe's."

Heron considered, his eyes unnervingly steady on my face. "You believe the man threatening Bairstowe set the spirits on you to frighten you off?"

That's him, they had said.

"The fellow – whoever he is – would have done better to leave well alone," I said. I drained my coffee and struggled to drag myself up from a chair that was far too comfortable. "Forgive me, I must go. I have an appointment on Westgate."

Heron also rose. "I say what I said to you before. Give this up."

"It's worth thirty guineas, sir," I reminded him.

"But not your life."

I hesitated. "I thank you for your advice, sir – "

"But you do not intend to take any notice of it." Heron put out a hand to steady me as my knee buckled under my weight. "Go home and rest."

"I have a lesson at the Assembly Rooms. With Mrs Jerdoun."

His face hardened; I said cautiously, "You are not on good

terms, I think."

We walked to the door. "She is a sensible enough woman," Heron said, hesitating on the doorstep. He made the words sound like condemnation rather than praise. Outside, the drizzle was still darkening the cobbles. "She was at Jenison's dinner on Saturday, castigating him for refusing you a benefit concert."

"I had heard she mentioned the matter," I said diplomatically.

Heron stared across at the bedraggled fish stalls. "As a matter of fact, I agreed with what she said. But she was wasting her breath. There is no arguing with Jenison once he has made up his mind. He put her down as a hysterical woman with no comprehension of the practicalities of the matter. I mean, of course, from the economic point of view."

"My experience," I said, rather too sharply, "is that 'hysterical' is the least appropriate word to apply to Mrs Jerdoun."

"But you must agree that it is not a woman's place to argue with a gentleman's assessment of his business affairs."

I turned for the Side; Heron walked with me in silence. As we passed Holloway's shop, the chatter of voices drifted out of the open door and I glanced in to see Richard Softly proffering advice on the rival merits of two walking canes.

I glanced at Heron. "Do you know John Holloway, sir?"

"I have spoken to him once or twice."

"And your opinion of him?"

He was staring at a carriage driven by a careless and laughing young man; the carriage was hurtling far too quickly down the hill. "Do you wish for an honest assessment, or a polite one?"

"An honest one."

"I ask," he said dryly, "Because it is my experience that most people do not like honesty." A stray lock of his fair hair fell across his brow. "Very well, you may have an honest assessment of John Holloway. He is a posturing incompetent whose shop lads keep him solvent. That is to say, the shoplads know exactly how much of his takings to pocket. A little more and Holloway would go bankrupt; a little less and it would not be worth their while."

I had forgotten how jaundiced a view of the world Heron has. He was studying my face.

"You disagree with me?"

I said carefully, "Not everyone is corrupt."

He shrugged. "There are a few exceptions, I daresay." He bowed to a lady of his acquaintance, walking past us. "But I would find it difficult to name more than one."

He returned his gaze to me. "I know Holloway is Bairstowe's brother-in-law, Patterson. I advise you again – give up the matter."

Of course, having struggled up Westgate Road, and stumbled into the Assembly Rooms, I had to face scrutiny again, not once but twice. The Steward, who paused at the door of his rooms to stare, was satisfied with my tale of slipping, but Esther Jerdoun was not. She stood at the top of the first flight of stairs watching as I limped from step to step, heard my story of a fall, and said coolly: "I am no fool, Mr Patterson. Give me a round tale, if you please."

Honesty seemed to be the fashion today.

We sat on the chairs that lined the walls of the small Assembly Room, while Mrs Jerdoun's maid at the other side of the room bent her head over her needlework. I told the tale yet again. Mrs Jerdoun heard me out in as great a silence as Claudius Heron, steadfastly looking at my face the whole while. I finished rather lamely, trying to reassure her that it had been a casual assault occasioned by my own foolishness in venturing into dangerous alleys.

What did I see in her eyes? Fear? Anger?

"Well," she said at last, in a calm voice. "You can at least avoid a repetition of the attack. Keep away from that alley."

"I intend to," I said dryly.

"Is it of any use to advise you to let the matter drop?"

"Claudius Heron has already tried," I said. "I cannot and, if I could, I would not." Perhaps it was pride speaking – no man likes to be humiliated. But it was anger too, that some unknown man thought he could do what he chose to obtain his own ends.

"Men are so obstinate!" Mrs Jerdoun said with an exasperated sigh. "Very well, I will say nothing more. But if you are in need of assistance, Mr Patterson, you have only to ask for it."

There was one matter on which I thought she might be able to help. "Do you know Mr John Holloway, madam?"

She shook her head. "I know of him, certainly, but we have never had dealings."

It had been worth a try. I limped across to the harpsichord, opened it for her and checked the tuning.

Mrs Jerdoun had brought some music, a piece by Domenico Scarlatti, and played through it with much skill. She was unexpectedly good in the lighter pieces, displaying a mischievous sense of humour that surprised and delighted me. And in sitting close to her, I lost for a short while the anger I had felt. I smelt her perfume, saw pale strands of hair curling on her smooth neck, watched her supple fingers on the keys. I found myself a little giddy and was forced to make a severe effort to be my usual detached self, and to listen for, and correct, her faults.

An hour passed all too quickly. Mrs Jerdoun rose, saying that she must not keep me from my other pupils. I refrained from telling her that I had no other pupil that day, thanked her and asked her if she wished to have her lesson at the same time next week. She paused in the act of folding up the music.

"Next week, Mr Patterson? I'm afraid you have mistaken me."

My heart sank. She had decided not to repeat the lesson.

"I wish for a lesson every day."

Every day?

"There is no profit in doing something half-heartedly, do you not agree?"

"I – you – no, no profit at all."

"And there is no point in my practising, if I am merely perpetuating errors."

"No – "

"Which you could correct if you saw me on a regular basis. Is that not so?"

"Yes."

"Therefore, if your time is not otherwise entirely taken up – "

I hesitated; she raised an eyebrow.

"No, not at all. Not in the least." It crossed my mind that she might be trying to distract me from other activities. "Apart from this business with Bairstowe, of course."

Her face set in disapproval; she said: "Of course."

A little awkwardness lay between us.

"At what time then?"

"Time?"

"My lesson tomorrow." She handed the music to her maid. "Unfortunately, I am engaged all the morning with Mr Armstrong."

"The lawyer? I trust there is nothing wrong."

"Just a tangle connected with some land in Norfolk. What do you say to early afternoon? Perhaps at one o'clock?"

"I would be honoured, madam." And I bowed mistress and maid out of the room, shook off the intoxication of the lady's presence, and prepared myself for less pleasant matters.

13

This is to give Notice That a fine CHAMBER ORGAN,
containing six stops and 335 Pipes, will be raffled for by
One Hundred Gentlemen and Ladies, at 10s. 6d. each Lot.
Tickets will be sold by Mr William Bairstowe,
at his House on Silver Street, at the Cordwainers' Hall,
or of the Printer of this Paper.
[Newcastle Courant, 27 February 1736]

I went straight back to Holloway's shop, limping less than I had before, the pain in my knee now only a dull ache. Richard Softly was alone in the shop. He told me that Holloway had ridden out to talk to a farmer about some skins and was not expected back until nightfall. I left in some irritation – Softly was politely spoken and respectful, but under all the politeness was an edge of resentment that grated.

If I could not talk to Holloway, I would find William Bairstowe – I sensed he was not telling me everything he knew. And I knew where he would be – at the Cordwainers' Hall where his organ was being exhibited.

The doors from the street were open into an entrance way and the notes of a chamber organ echoed from the hall. The bell-like notes were sweet and clear, a slow progression of chords, beautifully tuned and voiced, in plangent heart-breaking dissonance. From the door of the hall itself, I saw, between tall windows, the glossy varnished case of the organ. It was smaller than the one Claudius Heron had envisaged for his gallery, perhaps twelve feet tall and five or six wide; a rectangular case displayed a graduated rank of pipes painted with swirls and curlicues.

Bairstowe was seated in front of the manuals, which appeared to be two in number. I saw his head turn – he had clearly sensed someone at the door though I doubted he could see who it was. He nodded to a small boy who pumped the bellows' handle; his hands plunged down and the plangent chords began again. The same tune as before. Bairstowe knew how to make an organ but, like most builders, he didn't know how to play one; he merely had one tune off by heart to show the instrument to its greatest advantage.

I stayed behind him, where he could not see me, and glanced around at the ornamental splendour of the hall, the painted coats of arms and gilded roof beams. Two straight-backed middle-aged ladies, both in pale yellow, were sitting on chairs set against one wall. A notice on the door advertised the terms of sale for the organ; Bairstowe had priced the tickets at half a guinea each and notified the public he would wait until he had sold one hundred tickets before making the draw. A chamber organ for half a guinea was a good bargain for the lucky winner, but fifty guineas was setting the value of the organ low. I've seen organs not much bigger valued at twice the price.

I particularly liked the rider on the advertisement. "Any Lady or Gentleman who wishes to try the Organ may do so when the Hall is open." And then, in slightly larger letters below: "The Organist of All Hallows excepted."

Solomon Strolger had probably had a good laugh over that.

A gentleman walked into the hall, stood legs apart to contemplate the organ; when Bairstowe finished the tune, the visitor strolled forward to engage him in conversation about the instrument. I cursed, and dawdled about while he asked Bairstowe to play once more. Bairstowe began the same tune again.

The gentleman stopped him and asked for something else. As Bairstowe hesitated, I leapt forward. "Perhaps you would allow me, sir?"

He conceded his place on the stool with alacrity.

Despite my mood, I enjoyed myself. It was a long time since I had played an organ and I seized the opportunity to make a great deal of noise. Although it was small, the organ was capable of a surprisingly full blast. The small boy pumped the bellows enthusiastically and I played several of Signor Scarlatti's pieces then improvised a voluntary of my own; somewhat mischievously, given Bairstowe's hatred of Strolger, I put in a reference or two to the *Highland Laddie*.

The gentleman laughed and bought five tickets. Bairstowe saw him out with many begrudgingly expressed thanks; just before they reached the door, I saw Solomon Strolger, grinning, whisk himself away into the street.

Bairstowe came back swaggering, slipping coins into his pocket.

"You owe me some of that," I said, turning on the organ stool to face him. The ladies in yellow sat obstinately on – perhaps they thought it was still raining. "It was my showing off your organ that persuaded him to buy so many tickets."

"To the devil with that," he said. "You put yourself forward. I didn't ask you."

He was in a remarkably bad temper, even for him. "Creditors been round?" I murmured.

"That damned Heron."

"Claudius Heron's been here?"

"No more than half an hour ago. These gentlemen – " he sneered over the word – "always want you to leap to it and do as they bid, here and now."

"He has waited a long time for his organ."

"He's got the damned materials," Bairstowe snarled. "He can sell them, can't he?"

That was near enough an admission that Bairstowe would never get back to the project. I glanced at the bellows' boy but he was curled up on his chair, breaking apart a chunk of bread. "Did you tell him that?"

"Fellows like that never want to listen to anyone else. It's all *listen to me* and *do as I tell you.*"

"He wants the organ."

"Tried to sell him this one. Wouldn't buy even one ticket!"

I should imagine that as far as Heron was concerned, that had been adding insult to injury. Bairstowe was thrusting tickets at me. "Half a guinea. You've played the damn thing. Isn't it worth half a guinea?"

"I thought my services were worth *thirty* guineas."

Bairstowe's lip curled. "Thirty guineas? I wouldn't give you a shilling for what you've come up with so far."

"Oh, I've come up with a few conclusions. Like the fact that the notes never existed. Like the fact you wrecked your own workshop."

His face purpled to such an extent that I feared he might have an apoplexy. He started yelling, startling the two women who got up hurriedly and went out.

"But I do believe that you genuinely think yourself under threat," I said.

He fell abruptly silent.

"You must have some idea who might wish to threaten you."

He set his mouth in an obstinate line. I sighed.

"What's the point in hiring me to find out the truth and then not telling me what you know?"

He struggled with that, and mumbled.

"What?" I said, pretending to be deaf.

"Bloody spirits!" he roared.

I got the story out of him, eventually. He had been on the Key one night, 'visiting a friend' – apparently a euphemism for using the services of a brothel. He had just parted from the 'friend' when he felt an urgent need to piss. He'd ventured into one of the chares to do this more discreetly, and had been attacked by spirits.

We wasted some time arguing over why Bairstowe had so foolishly risked entering one of the chares off the Keyside. These are notorious resorts even in the daytime and at night they are not places respectable men would willingly venture. Why not simply piss against a wall, I wanted to know; there would be no respectable women to shock on the Key gone midnight.

Bairstowe hummed and hawed, and red-faced, admitted to a malady common to older men, the inability to piss at all except after long effort. He had not wanted anyone to see how long he stood there before achieving a result.

The spirits had at least let him finish before attacking him but they hadn't let him lace himself up again; his breeches had descended to his ankles and, all in all, he had felt not only abused and beaten but an old fool too. No wonder he hadn't wanted to tell me.

"But what makes you think it was not merely an opportunistic attack? How could they anticipate you would be there?"

"I heard 'em," he snarled. "One of them said 'He's the one.'"

That brought me up short, so similar was it to my own experience. The attack on myself *must* be connected to Bairstowe's affairs.

"And the notes?"

The notes, Bairstowe asserted obstinately, were genuine. He had received them, scoffed at them and burnt them. They'd come for the most part before the attack by the spirits and he'd thought them tomfoolery. He did admit, however, that he hadn't shown them to his wife, though he still thought he had mentioned them to her.

"And the workshop?"

"I did not touch it," he insisted, and continued to insist despite my disbelief. "I had nothing to do with the boy's death either. Don't you see, it was the spirits – if they can pummel me, they can heave over a piece of wood!"

"But there are no spirits in your yard," I protested. "Except the girl in the alley. And she's so old, she's not even sure where she is."

"Don't talk rubbish," he scoffed. "The yard's full of spirits. I hear 'em all the time – they're conspiring against me."

He sounded oddly convincing; I concluded he believed what he said.

"But *why* should they conspire against you?" I pressed.

"Damn it, I'm paying you to find that out!"

That was true enough.

14

Died. – Wednesday, suddenly on the Tine Bridge,
Mr Edward Bairstowe in the 52d year of his age.
[Newcastle Courant, 4 December 1731]

I left Bairstowe to a brace of interested gentlemen and went back out into the street. A chill drizzle fell on my face. Bairstowe's accusations against the spirits in the matter of Tom Eade's death were unbelievable – no spirit could have had a hand in it, because none lingered in the yard. It had to be either an accident, or the work of man.

Yet I knew, more than anyone else could, that the spirits were involved in this business somehow. I needed to talk to a spirit, one that might be able to enquire for me and find out why the spirits had attacked William. But which one? I was beginning to feel I could trust none of them.

I started down towards the Key, hoping the drizzle that spotted my coat would not harden to driving rain. As I reached the end of Silver Street, I saw the figure of a woman climbing Pilgrim Street towards me. The fisher girl.

She had seen me – she halted, staring with open hostility. Her hair was limp and bedraggled in the rain; her clothes, though much darned and patched, were clearly her Sunday best.

She folded her arms across her chest, marched up to me, nodded brusquely as if she was a great lady passing an acquaintance who was not quite respectable, then turned into Silver Street and walked on.

I lengthened my stride and caught up with her. At our last meeting she had been eager for help; now she plainly wanted to be rid of me. What had happened to change her mind?

"Good day," I said.

"Forgive me, sir," she said, not sounding in the least apologetic. "I have urgent business."

"So have I."

She hesitated as if she was about to confront me, then strode past the alley to the organ manufactory, and went on towards All Hallows Church. I paused by the entrance to the alley.

"You have missed your object."

She called back: "I am bound for the church."

I did not move. "I am going to question Tom Eade's spirit."

She stopped, close by the gate of All Hallows, then swung round and came back to me. Her hair and shoulders were bedewed by the rain, her face was twisted into something akin to a snarl. Perhaps that was understandable. Perhaps she wished to speak to her betrothed alone; at the first time since death, there is a grief that is difficult to face in the presence of others. I remember the case of my own dear mother...

The girl came back to me silently, went past me silently, into the alley. As I followed her, I caught a shimmer of light on the wall high above and shied away before I recalled it was only the girl's spirit. She called down to me. "Do you know Master Bairstowe, sir? Master Thomas Bairstowe? The carpenter?" We went on into the yard.

The house and workshop were closed up, the place deserted. For a moment, it felt as if it had never been occupied. Piles of broken wood and crushed pipes still lay about the yard; the two lengths of seasoned timber were still propped against the wall. I saw the girl shiver as she looked at them.

"Tom!" she called out. "Tom, are you there? Mr Patterson and me want to talk."

Silence.

"See," she said. "He's not here yet."

I shook my head. "It's nigh on four days since he died. His

spirit will have disembodied by now."

"We'll come back later," she said, turning for the alley. "Tomorrow, maybe. He'll be here then."

"He must be here now," I said, and raised my voice. "Tom Eade!"

No one replied. I knew I could not be wrong; no spirit took so long to disembody, yet there was no sound, no shimmer of light –

Was that a murmur? No, I must have been mistaken.

I raised my voice. "Tom," I called again. "I want to know who killed you."

"No one killed him," the girl snapped. She stared at me, defiantly contradicting everything she had said before.

"Then what happened?" I demanded.

"Wood fell on him."

"When he came to court the Bairstowes' maid?" I gingerly touched one of the wet baulks of timber. It slid along the wall and I stepped back quickly. Bairstowe was right in at least one respect; this yard was not a pleasant place. It was unsettling – gloomy and chill.

And I stopped, hardly daring to acknowledge the thought that had just come into my mind…

The girl was frowning at me. I gathered my wits. "I'm not surprised you want to speak to him alone. He was up to no good, wasn't he?"

A new voice high above me made me start. "That's between her and me," it said.

I looked up into the cold drizzle.

And saw overhead the night sky. I did not stand in the manufactory but in a graveyard under a speckled field of stars and the rich curve of the Milky Way. Tombstones stretched white on either side of me, casting impenetrable shadows across black grass…

Then the world righted itself and I was in the yard again,

in gloomy March daylight, looking high on the wall of the workshop at the faint shimmer of a new spirit and shivering in the residue of a great chill.

The girl had apparently not noticed anything; she was craning to look up at the eaves of the workshop.

"You've got explaining to do, Tom Eade," she snapped. "Like what did you see in that trollop?"

"Good manners, maybe," the spirit said.

"You weren't after good manners," she said. "You were after bad behaviour."

And so it went on, the insults going backwards and forwards. All so nicely done, I began to suspect they had spoken before. I was shaken, but this was no time to be distracted; I had questions to ask Tom Eade. I cut in on the girl. "How did you die, Tom?"

The spirit gave a sharp gasp, almost a cry of pain. The girl said hurriedly: "Tom, Tom – it's all right, love. Don't you worry, I'm still here."

My own shock had made me too outspoken, too brutal. The girl turned a look of such distress on me that I knew I was out of place and could not in all decency stay. I took the girl's arm, said: "Get the truth out of him and let me know it. You need help. You can trust me – "

She broke away from me, laughing bitterly. "Trust anyone of your kind? What d'you care about the likes of us?"

She fell silent, and stayed so until I had walked from the alley. I lingered in the hope of hearing their conversation but all I heard was the soft singing of the spirit in the alley.

I was for a short while unaware of what was going on around me. I walked through drizzle-dampened streets, oblivious of passers by. Shaken by events I had hoped never to experience again. Once more, as before Christmas, I had 'stepped through' from our own world to another. It had been a brief occurrence this time and without ill effects, but I was disturbed that it had happened at all. I had thought these worlds touched only in the region of Caroline Square – now it transpired that there were other places in the town where stepping through was possible.

I found myself on the Keyside, staring at sailors shouting over the loading of sacks of candles. At least this experience explained one thing that had been puzzling me. William Bairstowe had sworn that there were spirits in his yard when I knew there to be none; he had talked of hearing their voices. Spirits did not exist in the other world but perhaps Bairstowe had heard the voices of the living people there and mistaken them for spirits.

Turning along the Key, I made for the Tyne Bridge. Perhaps the existence of a link between the worlds in Bairstowe's yard also explained the confusion of the spirit in the alley. She had called Bairstowe a carpenter. Perhaps she too had seen the opening up of the other world and glimpsed there another William – not an organ-builder but a carpenter? Could she be less confused than I had imagined?

I put the matter aside for the time being. There was one further mystery that I might be able to clear up. Was the spirit of Edward Bairstowe, William's brother, on the bridge as the spirit in the alley said, or had he jumped into the river, as Mrs Bairstowe claimed, and was therefore lost for ever? Mrs Bairstowe had seemed anxious to avoid the subject – did Edward's fate have any connection with what was happening to William?

On the bridge, there was a busy to-ing and fro-ing amongst the shops. Pedestrians hurried against the drizzle; carts and horses clattered past, dogs and children ran underfoot. Hens pecked in every corner. Through a break in the buildings, I looked upstream into the murky drizzle that patterned the grey water. A miserable day.

I accosted a spirit gleaming on the timbering of one of the buildings.

"Edward Bairstowe?" she said scornfully. "A newcomer. He died a mere five years ago. How long do you think I've been here?"

I ventured on flattery. "Longer than anyone else here, I warrant."

"Forty years," she said. "Forty!"

"Heavens! I'd never have known." I heard a murmur, like a self-satisfied purr. "You must see everything that happens here."

"Everything," she said firmly.

"I'm told this fellow Bairstowe killed himself – jumped off the bridge. But in that case, wouldn't his spirit be in the river?"

"They lose courage, you know."

"He couldn't bring himself to jump? So what did happen?"

"Cut his throat," she confided, with glee. "Went all over the apron of his wife – terrible to wash out you know, blood."

"He had a knife, then?"

"A carving knife," she said. "A huge thing. But you don't want to hear about him. My own death – "

I extricated myself with difficulty.

I found Edward Bairstowe near the blue stones at the centre of the bridge though I had to look long and hard until I spotted a small patch of shine on a stone at the edge of the road, directly under the parapet. So he was on the bridge, not under it. And he was clearly a suicide – tied to one spot, unable to move even within the confines of the place where he died as spirits generally do; all he could do was move the length of that one cobble.

"Edward Bairstowe?"

A sudden convulsive movement in the stain. "Yes?" the spirit said eagerly. "Do you want to talk to me? Heavens, sir, do you know how long it has been since I talked to anyone? My dear sir, pray do not stand up there. Sit down here, next to me."

Reluctantly I squatted, with the parapet against my back; the cobbles were damp with rain. A cart trundled past. A thin cat hesitated a yard or two away, lifting its head to stare at me.

"You haven't introduced yourself, sir."

"Charles Patterson. I am a musician in this town. I have been asked, Mr Bairstowe, to assist your brother in a – a personal matter."

The spirit said sharply: "William?" The cat stretched to sniff at my arm.

"He believes himself to be in danger – he has received threats. I am looking for the culprit."

Another pause. "And you think I may have information? I have been five years dead, you know." His tone changed abruptly. "Will you please run that cat off!"

The cat was sniffing at the stone; cats are curious about spirits, unlike dogs, who give them a wide berth. I pushed gently at the cat, which took the gesture as an invitation to rub itself against my knee.

"I wondered if you knew of anyone who might have a grudge against your brother."

"Mr Patterson," the spirit said, apparently amused. "My brother's greatest talent is for rudeness. Dozens of people dislike him heartily!"

"Anyone in particular?"

"I have no recent knowledge." The spirit sighed hugely. "Alas, no one from the household comes near me."

I hate people who invite sympathy. I drew back, out of the way of a boy pushing a handcart. The cat yawned. "They cannot accept the manner of your dying, sir?"

The spirit sighed. "When I was alive my brother made my life a misery. It can be said that he drove me to my death. No, pray do not interrupt. I trust, sir, that whatever the wrongs done to me, I do as the Bible bids me and forgive my enemies."

His complacent tone set my teeth on edge.

"Tell me what happened," I said.

15

Mr KEREGAN, Manager of the Theatre, begs Leave of the Ladies and Gentlemen of Newcastle to announce a performance of The Apprentice, Or, The Temptations of Gambling.
[Newcastle Courant, 5 June 1731]

A cart rumbled past in the drizzle. I eased my back against the parapet; the old stone crumbled beneath my fingers. The cat eyed a cluster of hens then curled up next to my feet and showed every sign of intending to sleep.

"I was the oldest child," Edward Bairstowe's spirit said, rather pompously. "Then there was a sister but she didn't survive a year. Then came William. Then Thomas. After that, my mother gave birth year after year, and all the babies died." (This sounded all too like my own dear mother's experience.) "Of course, one year she died in childbirth. I was ten years old at the time and William was eight. My father never recovered from the loss – he dedicated himself to his organ-building and was often away from home visiting this church or that, repairing organs or installing new. We were brought up by my aunt, his sister. A good woman, but a maiden lady with no idea how to treat children. I was of an age to fend for myself, but William of course was spoiled. The baby of the family."

I shifted restlessly. This sounded like a recital that had been given several times before. The spirit laughed. "Now, now, Mr Patterson, don't tell me you are not interested in ancient history. It has relevance, I promise you."

It was not the ancientness I objected to, but the smooth sentimentality. I had a premonition that it was going to turn out to be one of those educational tales for children on the evils of indiscipline in youth. And that Edward Bairstowe in life had been one of those men who are always angling for sympathy, probably as a prelude to asking for money.

"William envied me from his earliest years," the spirit continued grandiosely. "I was my father's support, introduced to the business early and relied upon. I had no musical genius, but I had an excellent head for figures and managed my father's accounts. William, on the contrary, had the musical genius and helped with the manufacture of the organs." The spirit sighed. "But, alas, he had one fatal flaw."

Yes, indeed it was to be an educational tale.

"He dislikes effort," the spirit said. "He has always enjoyed spending money but working to get it – no, he does not like that at all. He saw me sitting in the house every day, with papers in front of me – he didn't call that work, not when he had to hammer and saw and roll sheets of lead. He saw me wine and dine elegant gentlemen, and thought I was taking my leisure when I was actually canvassing for business or settling a contract. He was envious, Mr Patterson. He thought he did the work and I reaped the benefit."

I suspected William Bairstowe might have had some justification for this point of view. "And when your father died?" A flock of sheep pattered on to the bridge from the Gateshead end, driven by one man and a brace of dogs. Headed for Butcher Bank, no doubt. The cat watched them pass.

"Father left the business to us jointly. He had been so bound up in his own concerns that he did not see how ill at ease we were with each other. The twenty years after that event, Mr Patterson, were the most troublesome of my life. William was so unreasonable. He always wanted the best materials even when I told him they were too expensive. He simply wouldn't make the slightest effort to understand! And then he married that harpy."

"Mary Holloway, as was?"

"Scheming bitch," the spirit said. "Only one thing on her mind. Money." It crowed with triumph. "Now there's the culprit for you!"

"You think Mary Bairstowe is threatening her own husband? Why?"

"Money!" he repeated, "Money, money, money! There are no children, sir, and no male relatives. She will inherit all!"

"But there isn't any money," I pointed out. "Your brother is in debt to half the town."

The spirit scoffed. "He'll have money hidden away. Or she'll have some under a floorboard. Or she's passed it on to that brother of hers."

He was accusing everyone at random, I realised, no doubt looking to pay back a few old scores.

"Wants to go off to London," he said snidely. "To get herself fancy clothes and set herself up in luxury. To buy a rich husband."

I had a ludicrous vision of plain, middle-aged, sharp-tongued Mary Bairstowe tricked out in satins and laces and ogling naïve young gentlemen with big fortunes.

"And of course there were the children that never came. Well, what can you expect? She must have been nigh on forty when they married." The spirit cackled with laughter. "No one else would have her! That brother of hers couldn't get her off his hands."

"She was living with Holloway before her marriage?"

"Ran away from home to do it. Walked out on her invalid old mother."

We were back to the sentimental tale; I felt like dashing home for my fiddle and playing a plaintive tune to accompany the story. But the spirit was in full flow, the stain on the stone shifting excitedly.

"William grew more preposterous by the day. If I failed to

appear at the manufactory every day, I was shirking my responsibilities. Even if I was out taking an order for an organ! If I so much as stopped to watch a thimble-rigger, I was accused of gambling away our inheritance. If he saw me talk to a woman in the street, I was spending a fortune on whores! I confess, Mr Patterson, that I grew very low under his tirades. And I suffered my own loss – the dearest of girls whom I had hoped to marry…"

Oh Lord, this grew worse. I hurried to bring him to the point; my irritation made me more brutal than I intended. "And how did you die?"

A pause. There was a new note in his voice when he said: "You do not sound as if you believe me, Mr Patterson."

"Forgive me," I said. "I am charged to find out who is threatening your brother and that must surely have its basis in something recent."

"You asked if I knew who might be threatening him," he said, offended. "I am telling you. Allow me to continue, sir."

I stifled a sigh, and stretched out to stroke the cat. Its fur was damp with the drizzle; it lifted its head and rubbed itself lazily against my hand. "Very well."

He continued. A note of querulousness had crept into his voice which told me that time had increased, not lessened, the bitterness of old resentments. When he talked of William envying him for being given responsibilities, it was plain it was the other way about: Edward had envied William for being the spoilt darling of the maiden aunt. And that might explain William's behaviour too – children who are spoilt often grow up bad-tempered when they discover the world in general does not treat adults with the same indulgence.

The cat dozed, children played in puddles, and I half-listened to Edward Bairstowe's litany of self-justification, the insults he had suffered, his grief at the death of his dearest love, the debts he had run up. William's refusal to pay those debts. Edward's despair. I had to remind myself that all this had occurred only five years ago and that Edward had been over fifty years old at the time. He sounded like an overwrought young man of twenty or so.

"And the day you died?" I said, losing patience at last.

"The night," he said. "Gone midnight. One November, a day or two after the birthday of his Majesty. We argued. William would give me no more money."

Two carts needed to pass; I pushed myself to my feet to leave more room. One of the cartwheels came perilously close to Bairstowe's stone; I let the cart pass then hunched down again. The cat butted up close to me. It was skeleton-thin, the bones showing through the fur. I wished I had food to give it, but I might be sharing its fate in a month or two.

"He said he had given me all the money he would, when he bought me out of the business."

"William bought you out? When was that?"

"A year or two before my death. And little enough he gave me for it. He said it was hard times, that no one wanted organs any more." The spirit's voice was scornful. "When will that day ever come? Churches will always need organs. Gentlemen will always buy them for fashion's sake. But no, he wouldn't give me any money. And I told him they were after me –"

"Your creditors?"

"Yes, yes," he said. "That's right, my creditors. You know what tradesmen are like. Always after you if you delay only a day or two after the bill arrives." There was something in his voice that suggested he was not being entirely frank with me. "Would William listen? Would that wife of his take any heed? Not a bit of it. So I told them. I couldn't bear it any longer, I said. I was going to kill myself."

They probably thought 'good riddance', I mused.

"And off I came here to do it!"

"To jump into the river?"

"And they came after me – "

I scratched the cat. "Why did they try to stop you, if they disliked you so much?"

"The disgrace of it," he said sharply. "The taint of self-destruction in the family." He plainly did not like the suggestion that they might have been glad to be rid of him.

"I daresay they could have covered it up," I said. Many a similar case has been glossed over by justices and constables with a murmur of 'no point in distressing widows and children with the thought of burial in unhallowed ground'.

He surprised me by chuckling; the gleam of the spirit slid right to the edge of the cobble. "As a matter of fact, there *was* something they wanted."

"Oh yes?"

"The deed to the manufactory. The deed of sale for the land. Father bought it off the vestry of All Hallows years ago, when he first set up in business. He gave me it to look after and I had it still when he died. They didn't know where it was. They still don't know!"

I stared with distaste at the oily stain on the cobble. Edward Bairstowe was plainly the vengeful type of spirit, the type that likes to keep what little power they have over the living. I heard in his voice a spiteful pleasure at thwarting his enemies. Or those he perceived as his enemies.

"What did you do with it?"

"Buried it."

"Where?"

Another chuckle. "No, no," he said. "You don't catch me out like that, sir. Not a word. I've kept quiet all these years and I won't say anything now. But you see the problem, don't you?"

I worked through the implications. "William can't prove he

owns the land."

"The church vestry wants to extend the graveyard," the spirit said gleefully. "My brother could get good money for that land. He could give up the business and live in idleness the rest of his life. If he could prove the land is his."

I sat, stroking the cat absent-mindedly. The drizzle had eased almost to nothing. Now I was embroiled in a hunt for buried treasure! Preposterous. Was this how William intended to pay me? But why had he not mentioned the deed?

I begged the spirit to go on with his story, since it would plainly put him in a good mood to tell it. They had come to the bridge, he said, all three of them. He climbed up on to the parapet and threatened to throw himself into the river. From the sound of it, I guessed he had been drunk. Mrs Bairstowe had advised him to make a good job of it. William Bairstowe had had more sense, had pleaded with him to reveal the hiding place of the deed. Edward had bargained for money and eventually won the day. He had climbed down from the parapet.

"But then how did you die?"

"It had been raining," he said. "Or sleeting rather. The first cold falls of winter, the ground was wet and slippery. As I climbed down off the parapet, my foot slipped."

At this late stage in the tale, he revealed that he had been carrying a knife. There had been a preliminary to the story. In the kitchen of the Bairstowes' house, Edward had seized a knife from the table and threatened to cut his throat. That had not frightened them – perhaps they knew he would not do it. So he had run out into the freezing cold of a November night, knowing that they would follow, must follow in case he meant what he had threatened. On the bridge, he had had the knife still in his hand when he had slipped and fallen.

"It was an accident," he said plaintively. "Not self-destruction – I had given that idea up entirely."

The fact that he was anchored to one stone gave the lie to that – Edward Bairstowe's tale was at the very least only half the truth. But it was plain I would get no more from him. I seized the bridge parapet to pull myself upright. The cat heaved itself to its feet and stretched luxuriously.

"You'll come back?" Edward Bairstowe said urgently.

"Why?"

"No one ever talks to me." Now he sounded like a sulky boy. Was this how he had worked on his family and friends when he was alive? The cat twined itself around my legs. I looked down at the livid stain on the cobblestone.

"I might tell you where the deed is," Bairstowe said, wheedling.

"Your brother tells me he was attacked by spirits."

"Really?" the spirit said, mockingly. "My dear sir, half of what William says is fabrication, the other half imagination. I warrant he was drunk!"

"I've no doubt of it. But he was attacked by spirits. As was I, yesterday."

Edward chuckled. "My dear Patterson, there are criminal elements, even amongst the dead."

"Yes, I know. I want you to find out who they are."

A silence, then the spirit said in a mock-humorous tone. "Me, sir?"

"I hear you had certain connections in life."

"Alas." He sighed. "I was young and foolish and didn't take too much care over my associates." I reminded myself again that he had been over fifty when he died. He added carelessly: "But I have long since lost track of them."

"Nevertheless, you could find them again, ask them a pertinent question or two."

A longer silence this time. He sounded annoyed when he spoke again. "Can you give me a good reason to help you in this, Patterson?"

"Yes. I'd have to come back to talk to you again."

A cart rattled past. The cat bounded away after an unwary hen.

"Very well," he said at last. "Though I tell you plainly, sir, a spirit should not have to barter for a little Christian charity."

I ignored this blatant attempt to put himself back in command of the situation. But there was no harm in being polite now I had achieved my object.

"Thank you." I dusted stone dust off my coat. "Just send word when you know what happened."

"All this fuss," the spirit said, snidely. "You'll learn better, sir. My brother is an out and out liar. You may believe nothing he says. Least of all any promises to pay out money!"

I thought of Tom Eade's death. Of the spirits' attack on me.

"It's gone beyond money," I said.

16

Every master has a duty to his servants, to care for them
and to educate them in the ways of a civilised Society.
And every servant owes a duty of obedience...
[Revd A. E., Letter to Newcastle Courant, 7 September 1734]

As I came off the bridge the female spirit called to me again. "Sir! Mr Patterson? I have a message for you!"

I hesitated, waited for two horsemen to pass between us. The cat came trotting up to me again; it was a remarkably unappealing animal, brownish in colour with a hint of tabby stripes.

"A message?"

The female spirit was lodging on a timber on one of the houses that clung to the edge of the bridge. "From a Mr Duncey."

I stared blankly for a moment. "Mr *Demsey*?"

"That's right, sir. He wants to meet you outside the shop."

"Which shop?"

"Your shop, sir."

"I don't have a shop."

"He said you did," she said in an offended tone. "He said it's a matter of money."

"What money?"

"You'll know that, sir."

I was silent. She plainly had no idea what Hugh had really said. Sometimes a message comes through garbled, muddled as it passes from spirit to spirit. Or perhaps, I wondered, deliberately confused?

No, I told myself, this will not do. I could not suspect every spirit of duplicity. I had never before had cause to fear any spirit. Occasionally they are tediously voluble, or irritating, but that is all. I must not allow one bad experience to prejudice me against them all. I turned away.

"It's urgent, he said," the spirit called after me. "He needs to see you straightway."

If it was that important, I told myself, Hugh could send the message again, by more reliable means.

I couldn't shake off the damned cat. It was at my heels every step of the way down the Key to the Printing Office, seizing every opportunity to rub itself against my legs or to look up at me in some kind of expectation. Perhaps I was the only person who had been kind to it.

It was otherwise totally wild. When it saw dogs it snarled them into submission; it even faced down a stray pig that was wandering along the Keyside, forced it on to the gangplank of a boat and sat placidly guarding the landward side while the sailors in the boat roared at the pig to be off. The pig struggled in the middle of the plank deciding whether to risk the wrath of the cat or the wrath of the men. In the end, it opted for the men as the lesser of two evils and stampeded on to the boat. The ensuing chase entertained an entire crowd.

I seized the opportunity to sidle away, *sans* cat, to the Printing Office.

Inside the office, with its pungent smells of ink and paper, Thomas Saint, the printer, a kindly Christian man who bears with the foibles of his fellow men more patiently than anyone else I know, had a sheaf of papers in his hands and was listening attentively to an elderly woman who wanted to tell him her life story. Fortunately the lady had to hurry off to a daughter who was lying-in and Saint gave me a courteous nod.

"How can I help you, Mr Patterson?"

"You keep back copies of the *Courant*, I think?"

"Indeed," Saint said with some pride. "Every edition. We have published since 1711, you know. Were you wanting something in particular?"

"Copies from five years ago."

Saint directed me into an office, spotlessly kept, and from thence into a tiny room made even smaller by shelves that lined the walls. The dull clatter of the printing room itself seeped through the walls.

The volumes lining the shelves were huge and leather-bound, with the year of publication embossed on the spine in gold lettering. I found the volume for 1731 and set it on the table Saint kept for that purpose. The *Courant* was printed on rag paper of the best quality; I turned the heavy pages until I reached the November editions. The layout of the paper had changed not at all over the years; advertisements still filled front and back pages, letters from London and abroad the second page. The local column was as ever on the third page.

In the second week of November, I found the tale of the old woman, with much ranting on the part of correspondents, as to the measures that ought to be taken concerning malicious spirits. One correspondent, a clergyman distinguished only by his initials, had also complained of men who had stood around laughing while the woman was battered by the spirits; he wanted those in question held for the Assizes as villains of the lowest order. The following week another note in the local column referred to the same incident, claiming that the names of the inhuman rogues who had stood callously by and even directed a kick or two of their own had been given to the constables in the town.

A glance ahead to succeeding weeks told me that nothing more appeared to have been done.

I found Edward Bairstowe's name in the edition dated 4 December 1731, in a very short entry under Deaths.

Died. – Wednesday se'nnight, suddenly on the Tine Bridge, Mr Edward Bairstowe in the 52d year of his age.

I guessed that the Bairstowes themselves must have written this brief notice. Reading through the column above the announcement, I found that Thomas Saint had published a more detailed account.

> *We hear that a certain gentleman of this town, in a sad perturbation of mind, threatened to jump from the Tine Bridge last Wednesday. He was persuaded down, but in an ensuing struggle cut his throat with a kitchen knife. His family did everything they could to assist him but he expired shortly afterwards. It is not yet possible to ask him what caused the great agitation that led to this dreadful act but it is to be hoped that this unfortunate occurrence will encourage others to inquire more deeply of those loved ones who appear uneasy in mind, and thus prevent such another awful scene.*

I went back into the Printing Office. Saint was alone, puzzling over advertisements that had been left for inclusion in the paper; he evidently could not read the handwriting.

"Do you remember the death of Edward Bairstowe, about five years back?"

He glanced up at me in surprise. "Indeed I do. I sat on the jury that viewed the body. Dreadful sight, dreadful."

"So you wrote the account in the paper from your own knowledge?"

He nodded. "It was all highly unsatisfactory," he said with unusual force.

"In what way?"

He put down his papers. "The Bairstowes were most unpleasant." He stared pensively into the air, as if into the past. "It turned out they'd known Edward was disturbed for weeks and had done nothing about it. 'Oh, he was always like that,' they said. 'He did things to be noticed. He was always threatening to kill himself.' They said they had more important things to do than worry over his tantrums."

I could hear William Bairstowe saying the words. Mrs Bairstowe would have said she was a stupid woman and couldn't think of anything to do about it. "And the event itself?"

"No witnesses but themselves. They agreed he tried to jump into the river but claimed the knife business was an accident."

Cutting one's throat by accident is a clever trick, I thought. "They wanted him buried in hallowed ground, of course."

"They didn't get their wish," Saint said tartly. "He was plainly a suicide. Though there was some debate as to who brought the knife to the bridge. William Bairstowe at first said his wife had it, that she had been using it in the kitchen and ran out with it when Edward dashed off to jump from the bridge. But she said Edward had snatched it up as he ran."

"And they ran after him."

He nodded.

"Despite knowing he was 'always like that'?"

"Apparently they believed him serious on this occasion."

"Was the spirit itself questioned?"

"Of course. But he was totally unreliable. First he claimed his brother had tried to kill him, then that Mrs Bairstowe had wanted him dead. Then he said he had done it himself 'by accident'. I never spoke with such a petulant fellow!"

The jury had decided for suicide and, given the spirit's confinement, that had to be the right verdict.

So why was I still uneasy over the matter?

The day was growing late and I was tired; my knee began to ache again. In the beginnings of a fresh drizzle, I turned for home.

And ran into Hugh, lounging against the wall outside the breeches maker's shop at the foot of the Side. He straightened with alacrity when he saw me.

"Where the devil have you been? I sent you a message an hour ago. An hour! I said it was urgent!"

I stared across the street. Directly opposite was John Holloway's establishment. "Your message was garbled. I had no notion where you were."

"I said the shop!" He was red-faced, tired and damp, but looked a hundred times better than he had when he had set out on that abortive trip to Paris.

"But not which shop."

"Who else in this business has a shop?"

"I'm here now," I said. "What's so urgent?"

Hugh embarked on a wild tale that seemed to involve half the town. He had been to Silver Street, All Hallows, the baker's on Pilgrim Street, the Flesh Market, the Fish Market and half a dozen other places as well. Eventually, I realised what he had been doing.

"You've been following the maid?" I said, incredulously.

He seized my coat. "Don't you see, Charles? She's at the heart of this business!"

"The maid!"

"I know, I know," he said, kindly. "She's a pretty little thing, you like the look of her – "

"If you're suggesting I'm being influenced by – "

"But don't you see how suspicious her behaviour is?"

"No, as a matter of fact – "

He tugged my sleeve. "She's the only witness that Bairstowe wrecked his own workshop! She's the only one that says the lad was courting her!"

I shook my head. "No, both the Bairstowes knew about Tom Eade. So did Holloway." Though it was odd, I thought in passing, that Bairstowe still insisted he had not wrecked the workshop.

"The maid told the Bairstowes the lad was courting her,"

Hugh said. "Do you know anyone who actually saw them together?"

I was reminded of Strolger's comment that the maid had initially tried to avoid Tom Eade. But Strolger had suggested the lad had eventually won her over. "I still don't understand what's so urgent, Hugh. You've been following the girl on a shopping expedition!"

"She's gone in there." He nodded at Holloway's shop and added, with heavy meaning, "An hour ago."

I looked across at the shop. Despite the late hour, two or three customers were lingering at the door and I could see Richard Softly lifting something down from a shelf.

"She's buying something."

He roared with frustration. "Upstairs, Charles! She went upstairs! She and Holloway." He jerked his head, winked, made a surreptitiously obscene gesture, smiling on an elderly woman who stared at him in passing.

I sighed. "So she's Holloway's drab. So? I hope he pays her well. I warrant the Bairstowes don't."

"They're conspiring together."

I looked at Demsey in silence for a moment. He was looking so much better, so animated, that I hesitated to discourage him. "You've heard them talking?"

"No, no," he said impatiently. "It's obvious, Charles! They're the ones plotting to kill William Bairstowe!"

"Why?"

He dug his fingers into my arm and almost shook me. "If Bairstowe dies, who inherits his property?"

"His wife. There are no children."

"And if his wife dies, who inherits from her?"

"As far as I know," I said cautiously, "Holloway."

"Exactly!"

"Hugh," I said sighing. "Holloway idolises his sister."

"He says so, does he?"

"I've seen them together." An unhealthy love in some ways, I thought, though I did not believe there was anything criminal in it. "How does Tom Eade fit in?"

"Who?"

"The dead shop lad."

"They thought he was Bairstowe, killed him by mistake."

"By all I've heard, the lad was slightly built. Bairstowe's bulky, Hugh. And if the maid is Holloway's mistress, why was she allowing Eade to pay court to her?"

I considered the matter, with some weariness I confess; it was all becoming damnably confusing. I rubbed my forehead and decided I needed more sleep. I was tempted to tell Hugh about my experiences in Bairstowe's yard but, thanks to his injuries, he had never heard the full tale of what had happened before Christmas and did not know of the existence of that other world. He would think me mad.

He was staring at me; with difficulty I brought my attention back to the present. "You think the maid and John Holloway are conspiring to kill both the Bairstowes."

"Exactly!"

"Hugh," I said, slapping him on the back. "You need sleep as much as I do. You'll see things in better proportion tomorrow."

"I'm right," he said, in obstinate annoyance. "I know I am."

I shook my head and turned to go on up the Side. And damned if the cat didn't trot out of an alley and race after me, following at my heels all the way up to my lodgings. Always just far enough away to avoid a kick.

I went to bed, disturbed only by the yowling of the cat in the street below. After a while, I heard someone shout, and throw a stone at it. Then I fell asleep and lay undreaming until I was startled awake.

I lay in the dark, staring at the unseen ceiling. A banging on the door. That was what had woken me. It came again. One of the miners in the house shouted in fury. I rolled over – my bed is under the window – and lifted the curtain. Below, in the street, craning to look up wildly at each window in turn, was John Holloway.

17

We hear that the house of Mr Gale the barber surgeon was broken into last night. The thieves were disturbed by a servant and ran off without taking anything. We trust that all householders will take steps to guard against similar occurrences.
[Newcastle Courant, 27 December 1735]

Holloway crashed into the Bairstowes' house before me with a clatter and a shout, throwing the door back against the wall. Mrs Bairstowe sat at the kitchen table, bloodstained and bedraggled – Holloway rushed to her side. He was a slight elegant tradesman of refined tastes; she was a big woman of rough habits and drab clothing, with a tongue as sharp as his was smooth. They had never looked like brother and sister to me. But there was clearly a link between them, proof that blood is indeed thick enough to endure many dissimilarities – there was genuine concern in his voice and gruff reassurance in hers.

Holloway had given me a garbled account of what he knew as we hurried through the dark, near-deserted streets. The maid had sent him a message, via the spirits, that his sister had been attacked, and he had hurried to my lodgings to enlist my help. This was plainly, he said, connected to William's affairs. No one seemed to have sent for the constable.

Mistress and maid were alone together in the light of one candle. Mrs Bairstowe sat stoically, her hands clasped on the table next to a bowl of reddened water; the maid stood behind her, eyes downcast as ever, dabbing at the back of her mistress's head with a bloody cloth. Blood had run down the back of Mrs Bairstowe's neck, following a line parallel to the braid into which her hair had been drawn for the night, and staining the neck of her nightgown.

"Well," she said. "Going to crow over this, are you?"

"Mary – " Holloway began.

"He's going to gloat," she said, with a nod at me. She winced, snapped at the maid. "Devil take you, girl, can't you do better than that?"

The girl murmured an almost inaudible apology.

"I said there was no villain out to get William and you said there was and it turns out you were right. Would you ever?" Mrs Bairstowe said sarcastically.

"But the villain has attacked you, madam," I pointed out. "Not your husband."

Holloway seized the candle upon the table, lit a stand of three upon the dresser and brought them back to better illuminate the scene.

"You should call Bedwalters, the constable," I said. Holloway and his sister exchanged glances; the maid continued to bathe her mistress's head.

"The fellow's a fool," Mrs Bairstowe said.

Bedwalters was far from a fool but I did not contradict her. And if they thought I was taken in by this affecting scene of injury, they were sadly mistaken; the girl should have finished dressing her mistress's injury long before I reached the house. This touching scene was staged – the question was: why?

But I might as well play their game; they might let something slip. "What happened?"

"I was attacked," Mrs Bairstowe said with contempt.

"Inside the house or outside?"

Between cursing the maid, slapping the girl's hands and sipping the ale her brother poured her, Mary Bairstowe gave me her tale. She had been woken in the night by a sound in the yard but had ignored it, thinking it was her husband coming in drunk.

Then she heard the noise a second time and came down to see what it was.

"Did you not look from the window first?"

"It was dark," she said, scornfully.

"No light in the yard?"

"Waste of money," she said. "Anyhow, I flung open the door, called to him to stop meddling and come in. He'd gone into the workshop, I thought, so I started out for it. And the next thing I know, someone brings an old piece of wood down on my head."

The maid lifted her head. "It's in the yard still," she said in her faintly Scotch accent.

"Quiet, girl!" her mistress snapped. "God, you'd make a saint full of wrath. Well, fool I may be but I still had the wit to grab him. And I yelled, my God, I yelled. I can tell you, it took some noise to rouse this slut!" She tugged at the maid's sleeve. "Get rid of this water."

The maid took the bowl to the door and threw the bloodied water across the yard.

"You didn't see your attacker?"

"Nay."

"Did he say anything?"

"Why should he do that?"

"Were you carrying a candle?"

"What's that to say to anything?"

"It was dark," I pointed out. "You said so yourself. If he could not see you properly, he might have imagined you to be your husband – you're much the same height."

She nodded begrudgingly, even though my words were hardly complimentary. "There was a candle in the house. On the table. But I left it there when I went to the door."

"Why not take it with you?"

"You're a fool," she said. "That's an old door, heavy – you need both your hands to pull the bolt and drag it open."

I looked round. The maid stood just inside the open door – a pool of light from the kitchen fell across the cobbled yard outside but beyond that all was darkness. Mrs Bairstowe was right about the door. But the ruder she became, the more determined I was to hold her to the point.

"Did the attacker run off?"

"Aye. I daresay."

"You didn't hear anything?"

"I was lying on the ground with my head split. Nay, I heard nothing."

"Did your maid see anything?"

"Not an ounce of sense in her head," she said.

I turned to the maid and caught an odd look in her eye just as she lowered her head. What was it? Distress?

"I saw the girl," she said in her soft voice, very flat, timid. "The fisher girl. Last night after you'd gone. She was talking to the spirit. They were arguing."

"I'm not surprised," I said dryly. Her lips twisted but she did not look at me. If she realised I was referring to her own dalliance with the lad she was not acknowledging it.

"But you didn't hear anything tonight – before your mistress shouted for help?"

She shook her head. At least she was looking at me now, carefully, from under her lowered eyelids. "I was asleep," she murmured.

"And when you heard your mistress shouting what did you do?"

"I came down."

"Aye," said her mistress. "But she stopped to put on her shoes and her robe first."

"And when you got down here?"

"I saw the mistress."

"Where was she?"

"At the door. On her hands and knees."

God, but it was hard, dragging the information out of her. "Did you see anyone else?"

"No, sir."

"Or hear anyone?"

"No, sir."

The attacker had probably run off as soon as the mistress started screaming. I looked back at Mrs Bairstowe. "I would like to search the yard."

"In the dark?" she said, scornfully.

"To begin with, yes." I looked at her steadily; she did not lower her gaze. "I'll come back when it's light enough to do the job properly but I want to check now too. There might be something that could blow away, or get carried away by a dog."

"I'll help," Holloway said eagerly, snatching up the branch of candles.

That was the last thing I wanted. "Indeed," I said, coolly. "I'd be grateful for you holding the lights."

He followed me out into the yard with a spring in his step. I stopped him just outside the kitchen door, said in a low voice: "Where's her husband?"

"Where he always is," he said. "Drinking and whoring. There's a place on the Keyside; he sometimes stays there all night."

I had expected something of the sort. The question was, did he have anyone to witness to his activities tonight? Could he have attacked his wife himself? And if so, why?

I asked Holloway to hold up the candles. The light was feeble and erratic, but it sufficed to show me the heaps of wood in the yard. One was piled on the other side of the yard near the alley, made up of ruined wood from the workshop – splintered fragments of pipes, the smashed soundboard. I glanced all around the yard but could see no trace of anything suspicious. No hint either of the graveyard I had glimpsed in that other world. No chill beyond the normal night chill. Might someone have 'stepped through' to our own world to threaten the Bairstowes? Heaven forbid that was the case!

In the flickering light of the candles, I saw a dark patch on the ground near the woodpile close by the alley; I beckoned Holloway closer. His hand was shaking and hot globules of wax sprayed on to the back of my hand. "Keep those candles still!" I bent and dabbled my fingers in the patch. Still sticky – unquestionably blood. Holloway made a choking noise.

One of the pieces of wood lay apart from the others. I left it where it was and squatted to look more closely. Yes, there was a splash of darkness on the end of it that looked like blood. Holloway gagged, but stood his ground. I shifted. and caught a glimpse of white under the debris.

"What is it?" Holloway asked.

"Just a shadow," I said, straightening. "I thought it was more blood."

We searched the rest of the yard as best we could in the darkness. Stars sparkled overhead, a waning moon gleamed. I saw nothing else of significance, nothing that the attacker might have dropped, for instance, no footprints or fragments of cloth torn from the attacker's clothes.

"You found nothing then," Mrs Bairstowe said, when we went back indoors. She had a tone of grim satisfaction.

"No," I agreed.

"I frightened him off."

"I think so, yes."

"Well," she said. "I daresay he'll be back."

I stood with my hands on the back of a chair, looking down at her. She met my gaze while Holloway fussed around her, placing his coat across her shoulders, patting her hand.

"Mrs Bairstowe," I said at last. "Why do you not leave your husband?"

That shook their composure, as I had intended it should. They stared at me, Holloway in outrage, the lady with a nod, as if to say 'what do you know of things like this?' It was the maid's reaction that interested me the most; she glanced up quickly, bit her lip, looked down again. As if I had promised her something, then disappointed her.

"Leave him?" Mrs Bairstowe said. "Abandon my duty as a wife?"

"A wife should not have to live in danger of attack because of her husband's quarrels."

"It's my duty," she said firmly. "A wife stays with her husband until death, his or hers. I swore that in the church and I stick by what I swear." Her lips curved in derision. "I am a stupid woman, Mr Patterson, but no one can say I am an undutiful wife."

I saw she meant it. I said: "Forgive me."

"Anyhow," she said, apparently deliberately spoiling her effect. "What would I do for money?"

"You know I'd look after you," Holloway said, earnestly.

"Aye," she said. "But I'm staying."

I stood up straight. "Then get yourself a vicious dog," I said, "and tether it in the yard. That'll stop this business."

She pushed herself up from the table. "Nay, I'd rather get the thing sorted here and now. And you're the one that's supposed to sort it, Mr Patterson." She glared at me in a kind of triumph. "So you'd better get on with it, hadn't you? If you want your money."

I insisted upon their sending for Bedwalters, pointing out that after this attack on Mrs Bairstowe, the death of Tom Eade took on a different aspect. They looked at each other at that; Holloway protested that Tom Eade's death had been an accident. But I stood firm, determined not to be bested by them, and they sent the maid off for Bedwalters.

When the maid went, we were left, the three of us, in the

kitchen, looking awkwardly about. Holloway started murmuring to his sister, privately, as if in confidence. I could not bear to stay with them; I went out into the yard, shutting the house door behind me.

In the darkness, I stood for a moment trying to sense the other world so close to our own. Nothing. It had been this way before Christmas; sometimes the world opened up, sometimes it did not. Others had said they could control it; I could not.

Reluctantly, I returned to more immediate matters. I scanned the walls for the faint gleam of a new spirit. Nothing. I wheedled and cajoled Eade, promised him justice if he told what had happened to him. No response. What the devil was the spirit doing? Or – the thought struck me suddenly – was he even in this world? Might he not have been trapped in the other world? It had happened before, with my unlucky apprentice, George.

I walked across the yard, paused by the wood pile at the entrance to the alley. Just at the point of dipping down for that white something I had seen before, I heard a noise behind me, like a cough. I turned, saw Holloway at the window, staring out at me. I strolled nonchalantly on into the alley.

Out of Holloway's sight, I called softly for the girl's spirit. She danced about me at once, sparkling faintly on the wall, laughing and crooning her ancient song.

"Did I see anyone?" she pondered, in answer to my question. "I've seen so many people."

"Tonight," I said. "Did you see anyone tonight?"

She mused, then said teasingly: "Shadows."

"Male or female shadows?"

"Both." She giggled.

"Mrs Bairstowe?"

"Oh, yes." She sighed. "So pretty. I was pretty like that."

She was plainly thinking of the maid, or some long-dead mistress.

"And the man?"

"Oh, yes, he was handsome too," she said.

"Did you see him hit her?"

"Oh he didn't hit her," she said, shocked. "I'm sure he'd not do anything of the sort. Such a handsome man. The other one was ugly – I didn't like him."

"Two men?"

"And then there's William, of course," she said. "He was such a nice child. He was the one who taught me to sing, you know. But – " (another sigh) "he died so long ago."

And she broke into a cry, a cry of pain and grief. "Where is everyone?" she said. "Oh please, where is everyone?"

And she began to weep, a terrible broken sound that came and went like the wind ebbing and flowing.

They did not enjoy talking to Bedwalters, whom Mary Bairstowe was so ready to castigate as a fool. He came remarkably quickly for such a late hour, still in his working clothes, ink staining one sleeve. He was accompanied by the streetwalker who dogged his steps at night, a watchful girl of about eighteen years old; she was so regularly in his company that I could not believe his wife was ignorant of it.

As Bedwalters questioned Mrs Bairstowe about her ordeal, listening gravely to the maid's quiet interpolations and Holloway's indignant outbursts, the street walker lingered in the yard. I went out to her; she was shivering in the cold, drawing a threadbare cloak around her shoulders.

"Will you not come inside?" I asked.

She smiled, wryly. "She'll not have the likes of me under her roof."

I glanced through the open door; Mrs Bairstowe still sat at the table, with an air of weary suffering. "She's not a woman overendowed with Christian charity," I admitted.

"No thought for anyone but herself," she said, with no trace of bitterness. "Funny how many ladies are like that."

We avoided each other's gaze; I knew she must be talking of Bedwalters' wife.

"And him," she said, nodding at Holloway. "You'd think he was meek enough, wouldn't you?"

"He isn't?"

"He likes a good beating."

I was startled. "He's hit you?"

She shook her head, vehemently. "Never! I'd not let him get away with that. No, the other way." For a moment, her young face looked infinitely tired. "Wanted me to tie him to the bed and beat him."

"Good God!"

She caught hold of my sleeve. "Don't tell *him*."

"Bedwalters?"

"It'll only distress him. He likes to pretend he's the only one. It hurts him to think what I have to do to earn a living."

"I won't say anything."

"Anyhow." She drew her thin arm back into the comfort of the cloak. "There is only him, in one way of speaking."

I was silent, staring into the house through the open door, through which light spilt. Bedwalters, stocky, grey-haired and sombre, had Holloway and Mrs Bairstowe under his thumb now; they were docile, answering every question although Mrs Bairstowe curled her lip as if in contempt. I knew hardly any man who would condemn Bedwalters for his liaison with the girl, though plenty of women would protest. And the difference in age would go unnoticed, whereas if the lady had been the older…

I dragged my attention back from my own affairs. There was no point in setting my heart on Esther Jerdoun. Better to concentrate on what I could do something about – my financial circumstances. And justice for a dead young man. "Did you know the dead lad – Tom Eade?"

She shook her head. "Only by sight. He was all taken up with that other girl. No eyes for anyone but her."

"The maid?"

She frowned. "The fisher lass." A slight smile. "She's a canny one. Like her brother."

"The fisher girl's brother?" I repeated to make sure I had heard her aright. "I didn't know she had one."

"Aye," she said. "Thinks a lot of himself, that one." Her tone told me the brother was probably another person Bedwalters would not want to know about. "And what does he look like? Nothing but a stick with hair on top. All grown up and not out." She gave me a tight smile. "And nothing much to interest a girl."

We shared a knowing look.

"Tall, is he?" I said, suddenly struck. "Does he work in Holloway's shop?"

"That's the one."

So Richard Softly was the brother of Tom Eade's discarded love. Which might give him reason to want revenge on Eade and, for that matter, on the maid. Was it possible that the mistress had received the attack meant for the maid? Surely there was not the slightest chance one could have been mistaken for the other. But if Richard Softly had found himself trapped in the yard, he might have panicked and hit out in order to escape. And that might explain the silence of Tom Eade's spirit, torn between revealing the identity of the man who had killed him and protecting him because he was the brother of his former lover.

Former? I wondered.

"She'll not be the same again," the girl said and, in reply to my frown of puzzlement, "The fisher lass. And the brother loves her

– the one thing in this world he loves, apart from himself."

She was watching me carefully and I knew she was trying to be helpful. "He likes you," she said. "He says you treat him like the good man he is." I knew she wasn't referring to Richard Softly any more but to Bedwalters. "One good turn demands another," she said.

I was a trifle depressed as I left her and went out through the alley into the street, musing on the sight of good men and women trapped by fate or circumstance. The night was pitch black, and sparkling with stars, the moon hidden by a trail of cloud. Glancing along the street I saw only one torch burning, on a house opposite All Hallows Church. I stepped out into the road, drawing my coat more tightly around me against the cold, and stopped.

Something was wrong. I could not quite place where or why. There was no sound, nothing moved in the dark night, not even a dog or cat. I stood, hearing only the sound of my own breathing. No, I heard something else too – a faint scratching noise. But where –

All Hallows' churchyard.

A stone clattered on to the cobbles at my feet.

18

It is outrageous that our churchyards are daily desecrated
by the most disgraceful goings-on.
Respectable men and women dare not enter them!
[LOVER OF ORDER: Letter to Newcastle Courant,
3 January 1736]

Only a fool ventures into a graveyard at night. We don't suffer much from graverobbers in this town, but there is always a chance you'll find thieves sharing the spoils of the day, or plotting tomorrow's depredations. Or drunks commiserating with each other. Even an adulterous couple, although a cold March is not the usual time of year for such sights. So sensible men walk past. Only fools venture in.

Fools, and men who already know what, or who, they'll find.

I pushed open the gate, whispered, "Hugh?"

It was damnably dark in here; the one torch burning in Silver Street hardly reached this far and served only to make the shadows darker still. The moon hid behind a cloud. Gravestones were pale tilted blurs; I tripped over two or three low wooden crosses of the type used by the poorer sort of people. There was a path leading round the church but I was damned if I could find it. I was oddly disorientated, reminded of the vision I had had in Bairstowe's manufactory, of the graveyard in the other world.

A figure rose up out of the dark; I gasped in alarm. A face gleamed, pale hands waved.

"For God's sake, be quiet!" Hugh Demsey hissed.

He retreated and I followed. A dark hole yawned behind him then I was on sloping ground, walking down into a low-ceilinged passage that echoed our heavy breathing and thudding footfalls. The air smelt earthy and damp. We must be in the entrance to the undercrypt; at the far end of the passage would be a vaulted room, supported by ancient pillars.

We did not get so far. I stubbed my toe against something hard and yelped. Hugh hushed me again. I explored the something hard with my hands. Several wooden boxes. "Hugh, this must be stolen property. What if the thieves come back for it?"

"Then you'd better let me talk, hadn't you?" he retorted. I saw his pale face move in the darkness; he seemed to sit down. On one of the boxes, presumably. "I'm glad I didn't go to Paris," he said, with some enthusiasm.

"Hugh," I said, with foreboding. "What have you been doing?"

"Watching the maid."

I felt for a box, sat down cautiously and resigned myself to a long tale. "So what did she do after seeing Holloway?"

"She was in there nigh on an hour. Then she comes out again, goes down to the Key to the chandlers and buys some candles, then goes to the Printing Office for the *Courant*, then to half a dozen other places before going home. Charles, I can tell you what the Bairstowes ate tonight, every last bone of it. Mutton..."

"What happened in the yard?" I asked hurriedly.

"I wish I knew."

"Hugh!" I said, outraged. "You bring me to this damp miserable place, for nothing!"

"I grew impatient," he admitted.

"You surprise me."

"No need to be rude, Charles. I waited in the churchyard here for hours, keeping my eye on that alley. Bairstowe went off somewhere just as it was getting dark but the other two didn't stir. So I crept into the yard to see what was going on in the house."

"And?"

"Nothing was going on. The lights were all out, except for the maid's in the attic. I was just about to go off home when I saw a flickering."

"Someone with a candle?"

"Coming downstairs, by the look of it. So I ducked down behind a pile of wood. I heard the door open and a woman call, as if she expected someone to be there. I didn't dare poke my head up in case she saw me but it was Mrs Bairstowe – I recognised the voice."

"And then?" I put a hand on a splinter and muttered a curse.

"Footsteps coming from the alley. And a man. I heard him talking with the Bairstowe woman though they were quiet – I couldn't make out a damned word. Then there was a thud and a clatter and I heard him running. The woman was shouting – God, she can yell when she chooses, Charles."

"What did you do?" I thought I heard movement outside – were the thieves returning for the booty on which I was sitting?

"I ran for it myself," Hugh said. "Only it was pitch-black of course and I fell over in that filthy alley. This coat is probably ruined!"

"You shouldn't have come out in anything so fine. You didn't get a glimpse of this fellow?"

"I didn't see so much as his foot."

"Or recognise his voice?"

"He spoke too low." He paused. "You think this is the villain who is threatening Bairstowe?"

"Who else?" At least, I thought, considering the matter carefully, the attacker had plainly come from our world. From the alley, Hugh had said, and therefore from the street. Anyone from the other world would have come from the direction of the workshop. I felt an immense relief. I had visited that other world once before in search of a murderer – I did not wish to have to do so again.

"She knew him," Hugh said. "I'd lay odds Mrs Bairstowe knew him."

I contemplated the darkness and the pale blur of Hugh's face. "She told me she saw no one, that the attacker took her by surprise," I said, thoughtfully. "She also swore she went out without a candle but I saw one under a pile of wood in the yard. She must have dropped it and it rolled under the wood. I tried to retrieve it but they were watching me too closely."

"So what now?" Hugh asked. "Do you have any idea who the attacker was?"

"No," I said. "But I mean to find out."

And at that moment, we heard voices in the churchyard.

Hugh clutched at my arm and cursed. We rose together, holding on to each other. Trailing our hands along the walls of the narrow undercrypt, we edged towards the entrance. Hugh whispered. "Do you have a weapon with you?"

"Yes," I whispered back. "I wear a sword day and night."

"Don't be sarcastic, Charles," he hissed. "It doesn't suit you."

We crept forward, more nervously than I would have openly admitted. The voices were louder now, but they seemed to have stopped a few yards away. At the entrance to the undercrypt, we peered out into the darkness. Nothing could be heard. I glanced up; heavy cloud was rolling in, obscuring the moon.

A shifting in the darkness.

"They're going towards the church," I whispered.

"Thieves?"

"How do I know? Let's get to the churchyard wall. Then we can work our way round to the street gate."

We edged into the open. And at that moment, I heard a woman's voice, sharp, decisive. I knew that voice.

"Wait here!" I said.

Hugh grabbed at me but I was away, creeping on all fours

from one dimly-seen gravestone to another. I could just make out two shapes at the side of the church and the outline of a man's pale coat. The fellow had on white stockings too, much too fine for a night's dalliance in a churchyard.

I caught the woman's words now, spoken fiercely. "It's no use trying to stop me – you can't do it."

The fisher girl.

"Don't be a fool," the man hissed. "He's dead."

Richard Softly. This was brother and sister arguing – but why for heaven's sake in a churchyard? Why not talk in the warmth of their own rooms?

"You don't stop loving someone because they're dead," she said. "There's no one else to match him. There never could be."

"For God's sake! He betrayed you – he was courting that Scotch maid!"

"Richard," she said. "You know nothing. Go home."

"He's lucky he died before I laid my hands on him." Softly's voice held a trace of sulkiness that made him sound very young. Well, I thought, that was one of my suspects eliminated.

"I asked you not to interfere," she said. "And I'm asking again. Leave me be."

"You'll get yourself into trouble!"

"What can be worse than Tom's death?"

She was coming back towards me. I flattened myself behind a gravestone, and she passed so close I felt the breath of her skirts moving. She was rough and harsh-voiced, badly-dressed and poor, whereas her brother had smoothed out the rough vowels in his speech and dressed in the smartest clothes he could afford, but I would wager that she would be the one to do better in life. Then she was out of the churchyard and running lightly up the street, keeping to the shadows. Behind me, I heard her brother swear.

I crept back to the wall where Hugh was crouching.

"She didn't see you?" I asked.

"Didn't look my way. What was all that about?"

"I think she must have come to speak to her dead lover and found Bedwalters here and the whole house roused. She'll be back."

Hugh hushed me. "The other one's coming!"

We waited until Richard Softly had let himself out of the gate. He turned down the street towards the Key, muttering irritably. The one lantern in Silver Street illuminated his back.

"Good clothes for a shop lad," Hugh commented.

"Claudius Heron thinks they rob Holloway – they take just enough not to be noticed."

"Heron always thinks the worst but I'd say he was right in this case. Pity the lad has no taste."

I cast my eye up and down Hugh's well-clad figure. Despite a few mud stains here and there, he contrived, as always, to look both devil-may-care and respectable. The big buttons on his coat gleamed in the lantern light.

We walked out into the street in our turn. I was intent on going home and sleeping well past dawn.

"You don't think either of those two attacked Mrs Bairstowe?" Hugh asked.

"I don't think anyone attacked her," I said, grimly.

On my way home I crept down the alley into the manufactory. The yard was deserted, the house and workshop shut up. No gleam of spirit or hint of anything else not solidly of this world. I ducked down to look under the pile of wood.

The white candle had gone.

19

Despair is the ultimate sin, against God and against ourselves.
[McDonald's Sermons, Sixteenth edition,
published Edinburgh, 1722]

I did not wake until some miners made a rumpus in the street outside. The sun was as high in the sky as it ever gets in March, though it was blurred by a thin hazy cloud. At least there was no rain. As I dressed, I considered the events of the previous night – I had no doubt that a charade had been played out for my benefit, that Mrs Bairstowe had been in no danger at all. But why should they try to convince me she had been? And how did what Hugh had seen fit in?

One thing I was sure of, they'd not get the better of me. I was promised thirty guineas, Tom Eade demanded justice, and my lingering aches and pains spoke for my own grudge against whoever was doing this to William Bairstowe. The bills the culprit would have to pay were mounting up, and I would make sure he paid them.

I went down to Nellie's coffee-house and bought ale and a slice of game pie. I had broken into William Bairstowe's guinea long since – God but I needed those guineas of Bairstowe's! And I still could not make head nor tail of the situation; I was merely accumulating questions.

It was, I discovered, mid-morning. William Bairstowe must have torn himself from the arms of his whore by now and dragged himself up to the Cordwainers' Hall. I marched off, armed with a dozen questions for the organ builder, along the lines of 'where were you last night?' and 'is there any witness to your activities at the time your wife was attacked?' But when I reached the hall, I discovered Thomas Saint's errand-boy, dressed in his Sunday best, being very grown-up in showing gentlemen the organ. I also discovered Claudius Heron standing at the back of the hall impatiently tapping his thigh with his fingers.

He nodded at me, looked me up and down.

"No lasting ill effects," I said, lightly. "The knee is healed."

Heron watched the boy's enthusiasm with some cynicism. "I take it you have come to see Bairstowe."

"His wife was attacked last night."

One eyebrow went up. "As a warning?"

"Possibly." I did not want to commit myself to any theory at this moment. Nor, I discovered, did I want to tell Heron – the one man who might understand – about my new encounter with the world lying next to our own. That must keep for later, when I could give the matter the consideration it deserved. I was tolerably certain now it had no connection with this matter of Bairstowe's.

"Well," Heron said, "You will not find him here. He says he is otherwise occupied. As you can see, he is paying Saint's boy to stand in for him. He also sent me word to sell the timber and pipes in my possession in order to pay for the damage to the room. In short, he has abandoned the commission. Perhaps I should lay out a guinea or two on this instrument." He nodded at the chamber organ.

"A trifle too small for your gallery, I should think."

"I could sell it. The song school at Durham Cathedral is in need of an organ and the prebendaries there are careless with their money. I might get a hundred guineas for it, maybe more."

His casual tone in referring to such a large sum of money took my breath away.

"You do not buy a ticket yourself?" he asked.

I felt the few coins in my pocket wryly; I could not afford even one ticket. "I trust Bairstowe will pay me, not the other way around."

I left Heron waiting for the boy to finish with the other gentlemen, and went in search of Bairstowe. I chased his trail through coffee houses and taverns, through chandlers' shops and into the printing office and out again, and finally ran him to ground on the Key, looking over a stock of Baltic timber, newly unloaded.

His clothes were grubby and creased, his shoulders slumped. He did not see me at first and when he did look up there was no recognition in his eyes. I addressed him by name, and only at the third time did he say heavily: "Patterson. Yes. Patterson."

I drew him aside, nodding apologetically at the timber merchant, and pushed him down on to one of the timber baulks. We sat looking across the river. Seagulls wheeled over the moored keels, a faint twist of smoke trailed upstream. Looking downriver towards the coast, I saw a murky haze gathering over the salt works at Shields.

"I know why you're here," Bairstowe said, at last.

"Your wife was attacked."

"It was meant for me."

In the darkness, an attacker might just have confused the two. But I knew that was not what had happened. I intended to question Mrs Bairstowe again in the light of Hugh's revelations but not quite yet. She would simply deny my accusations and stick to her own account of what had happened; I needed more evidence before confronting her.

"It's my turn next," Bairstowe said, dully.

God, he was in a self-pitying mood. I reminded myself of the thirty guineas. "Where were you last night?"

Again, I had to repeat the question before he answered. He had indeed been with a woman although he grew coy when I pressed him for a name. Was the lady more respectable than I had thought? I began to wonder if Mrs Bairstowe might have set the spirits on him as punishment for a wandering eye.

But simple jealousy could not explain this affair. It could not explain the attack on Mrs Bairstowe last night, or that charade brother and sister had played out for my benefit. Perhaps Mrs Bairstowe had a lover. They had met, argued and he had hit her. She didn't want to reveal his name, out of love, and Holloway was helping her to conceal the affair. No, I could not envisage Mrs Bairstowe swooning with passion.

Bairstowe started to shake. "It's me next," he said again. A pair of merchants strolled past behind us, discussing the latest taxes; a seagull pecked at the remains of a gutted fish. I was afraid that if I questioned Bairstowe too closely he would break down completely, so I hunted round for an unexceptional topic of conversation to calm him.

"Your brother – "

"Edward?" And then he was off, the words tumbling out of him so quickly I could hardly catch half of it, as if his fear and anguish had to find some outlet, no matter how trivial.

He told the story of his childhood and he told it, as I had anticipated, from the opposite perspective to his brother. Edward had called him a spoiled, indulged child who had never had to do any work; William said he had never been allowed to do anything, that his father had not trusted him with any responsibility.

And, of course, Edward had never done a day's toil. He had spent money like water, had never done the accounts, had wined and dined the gentlemen customers, and whored with them, and left William all the hard labour, the searching out of supplies, the buying and selling. I thanked God that none of my baby brothers and sisters had survived, if this was what siblings came to.

Bairstowe caught hold of my sleeve, gripped so hard that I

feared the cloth would tear.

"What is the point?" he said.

"Of what?"

"Of living? There's nothing but labour and misery, from childhood to grave. Nothing but wretchedness and persecution. The spirits are after me, Patterson. And there's no point in dying," he added, bitterly. "I'd kill myself like Edward did, except there'd still be misery. Just a tiny stone to be trodden on and pissed on and laughed at. What's the point of dying?"

Tears glistened in his eyes.

"What's the point in looking for meaning?" I responded, after a moment. "We're here. We can't do anything about it. And that being so, we might as well be happy as not."

Bairstowe sneered with a touch of his old insolence. "That's easy for you. You've got money and friends, a rich patron. What chance have I got? Nothing."

He pushed himself clumsily to his feet. "I'll you what I am going to do. I'm going to give you three days."

"Three days?" I echoed blankly.

"Find me the fellow who's threatening me before the end of the week, and I'll pay you your thirty guineas. But if you can't, I'll take the money and go off to London. And I'll spend every last penny I have, on whoring and gaming and drinking and any other pleasure I can think on, and to hell with the rest of the world and what happens afterwards. And especially to hell with my wife!"

And he turned sharply away, stumbling as he tried to stride off.

I watched him go, torn between the irritation that always possessed me after my dealings with him, and a reluctant pity. What was this obsession with London? Holloway, Mrs Bairstowe, then her husband. It had the air of an old argument between them. They would find the city a sad disappointment if ever they got there. And the fifty guineas Bairstowe would receive for the organ, which seemed so much here in Newcastle, would hardly last a month there.

William Bairstowe had decided against suicide, but he was still in a self-destructive mood. I had an unpleasant feeling that, unless I was very careful, he would drag me down with him.

Three days. What could I do in three days?

20

Let me recommend Armstrong of Newcastle to you if you are in search of a good man of business. I have always found him most efficient. But he does like to talk.
[Sir John Carlisle, Letter to his brother, 6 July 1730]

"You've come about this business of Bairstowe's." Armstrong looked at me over the top of his wine glass, lines wrinkling his forehead in a hint of a smile.

I had half-expected to meet Mrs Jerdoun at lawyer Armstrong's office – I recalled her telling me she had a meeting with him. But she must have finished her business and gone, for when I sent my name in to Armstrong he agreed to see me at once.

He was a tall, lanky individual with the ungainly gait of a boy, which sat oddly with the face of a middle-aged man. His room was a miracle of papers; books and boxes on a multitude of shelves were neatly ordered and labelled with not a speck of dust anywhere. In the middle of all this, he sat at a table that seemed too small for him, a bottle of wine and two glasses before him. "Claret, Mr Patterson?" He was already pouring. "I'm glad of your company, sir. Legal work is more paper than people, I regret to say."

I sat in the chair opposite him and sipped my claret. It was of a quality I had previously sampled only at Claudius Heron's house and no doubt extremely expensive.

I answered his first question. "Which Bairstowe do you mean, Mr Armstrong – William or Edward?"

He nodded slowly, as if in compliment. "I agree with you, Mr Patterson. The matters are connected."

It was rumoured that Armstrong knew the business of the

entire town and I was quite prepared to believe, from his expression, that he knew everything I had already discovered. I cast an uneasy glance around for a spirit, the most likely informant; if Armstrong had such a spirit, however, it was not in this room.

"I hoped for information, sir," I said. "If, however, you cannot give me it – for reasons of confidence and so on – I would rather you told me at once and saved us both time."

He considered me. "There may indeed be one or two private matters I cannot divulge but I suspect there is much information that does not come into that category. May I first say, sir, how impressed I was with your conduct of that matter several months ago."

He had thrown me off balance again. Armstrong waved away my protests. "Nothing to know, you say? That is precisely my point. You dealt with the matter and most of the town is ignorant of anything untoward having occurred. Most impressive. May I also say that I was most surprised that the gentlemen directors of the concerts did not give you a benefit?"

I hesitated over that. There was a significance in his voice that told me he meant the comment as more than mere politeness. Armstrong is no fool; he knows that a benefit concert can supply a musician with enough income to last a year. As, I suspected, he knew that William Bairstowe had offered me a large sum to find the man threatening him.

"Now," Armstrong said, "Edward Bairstowe first. We'll come to William later. I presided over the inquest on Edward, you know."

"I wondered if you had, sir." Armstrong is one of the two coroners for this town.

He got up, unfolding his long legs from the ludicrously small table, and mused over the shelves behind him. Drawing down a box, he lifted some papers out of it, and folded himself back under the table. He read through the papers carefully, murmuring to himself.

"Now, Mr Patterson," he said, looking up, "I think we may proceed best if you tell me how you understand Edward Bairstowe's death to have occurred, and I will inform you if your account differs from that discovered at the inquest."

It was, I found, a very good exercise. Making a concise statement of the facts required careful thought, and cleared my mind. I recounted what Edward had himself told me, detailed the *Courant's* account and finished with Thomas Saint's comments.

"There are," I said, "a number of points to consider. The first is the matter of the knife. At the inquest, both William Bairstowe and his wife said that Edward snatched it up before leaving the house. Yet when William first talked to Bedwalters about it, he said that his wife had taken it with her."

"That, I think, is easily dealt with," Armstrong said. "The postboy was on his way to his lodgings after having been delayed, and gave evidence that he saw Edward Bairstowe at the foot of the Side with the knife in his hand, and his sister and brother hurrying after him."

"Why then did William Bairstowe lie when he spoke to Bedwalters?"

"He said later that he had simply been mistaken. The agitation of the moment and the dreadful distress of the unhappy outcome confused him. Not an unreasonable supposition, I think. What were your other matters?"

"The death itself. It was plainly suicide. The spirit is anchored to a single stone."

"And railing against his fate, no doubt," Armstrong said with a chuckle.

"Endlessly," I said. "But I cannot fathom the state of his mind at the time of his death. He snatched up a knife from the kitchen – "

"To cut his throat."

"Then why did he not do so at once? Why rush out on to the street?"

Yes, this was a most useful exercise; I had been thinking all these things yet not acknowledging to myself how important they might be.

For the first time, Armstrong looked uncertain. "Perhaps he had changed his mind. Perhaps he hated the thought of the pain, and believed throwing himself from the bridge would hurt less."

"Then why take the knife with him?"

Armstrong began to show signs of enjoying himself. "He forgot he held it," he speculated. "Or he feared that his brother would overwhelm him before he could get to the bridge. Edward was a slighter man than William."

That theory I could accept. I could imagine Edward Bairstowe brandishing the knife and threatening to use it if they came near him. "So he rushed down to the bridge, climbed up on to the parapet and threatened to throw himself into the river."

"Indeed."

"How did he climb up on to the parapet with a knife in his hand?"

Armstrong started to speak, changed his mind. "Ah," he said.

"Indeed, I'm not sure how he could pull himself up on to the parapet at all, even with the use of two hands." I tried to picture the scene. "To clamber over the parapet is one thing, to stand on it quite another, particularly for any length of time. It is very narrow, and just at the point where Edward must have stood there is nothing to hold on to."

Armstrong perused the papers again with pursed lips. "I have been most remarkably remiss. You have a very practical mind, Mr Patterson."

I was in my stride now. I did not know precisely how Edward's death related to his brother's present predicament but I sensed it must do. Perhaps both brothers had been the victim of one malevolent attacker? "Let us suppose Edward did climb up on to the parapet. According to all the accounts, his brother persuaded him to abandon his scheme and climb down."

"With the knife in his hand," Armstrong murmured.

"Edward says that the ground was slippery."

"The first sleet of the year."

"He says he lost his balance and fell forward on to the knife. But in that case, his death must surely have been accidental. Yet the confinement of the spirit tells us otherwise. For the spirit to be anchored to the stone, there must have been some element of intention in his death. And that is not explained by any of the accounts. If William had indeed just persuaded Edward not to jump, why should he set his feet on solid ground and immediately cut his throat?"

"He was – " Armstrong paused, and chose his words carefully. "An unstable man. One never knew what he would do next. I had dealings with him over various business matters and could never predict how he would react. He was capable of great vindictiveness." He chuckled dryly. "He and his sister-in-law were a matched pair."

"Perhaps that's why they hated each other."

He stretched against the confines of the small desk. "Oh, that is relatively new. There was a time when they were thick as thieves. Kindred spirits. She would excuse him anything, tell you he was only a lad. A lad! He was a mere year younger than she – both of them in their forties when she married William."

"What changed?"

He shook his head. "I have long since given up fathoming the ways of women, and Edward Bairstowe, as I have said, always confounded me. He had but one guiding principle."

"His own interests?"

"Precisely." Armstrong refilled his glass. "Mr Patterson, I do not find the behaviour of the Bairstowes at the time of the inquest difficult to understand. They were shocked by what had happened – confused, puzzled, distressed. And relatives in that situation always plead for a verdict of accidental death. Then they may bury the deceased in hallowed ground."

"But in this case there was a verdict of suicide."

He looked at me over his newly-filled glass, nodding slowly. "You want the truth, Patterson? There were too many men on the jury who were owed money by Edward Bairstowe, and had been for years. They seized their chance for revenge."

We sat in silence for a moment or two. "The bridge," I said at last. That is the part of the story that sticks in my craw. I cannot believe Edward climbed up and stood there. Yet he said he did. Why should the spirit lie?"

Armstrong said nothing but sipped his wine. After a moment, he stirred. "Now, this matter of William Bairstowe. I have heard little of it, barring some rumours that he is being threatened."

I outlined the story as quickly and accurately as I could, summarising at the end. "William Bairstowe swears he did not wreck his own workshop, write the notes, or attack his wife."

"And there is no hint as to who hit her?"

"I have a witness to the attack who heard Mrs Bairstowe talking, apparently calmly, to her attacker."

"She knew him, eh? What does she say to that?"

"I have not yet had time to ask her, sir."

Armstrong chuckled again. "She'll deny it, of course. You think it was Bairstowe and she is simply being loyal?"

"She says very firmly that she knows her duty."

"Oh yes," he said grimly. "I've heard that tale from her too, at the inquest. She is very keen on her duty."

"She is sister to Holloway, the leather merchant, I understand?"

He nodded. "Of a farming family somewhere Berwick way."

"I cannot imagine why she and Bairstowe married."

"Expediency, my dear sir. She had money, or her father did – he was fond of her and gave her a big dowry. William needed money for the business which was in difficulties at the time. William has never been good with financial matters and Edward was less than honest. He had friends I would not allow near my dog. Ruffians and villains."

He mused over his wine. "The Bairstowes have been married around ten years and she was forty or more when the marriage took place. That's why there's no children – she wasn't quite beyond child-bearing, I fancy, when they married but nothing came of it. Her money's all spent, long since. Now there's this matter of the land. An unlucky family, I fancy, very unlucky."

"The land?"

He regarded me for a moment, in careful assessment. "Do you mean to tell me you know nothing of the deed, Mr Patterson?"

I gave up on playing my hand cautiously. "The one Edward Bairstowe buried?"

"Ah-ha," he said. "Is that what he did with it? Mr Patterson, I congratulate you. I have been chasing this matter for the past six months and never even knew for certain that the deed does indeed exist."

"Edward could be lying," I pointed out.

Armstrong poured yet more wine – he was clearly used to a large intake. "Let me be plain, Mr Patterson. I am acting for the vestry of All Hallows in the matter of the deed. They want to extend their graveyard, and the land on which the manufactory stands would be excellent for the purpose."

That startled me. I had seen that events in that other world mimicked ours, though they did not necessarily repeat them exactly. Could it be that in that other world Bairstowe's manufactory had already been done away with and the graveyard extended? That would explain the tombstones I had glimpsed.

Armstrong was consulting his papers. "William Bairstowe – I'm talking about the old man now, William and Edward's father – he acquired the land from the church fifty years ago. Bought it for almost nothing, I'm told. But the devil's in the detail. The matter's not in the parish books – not a record of it anywhere. The parish clerk was drunk most of the time, I'm told, and never wrote anything up. So unless the Bairstowes can produce the deed there's nothing to say the transaction ever took place. And if it didn't take place – "

"The vestry can reclaim the land at no cost, making the Bairstowes homeless and penniless."

"Exactly."

"What does the spirit of the old man say? William Bairstowe senior, I mean."

"Absolutely nothing. He collapsed in the street on a visit to Dundee – he was building an organ there. The Bairstowes do not have the money to visit and ask him. Or so they say."

I would have thought the prize worth the expense, but the information suggested that the Bairstowes' financial situation was worse than I thought. Either that, or they knew William senior would not give the answer they needed.

"In any case," Armstrong pursued. "The unsupported word of a spirit would be not be sufficient in a court of law. There must be documentation, good written proof of ownership."

He leant forward, the small table shifting as his long legs straightened. "Mr Patterson, I have a proposition. Find that deed and I will pay you ten guineas."

I stared at him, astonished. "Forgive me sir, but is it not an advantage to your clients if the deed is never found?"

He shook his head. "Not at all, Mr Patterson. Consider what might happen. The vestry claims the land, demolishes the buildings, buries half a dozen people there. Then the deed is found, showing that the Bairstowes did indeed own the land.

What a mess that would be! Besides, William Bairstowe is threatening to take them all to court over the matter. If he does that, nothing will ever get done – these things drag on for years. No, sir, find me that deed, then the Bairstowes will have their claim, the church will buy the land off them and everyone will be happy."

Ten guineas. And Armstrong would keep his promises, while William Bairstowe might not.

How could I say no?

21

The Divine Art of Music has powers to draw all the Cares from our Shoulders, to soothe the evil Passions and to encourage the good...
[Abbé de Troyes, De l'art divin de la musique, Paris, 1721]

"You look tired," Esther Jerdoun said.

There was a caress in her voice, a tilt to her head, the slightest of smiles that made me breathless. I glanced across the Assembly Room but the maid, Catherine, sat bowed over her needlework.

"I had a disturbed night."

She turned in a flurry of rustling skirts, lifted a basket from the harpsichord stool and showed me a bottle of wine and three glasses. I had not long since come from Armstrong's claret but not for the world would I have refused this wine. She poured the sparkling pale liquid and took a glass to the maid, who accepted this generosity, I saw, with no sign of surprise. I could not imagine the Bairstowes treating their maid with such courtesy.

We sat on chairs at the side of the room, in a weak patch of stray sunshine. I felt lazy and contented, the anger and frustration over this matter of Bairstowe's seeping out of me. I recounted the tale of my night. In retrospect, it seemed funnier than it had at the time – Holloway's dishevelled appearance, Mrs Bairstowe's rudeness, the abortive attempt to retrieve the candle, Hugh and I hiding in the undercrypt at All Hallows. Perhaps my contentment made me look at it all more favourably.

Mrs Jerdoun listened to everything with attention, smiling at times, raising her eyebrows now and again. "You say William Bairstowe was not there? Might he not have attacked his wife and hurried away again? Perhaps she railed at him for coming home late!"

I shook my head. "I've spoken to him since. I'm certain he had nothing to do with it."

"I saw him myself this afternoon," she said. "At the Cordwainers' Hall. I was intrigued, I confess, at what you told me of him and wanted to see if he was as rude as I remembered."

"And was he?"

She laughed. "He trapped me into buying some tickets for his wretched organ – I could not think of a way out of it without being offensive. He was worse than I remembered."

"You could always sell the organ if you win it. The song school at Durham evidently want one."

"I shall bear that in mind."

"Was he – " I hesitated. "Was he disturbed in manner?"

"No. At least, no more than usual."

I regarded her with pleasure; the sunshine seeping through the windows silvered her pale hair, gleamed off the silk of her gown and highlighted a myriad tiny embroidered flowers on the fabric. How much had that gown cost? More than I could earn in five years, no doubt. There was no question – Esther Jerdoun was not for me.

She said, "Are you well?"

I shook myself out of my introspection. "When I saw Bairstowe this morning, I feared for him." I searched for words. "I thought he was... descending into a lethargy that is unhealthy in the extreme."

"His brother killed himself, did he not? Do you think William might do the same?"

I shook my head. "He thinks death is even worse than life and he finds that intolerable enough."

"The father died young, I'm told."

"Of an apoplexy. Dropped down dead in the street." The wine gleamed in the glass, the sunshine warmed me, Mrs Jerdoun's regard pleased me. Well, a man can dream – what is wrong with dreaming?

"It's the maid I feel sorry for," she said. "She is in an unenviable position."

"Most maids are."

Mrs Jerdoun cast a glance at her own maid, sitting placidly across the room, a neat figure in a neat dress with even a little lace at cuffs and collar, industriously sewing, and sipping at her mistress's freely offered wine. "I have never understood why servants are treated so badly. We rely on them so much; it seems only sensible to keep their goodwill. And why be at outs with any of our fellow creatures, except the most evil of them?" She finished her own wine. "So you are no nearer discovering the identity of the man threatening Bairstowe?"

"Further from it," I said. "The matter gets more complicated, not less." But at least, I reflected, I had Armstrong's offer to fall back on now; retrieving the deed might be easier than disentangling Bairstowe's affairs. And why spoil the pleasant hour with unpalatable thoughts? I finished my wine. "Shall we proceed with the lesson?"

I was walking on air when I left the Assembly Rooms late in the afternoon, although I would not for the world have admitted it. The late sun was just touching the tops of the houses opposite in a red flare of light; the street itself was shadowed and chill. I sauntered along in a pleasant haze. Esther Jerdoun combined the delights of a diligent pupil and an attractive woman, and no teacher could ask for more. So I would enjoy the memories of the delightful hour just past, and the anticipation of such an hour every day, and banish discontent.

A whisper made me stop in my tracks, a tiny apologetic cough from a spirit lodged in one of the trees of the vicarage garden, which I was just passing. "Mr Patterson sir?" It sounded like a very elderly, very prim lady. "Forgive me for disturbing you, sir, but Mr Demsey was asking to see you."

I listened to Hugh's message and found myself wondering if it was genuine. The spirit was plainly an old lady of timid disposition, yet I was listening for something in her voice, in her manner, something untoward, something threatening. I must not do this, I told myself. I must not allow one incident to make me doubt all spirits. I was in danger of becoming like one of those young women who fear that all gentlemen will try to take advantage merely because one has been over-familiar.

How ridiculous to doubt!

But how irresistible.

22

There were bystanders, sir, who never raised a finger to help the poor woman. What can be said of present day society, when so many stand callously by?
[Rev. A. E., Letter to Newcastle Courant, 27 November 1731]

The spirit had told me the truth. Hugh was leaning against the wall of the breeches shop and scowling, looking like the sort of fellow you'd cross the street to be away from.

"Hugh," I said, glancing across the street at the leather shop. "Why are you haunting John Holloway?"

"Because she is."

"The maid?"

He seemed to slide lower against the wall. "God, she leads a dull life, Charles! Cooking, cleaning, shopping – the highlight of her life is staring at ribbons in shop windows. Oh, and at the engravings of rich ladies prancing in the streets of London."

"Damn London. Why are people so obsessed with it?"

I leant beside Demsey and we stared at the façade of John Holloway's house, ancient and timbered, slightly leaning, touched by the last of the sun. The door was out of true – I wondered how it shut. It was only mid-evening yet the place was already shuttered. "Why is the shop closed?"

"They all went off to the Eade lad's funeral. Holloway told them not to come back tonight." Hugh shivered in the cold. He was dressed in his finest for some reason, in the dark blue coat with huge buttons, turquoise knee breeches, and shoes with big buckles. And here was I in drab green and threadbare brown.

"I was following the girl and she got here too early – Holloway was just seeing them off from the doorstep. So she hid round the corner."

I frowned at the tipsy windows, flashing back the last redness of the setting sun. "That doesn't make sense. The other day she went in bold as brass while the lads were there, yet today she doesn't want them to see her. Why not?"

He wasn't listening, stamping his feet against the evening chill. Two children ran past, giggling over some escapade. "She's been in there three hours, Charles, three hours!"

Well, someone's having a good time at any rate, I thought, then castigated myself for my flippancy. In all likelihood, the maid had no choice in what she was doing. If she offended Holloway, he had the power to get her dismissed without a reference. No reference meant destitution. And there would be only one profession left to her then.

"Hugh," I said. "That girl's situation is abominable and if I could help her I would, but – "

A woman's scream tore the air.

We were both startled into immobility. I stared at the ancient, leaning house, the blank reddened windows, the shuttered shop, the slant of sunshine across the lichened tiles.

"In heaven's name!" Hugh said.

Then we were both running, dodging carts that trundled down the hill. I stumbled on a projecting cobble, and Hugh drew ahead, dashing up to Holloway's door and battering on it.

"The back of the house!" I called. Hugh spun for the alley between Holloway's shop and its neighbour; I was so close behind, I almost trod on his heels. The alley was narrow and dark, the yard at the back small; the bulk of the Castle mound reared up suddenly behind the house, overshadowing the yard and making it gloomier still.

The back door was open. Hugh ran inside. I followed, stopped.

Whispers…

It was as if a crowd of people were all trying to talk to me at the same time, muttering, whispering, moaning. I gasped and put up my hands to stop my ears, thought I caught a glimpse of brightness, spun round, saw a flicker of light sliding from an overhanging beam. My heart raced...

The noise ceased. A great silence. Then the whispering started again, ebbing away from me. I saw a flow of light like water, over the walls, on to the ceiling, up the banisters of a stair at the back of the room. The light ebbed away and left me, shaken and alone, in near-darkness.

I was in a small room, low-ceilinged with timbers. One tiny window gave on to the gloomy backyard. The room was evidently used for storage; it was piled with boxes and parcels, and mysterious rolls of material. A strong smell of tanned leather made me cough.

Voices upstairs: Hugh's voice, Holloway's. Gathering my wits, I ran for the stairs. They rocked under my feet as if about to give way. The upper floor was brighter; a night light burned on a table, the reflections of a branch of candles gleamed in a mirror.

Two rooms. The first was the room Holloway and I had talked in before. The voices were coming from an inner room. I ran through into a bedroom.

Across the bed, with his breeches round his ankles and his bare knees to the ground as if he had been caught in the act of praying, was sprawled John Holloway. His hands were tied to the brass bedhead, and his back was reddened with blows.

There was no sign of the maid.

Hugh was shouting at Holloway who was groaning inconsolably. I pulled Hugh back.

"For God's sake, leave him alone!" I bent and picked at the knots that tethered Holloway's hands to the bedhead. My hands were shaking and I fumbled ineffectually. A spirit slid on to the bedhead, on to the rope, across the back of my wrist. I jerked back, tried to shake it off. It slid up my arm and back on to the bedhead.

"Ravisher," Hugh was raging. "Where is she?" Holloway merely groaned. "Damn it, tell me!"

"Hugh," I began.

He was past listening. "She must have run off."

"Hugh – "

"I'm after her, Charles." He was already running for the door, yelling back over his shoulder. "Don't let him go!"

The spirits were gathering again, humming like a river in full flow. I pulled back, heart pounding, took a step towards the door.

"Don't leave me!" Holloway groaned.

"Keep those damned spirits away from me."

He groaned again.

"I mean it, damn it!" I was shaking with anger. "Keep them away from me or I'll leave you here. And it'll be morning before the shop lads come back and who knows whether they'll find you even then?"

He muttered, but he must have known he could not refuse me. If the lads came up here tomorrow and found him bare-arsed and freezing cold, all shrivelled and bruised, he'd never be able to face them again.

"Go away," he said, to the spirits. "Yes, yes, I know he doesn't like you. Devil take it, do as I say!"

The flecks of light withdrew and clustered together on the crumbling wall. I steeled myself to cross to the bed.

"Untie me," Holloway moaned.

"Tell me first why you set those spirits on me."

He twisted to stare up at me. "Set them on you? Patterson, they do as they wish. I can't order them about!"

I realised he thought I meant the spirits in his house. "The spirits in the alley, damn it, the ones who attacked me when I came in answer to your message."

He stared. "Which message? Spirits in the alley? No, no, he doesn't mean you. What?" I wondered he didn't strain his neck as he struggled against his bonds to see the spirits on the wall above him. "Oh, the press gang victims? No, no." He twisted back to me again. "Patterson, I had nothing to do with that!" I heard panic in his voice. "Ruffians like that – do you think I'd associate with riff-raff!"

There was no mistaking the sincerity in his voice. Gritting my teeth, I reached for the knots that bound him. They were tightly bound and took some unravelling; I tore my nails and fingertips. But at least the spirits made no attempt to approach me again, although they continued to hiss and mutter on the wall above us.

Holloway's hands were at last free. He lifted them to his head. His wig had dropped off on to the bed and his scalp was covered by a dark stubble scattered with grey. He looked older, gaunt.

He gathered his shirt-tails about his loins in a pathetic gesture of modesty.

"For God's sake, man, pull your breeches up!"

He struggled to make himself presentable. "Damn woman."

A spirit glided along the bedhead, slid down the rope that had tethered Holloway's hands and glistened on the bedclothes. I stood very still, trying to ignore it.

"I take it she didn't like your attentions?"

"I pay her enough." He twitched his head as if the spirit was saying something to him.

I was hard put to disguise my contempt for him. "Not the first time, then?"

"She's a servant, Patterson. What else is she good for?"

"Your brother-in-law thinks the same way, does he?"

He snorted. "William's been enjoying her for years! Since she came to the house."

"How old was she then?"

He mumbled irritably. I wasn't sure if he was talking to the spirit, or trying to justify himself. His fingers pulled at his clothing, trying to rearrange it. I leant forward, grabbed his shirt. "How old?"

"Ten, twelve? Who knows?"

I let him go, feeling dirty. The spirit gleamed on his shoulder. "So why did she suddenly object to your attentions today?"

"Who knows? Damn it, Patterson, who asked you to come in here? Get out of my house!"

I did not move. "She tied you up very thoroughly."

He tried to regain his old arrogant, airy manner. "What I do in the privacy of my own house – "

" – is none of my business," I finished. "True, but tell me this, Holloway. If you were all tied up and at her mercy, what had she to scream about?"

For a moment, fear showed in his face. He started to shiver and splutter and twitch. The spirits were muttering now, louder and louder. I was shaking with fear again but, damn it, I wouldn't gratify them by running. "You like your spirits, don't you, Holloway? Talk to them all the time, like to share everything with them?"

"No, no. I mean – well – "

"Even your women?"

He burst out: "What's the harm? Why should they be deprived of a little pleasure because they're dead? You don't know, Patterson, you can't know!"

I turned my back on him and walked out. Out of that damned room. Striding quickly to escape the sudden roar of sound, and the rush of brightness over the timbers. Clattering down the stairs to the back door just ahead of the wash of light. Once I was out of the house they could not touch me. Into the yard and blessed cool air.

Damn them, damn them all.

The yard was shrouded in darkness; a last stray finger of sun touched a window in the roof above. Hugh was nowhere to be seen. Still breathing heavily, I turned back to the alley, then glimpsed another opening in the far corner of the yard. A second tiny alley, hardly wide enough to accommodate a man and low enough to force me to stoop. Through its turns and winds, I came out on to the twilight Sandhill and stood looking at the remnants of the Fish Market. This must have been the way the girl ran when she fled from Holloway, but where had she gone from here?

And where was Hugh? In the gloom, I walked up to the Cale Cross that stood at the foot of Butcher Bank. From the Bank opened a dozen or more chares, narrow stinking alleys packed with sailors and keelmen and their families; a small band of children stood at the entrance to one of the chares with a dog whining miserably about their heels. The dog was tethered by a piece of string to one of the children, and looked very much as if it was trying to get away.

Standing irresolutely on the corner of Butcher Bank, I looked down on the Sandhill again where a man was hanging a lantern outside the coffee house, creating a small pool of brightness in the dusk. Was there any point in trying to find Hugh and the girl? She must have been long gone before he came out into the street.

I started back down to the Sandhill.

And heard Hugh shout.

I turned on my heels. The children had scattered; three were running up the dark street, another two dived into the chare with apparent glee. The dog, accidentally released, had loped across the road to the far side where it hunched against a wall, shivering and whining, ears flattened against its head.

Hugh yelled again.

I ran, panting and struggling for breath as the street steepened, and swung into the chare.

I stopped. In a gloom relieved only by the flicker of candlelight behind a window, a group of men, ten or twelve strong, were grinning at me. I turned back. Another three or four were lounging at the entrance to the chare. Damn. Cursing myself for an impetuous fool, I put my back to the wall of a house.

Hugh's voice came again – from one of the houses. The men were still grinning. They were savouring the moment, I thought, enjoying my fear and anticipating the pleasure to come. I pressed myself back against the house wall. My hand touched something cold. It clattered to the ground.

I risked a glance down. It was a stick, rough-hewn from a branch and sharpened to a vicious point at one end. I dipped for it, held it in my hand like a sword.

One of the men laughed. He was of middle-years, grey-haired, lean and hard. His clothes were torn and as he shifted I smelt the reek of gin.

"Now, lad," he said, chidingly. "Give us the stick. No point in mekking things worse."

"I'll give you it when I'm out of here," I said.

"Well, lad." He shook his head. "You were the one that wandered in. No one brought you."

I was in a mess, no denying it, but I had a weapon in my hand and the reassuring roughness of old brick at my back. They would not find me easy meat.

"I want my friend."

"The fellow with the fine coat?"

A woman on the edge of the crowd said something indistinguishable; they all roared with laughter.

"Aye," said the man. "Our coat now. It's a simple matter, lad. We've no use for your body – "

"Speak for yersel," the woman shouted. Another roar of hilarity.

"But those clothes are another matter. They'll bring in a pretty penny."

I regarded the men with wry gloom. The clothes that I wore were old, much darned and not expensive even when new. Compared to what Claudius Heron or John Holloway wore, they were rags. Yet for these destitutes, they would pay for a month's food. Or gin.

Two or three men blocked the narrow entrance to the chare. The children had crept back and the dog had been recaptured; it was whining and squealing and desperately trying to pull away. I stared at it. The dog – what was worrying me so much about the dog?

The middle-aged man was sauntering towards me, pushing up his ragged sleeves. Behind him came three or four others. One of them gave the distressed dog a kick.

I lifted up the stick, backed myself into a corner where two crumbling walls met, swung the stick to cover their approach. I was merely delaying the inevitable, but damn it, if they wanted me, they would have to come and get me. The first man came at me, lean, hard-faced, plainly used to scrapping. I swung the stick wildly. It cracked against his arm and he let out a great roar of pain. Half a dozen of the other fellows thought that a great laugh. He lunged at me, snarling.

Then I heard the dog squeal as if in pain. Someone shouted in alarm.

I remembered what dogs feared almost above anything else.

23

No respectable Lady or Gentleman would walk on
the Key at night for fear of being abused.
This is a situation which cannot be allowed to continue.
[LOVER OF ORDER, Newcastle Courant, 3 January 1736]

I glimpsed a great flickering light in the evening darkness. Then a blow from the air knocked me sideways. The men scattered in alarm. A gleaming cloud swarmed over me, hissing in my ears, crawling in my hair. The dog howled.

I swung my arms, tried to bat the spirits away. A silvery gleam slid over my sleeve, across the back of my hand. Something cold slipped along my spine.

Walls reeled. I hit hard stone, squeezed my eyes shut. Something, some*one*, crept across my eyelids. There was an enraged screeching in my ear.

A distant voice; the men shouted. Warm living fingers gripped my arm, pulled –

And I felt a kind of flowing, like water receding, ebbing away.

Silence.

I opened my eyes. I was on the Key, at the far entrance of the chare. Lanterns burned with comforting brilliance over shops and brothels. Seagulls screeched overhead; passers by looked on curiously. And behind me in the dark chare stood a knot of men, regarding me with fear and anger.

The maid, Jennie McIntosh, was ranting at them. Hair and cap askew, she was flushed with exertion and bright-eyed with fury, screaming at the men, calling them cowards and idiots and a dozen other names beside. I remembered a hand in mine, an unexpected scent of lavender. The maid must have seized me, dragged me out of the chare...

The cold hard wall of a house at my back was the only thing keeping me standing. I stared at my hands, at the unsullied cloth of my sleeve. My scalp was itchy; I ran my hands through my hair. This hateful itchiness of the scalp is precisely the reason I wear my own hair rather than a wig – I cannot endure it. Now I wanted to scratch and scratch and scratch, and there was no relief.

My legs gave way; I sat down on a coil of thick rope, buried my head in my hands. The dog. I should have taken heed of the dog. Dogs don't like spirits. This had been another trap, though the men could not have been a part of it – they had been as alarmed as I.

I raised my head. The men had gone, but Jennie McIntosh sat on a box in front of me, trembling hands clasped in her lap, the lantern light gleaming on her dark curls.

"Thank you," I said.

Gone was the termagant that had raged at the ruffians. She said shakily: "Men! They boast about their great deeds but can't face a few spirits!"

I had been frightened of them too, very frightened. I admired her courage in rescuing me and said so. She flushed and lowered her eyes.

"It's my fault you was there."

I nodded. "We heard you scream, in Holloway's shop."

She bit her lip. "I couldn't bear it." She was shaking more noticeably now. "Not a moment longer. I couldn't." I thought her bravery in helping me all the more admirable for her experiences with Holloway.

"He could do you a great deal of harm," I said, breathing deeply. "If he takes offence, he could persuade his sister to dismiss you."

There were tears in her eyes, sparkling in the lantern light.

She said, in almost inaudible tones, "I'm scared."

"Of Holloway?"

"Everything."

"You mean Tom Eade's death?"

"It might have been me," she burst out. "I could have been the one in the yard."

"It was an accident."

She shook her head. "It's her. The fisher girl. She's not forgiven me for taking Tom from her. She killed Tom and she's going to kill me!"

For a moment, my mind went back to All Hallows' graveyard. "You don't stop loving someone because they're dead," she'd said. I was almost certain Tom Eade's death had been an accident, but could the fisher girl blame Jennie McIntosh for it? After all, if Tom had not succumbed to her charms, he would not have been in the yard.

"I can't go back there," Jennie McIntosh burst out. "She'll kill me if I go back."

I hesitated, trying to think of reassurance and finding none. This is not a big town like London; if the fisher girl was determined to kill Jennie, she could find her, no matter where she was.

And then, like a firework bursting, I remembered. Hugh!

In God's name, how had I forgotten him? He was still in that chare, still held by those men, still in danger. I needed to find him!

"And someone's after the master now!" the maid said wretchedly. "They're after him, and after the mistress, and next they'll be after me! I don't want to go back there. I can't bear to go back!"

She was beginning to work herself into a frenzy. I was only half-listening. I had to find Hugh! I said hurriedly: "Your master will look after you," and started to get up. But the knee I'd injured in the spirits' first attack gave way; I collapsed back on to the coil of rope.

Jennie McIntosh laughed hysterically. "I'll be turned off without a reference! And then how will I get another place? I'll have to live – *there*." She cast a glance at the chare. "And there's only one way for a woman to earn her keep there!"

She began to weep, silent tears that drained down her cheeks, dropped on to her hands and left translucent marks on the thin material of her apron.

The thought of Hugh's plight was beginning to panic me. I struggled to my feet at last. The Key swung around me; I put out a hand to the wall for support. The knee held, though it ached.

Tears were streaming down Jennie McIntosh's cheeks. "What can I do? What can I do?"

Damn it, I could not abandon her. I forced myself to say, "I'll find you somewhere safe."

She looked up at me in alarm. "Sir!" She hesitated, said indistinctly: "My reputation…'

I was desperately trying to think what to do. "Unless you're married," she said hopefully. "If there was a lady in the house, that would be all right."

"A lady," I said. "Yes, a lady."

Mrs Jerdoun. Could I deposit the girl with her? What would she think? It was obvious what she would think. But I had to get back to Hugh!

I began to give the maid instructions on how to reach Mrs Jerdoun's house but she stared at me miserably. "She'll turn me away," she said. "How's she to know you sent me?"

I could not argue with this; a girl arriving on the doorstep with such an odd story would not get past the servants. And she fell to weeping again and twisting her apron to shreds, and in the end, I had to take her to Mrs Jerdoun's myself. Fretting constantly over Hugh, desperate to get back to him, trying to calm my fears. Hugh was a grown man who could take care of himself; Jennie McIntosh was a young girl, a brave one certainly, but in need of help. I had to do what I could for her. I had no choice.

I approached Mrs Jerdoun's house in Caroline Square with trepidation; it was the first time I had been there since the events of last November. Old fears and memories of stepping through to that other world still lingered, but somehow, I realised with momentary surprise, they were losing their sharpness. This business of linked worlds was beginning to intrigue me – I wanted to get to the bottom of it.

But for the moment there were more pressing matters I had to be rid of this girl and get back to find Hugh.

I marched up to the door, rapped smartly and asked the servant who answered if Mrs Jerdoun was at home. She was, and we were shown into the library, accompanied by the servant's scornful looks at Jennie.

Mrs Jerdoun was seated in an elegant chair with a book of music in her hand. Flickering candles cast uncertain shadows in the far corners of the room. As the servant announced us, she looked up in surprise. Then her gaze settled on Jennie and I saw a look of cynical understanding, succeeded by a flash of anger.

"Mrs Jerdoun, madam. I have come to beg your assistance."

"Indeed?" she said frostily.

Her inference was obvious – she thought the girl my mistress. I could not bear that she should believe such a thing. Despite my eagerness to be away and look for Hugh, I hurried to explain everything that had happened since we had interviewed Mrs Bairstowe together, though I glossed over some of the abuse to the maid, out of consideration for the girl's feelings. Mrs Jerdoun looked at me sharply when I mentioned the attack by the spirits in the chare and said, "Again?" I tried to reassure her it had been of much less significance than the first attack but I was far from sure she believed me.

When I at last stopped, Jennie said in her low voice, "Begging your pardon, my lady, but I won't be any trouble. I'll work hard."

There was silence. Esther Jerdoun looked searchingly at the girl then at me. Then she stood up, walked over to the fireplace and rang the bell. We stood unspeaking until the servant arrived.

"Find this girl a room," Mrs Jerdoun said. "She will be staying a few days. And give her work to occupy her hands."

I realised I had been holding my breath. The two servants went off together, he in high dignity, she timidly.

Mrs Jerdoun smoothed her skirts. Tendrils of pale hair lay across her neck and gleamed in the candlelight. She was dressed in pale green, a colour particularly flattering to her; if it had not been for my growing anxiety about Hugh, I would have been content to admire. As it was, I was searching my mind for a reason to hurry off.

"How long do you wish the girl to stay here?" she asked. Her tone was still cool.

"For as short a time as possible. This matter must be dealt with quickly, for the sake of all concerned."

She nodded. "Her treatment has been appalling – I am assuming you did not tell me all the detail of it?" She was still holding the book and set it carefully on the mantelshelf. Firelight gleamed on her gown. "You still believe William Bairstowe the author of the threats against himself?"

"I'm certain he wrecked his own workshop."

"And the attack on Mrs Bairstowe? You think he did that too?"

"I think it possible. I think he may have come to do more damage to the workshop or house, and she went out to stop him. They argued and he struck her, perhaps harder than he intended. He wouldn't be the first husband to hit his wife. He is after all entitled to do so."

"And she stays silent out of duty."

I met her gaze and the dryness in her tone. For perhaps the first time I gave thought to the practicalities of her situation. A single woman over the age of majority has some independence provided she has money, and Esther Jerdoun had a great deal of money, and the power of governing what she did with it. Were she to marry, however, that power would pass out of her hands. Why should she do anything so foolish? Particularly with such examples as the Bairstowes to guide her?

She was waiting for an answer, the satin of her dress gleaming rosily in the firelight. I said, "Mary Bairstowe stays where she is because she has nowhere else to go and no money to live on except what her husband allows her."

Esther Jerdoun nodded. "She suffers, in short, the common lot of women." She stirred, walked to the table to trim a candle that was guttering. "Well, Mr Patterson, I will shelter the maid until she can be assured of safety. But I suggest you go down to the manufactory and speak to the mistress, or the master if you think it more appropriate. It is abominable that she should suffer such abuse. It must stop."

She straightened and added, "I trust you have not forgotten our lesson tomorrow?"

She stood before me in the shifting candlelight, a tall slim figure of presence and authority that almost intimidated me. And yet I felt exhilaration too. I could not conceive that she would ever disappoint me. I left the house with an unbounded sense of regret and the words *if only* running through my mind.

But I had wasted too much time. I needed to find Hugh, and quickly.

24

Brawling is a regular occurrence and cannot be tolerated.
[LOVER OF ORDER, Newcastle Courant, 3 January 1736]

Halfway down Pilgrim Street, the cat came trotting up to me. I kicked at it but it merely sidled away, then came back again at a more cautious distance. I was frustrated by the delay forced upon me but I was sensible enough to know that I could not simply walk back into the chare and demand Hugh's freedom.

Commonsense told me that Hugh must be in the hold of the ruffians in the chare and had probably been bundled into one of the houses so they could deal with me. Was he still there? And was he uninjured? Damn it, if he had been hurt again because of my dealings, I would never forgive myself.

I walked along the Key towards the first of the chares. There were fifteen or sixteen of them, some broader and more civilised than others; it was the furthest one I wanted, the one nearest the Sandhill. Night had gathered while I was in Esther Jerdoun's house; trails of cloud drifted across the bright curve of the Milky Way above and the dog star sparkled. Sailors stood talking and smoking; whores sauntered brazenly across to join them.

Cautiously, followed by the cat, I hesitated at the entrance to the chare. Ratten Row, it was called, and from the lamp-lit Key it looked like a black hole into hell. Not a light shining in it, not a glimmer of brightness or movement.

"You're a fool to come back," a voice said.

I swung round. The man stood a little way off, outlined against the glow of lanterns, pipe in hand, still reeking of gin.

"I don't desert my friends," I said.

He considered. "Don't seem it's your friend you need worry

about." There was a calculating look in his eye. "Never seen spirits act like that afore."

"There's a first time for everything."

"Nuisance, the lot of 'em." His lean face was shadowed, grotesque. "Poke their noses into everything. Ye can never plot in peace for fear they'll hear you. But vicious like that – never. Ye must have annoyed 'em plenty."

I could barely control my temper. "Tell me where my friend is."

He shook his head. "Can't." He sneered. "Ye see, I can't betray *my* friends."

"Thieves and rogues," I said bitterly.

"Aye. What else is there to do?"

I said nothing.

"Well," he said, "At least you don't insult us, by saying what all the other gentlemen say. 'You could do an honest day's work.'"

I knew how hard it could be to earn a living. "I don't care about Hugh's possessions," I said tightly. "I just want my friend safe and well. All else you can have – his clothes, his money…"

He shook his head. "What's done's done."

Cold fear gripped me. "What the devil do you mean by that?"

"It was all dealt with. While the spirits were having their fun."

"Where is he?!"

He looked at his pipe, as if he was seeking the answer there. "Nay," he said eventually.

I threw myself at him. The suddenness of my attack caught him by surprise. He staggered backwards, dropped his pipe. The cat skittered away in alarm. I got a handful of the fellow's rough coat in my hand, bore him against the shadowed wall of the chare with a force that snapped his head back against the stone. He groaned.

"Tell me or I'll break your neck!"

He gasped for air. "Then ye'll be a dead man."

I gathered the rough material tighter. "Tell me where he is!"

He grunted. I sensed his punch coming, twisted out of the way, took it on my left arm. I swung my own fist but he slipped from my grasp, into the glare of the lights. He stumbled; I hooked out a foot, caught his ankle and tipped him over. He sprawled on to hands and knees.

Like a fool, I went to grab him. His fingers curled around my ankle and tugged. I crashed into the wall of the chare with a force that took the breath out of me. The nearest lantern swung wildly. I went down.

We were both on the ground now. My head rang. I was gasping for air, but scrabbled desperately out of his way. His face loomed over me, grimy and unshaven. He was snarling obscenities.

I raised my hand, fingers outstretched, and jabbed at the ugly, vicious face. Into the eyes. He screamed.

Scrambling backwards, I pushed myself upright. The fellow was on his hands and knees, screeching threats. I said thickly: "Go to the devil," and staggered away.

I was not proud of myself, but not ashamed either. Anger still filled me but it was colder, more calculating. I had made another enemy; I did not care. I had not found Hugh – that was what mattered.

I was aching. I had again aggravated the injury to my knee and it stabbed with pain at every step. Followed at a wary distance by the cat, I climbed up the slope of the bridge, stood heaving for breath by Fleming's stationery shop. Suddenly nowhere seemed safe. There were a dozen spirits on the bridge, perhaps more; the end tower had been used as a prison for centuries and hundreds of inmates might have died there. If they too chose to attack me…

I was damned if I'd let spirits get the better of me. I needed help and I'd take it wherever I could find it.

"An odd time of day to pay a social call," Edward Bairstowe's spirit said. In the darkness, I could just sense movement on the stone. There was an irony, I reflected, in seeking help against spirits from a spirit. Curbing my impatience, I eased myself down on to the cobbles, my back to the bridge parapet. Hardly a soul was about; two whores talked quietly in a shop doorway, and a timid, gangly youth hesitated outside Fleming's as if trying to summon up courage to approach the girls. A few lanterns burned outside the shops but here in the middle of the bridge there was only darkness and the faint gleam of the water far below.

"I would have sent my card in," I said, curtly. "But your servant said you were not at home."

The spirit cackled with laughter. "I like your sense of humour, sir. You do not sound well."

"I have recently had an – *altercation* with a man of the lower sort."

He tut-tutted. "Some fellows really have no idea of the social graces."

"He was more interested in my coat."

"Ah," he said. "An acquisitive fellow." A trace of doubt crept into his voice. "Forgive me, my dear Patterson, but you could hardly be called a stylish dresser."

I could forgive him criticising my clothes; his casual use of my name set my teeth on edge. But I had to humour him if I was to stand any chance of helping Hugh. "My friend Demsey is better dressed. He's a dancing master and you know how much care such fellows take of their clothes."

"Indeed, indeed," he said. But there was a strained note in the spirit's voice. I felt a surge of triumph – he knew something, he *knew* something.

"You had a wide acquaintance yourself, I think," I said, in as light a tone as I could manage, wishing I could see him better in this damned darkness.

"Well, you know how it is," he said. "A young man-about-town rubs shoulders with a host of interesting characters. Now, sir, about that deed I mentioned to you."

I was desperate to find Hugh but you cannot grab a spirit by the throat and demand he keeps to the point and damn well gives you the information you want. Edward Bairstowe needed to be wooed, to be wheedled and cajoled. I gritted my teeth and said pleasantly: "You want to tell me where the deed is?"

"No..." I sensed his indecision. In truth, I realised, he did not much want to talk about the deed but he had hoped to distract my attention, and it must have been the first subject that came to mind. "That is – "

"Yes?"

"I have been thinking the matter over."

"Yes?"

"I would like to speak to William about it. Would you ask him to come and see me?"

"I can ask. I cannot guarantee he will agree."

"Oh, indeed, indeed. But, well, one must let bygones be bygones, sooner or later, do you not think, Patterson?"

"I think," I snapped, losing patience, "that you know where Hugh Demsey is. And I am not going from here until you tell me."

It was a bow drawn very much at a venture. I had come to him because I thought he might barter information for my company. But his eagerness to change the subject, and his silence now, told me he knew more than I had anticipated.

"My dear Patterson," he said, with an effort at joviality. "What makes you think I know the whereabouts of – what was his name – Devlin?"

"Demsey," I snapped, then restrained myself. The cat butted up against my feet. I shifted on the cobbles and tried to push it away. "If you do not know, why not say so?"

"If that's your wish, sir," he said, plainly intent on humouring me. "I do not know where your friend Devlin is."

"Demsey!" I roared with fury.

It was the very worst thing to do; I heard his self-satisfied chuckle.

I set my head back against the parapet of the bridge, breathed deeply, clenched my fist to steady my temper. "Forgive me," I said. "I am not a patient man at the best of times, and the events of today have tried me sorely. I have been attacked and my friend has been taken prisoner by a band of rogues. He may be in danger of his life." God, might I already be too late? "All I want is to know where he is so I can find and help him."

There was the sound of shouting and singing from downstream; women shrieked and laughed. A dog barked. The cat lifted its head then settled down again.

"I think, my dear Patterson," Edward Bairstowe said, with obvious care, "I might be able to do something for you…"

There was obviously a price to be paid. "In exchange for what?" God, but it was hard not to shout at him.

"This business of William's," the spirit said. "It wouldn't surprise me if there was nothing to it."

"Just a few spirits getting frisky?"

"Alas." He sighed. "Some people are as unruly in death as in life."

"So I perceive."

"In fact," he said, "I'd be surprised if the whole matter was worth pursuing at all."

"It's worth thirty guineas to me."

"But will William pay, sir?"

I shifted on the hard ground. More shouting from the revellers downstream, a scream or two. "Let me see if I have you right," I said. "If I cease to work on your brother's behalf, you will tell me where Hugh is."

"That's the sum of it, sir."

"Tell me where he is."

"When I have your promise," he said coyly.

"No," I said.

"Then you will not get the information, sir," he said.

"On the contrary."

"No, sir," he chuckled. "Not at all."

"Because," I said, unable to restrain my fury any longer, "if you don't tell me, I shall dig up your stone and toss it in the river, where it will sink beyond trace and you'll never see another living man or talk to another spirit ever again!"

"Sir," he said, with good humour. "You should never make threats you have no intention of carrying out."

"Believe me," I said. "Believe every word I say. Because my closest friend is at the moment in the direst dangers and I have no intention of sitting back and doing nothing. Now tell me!"

"No." The spirit's voice subsided. "No, you wouldn't. Not a law-abiding man like you." But he did not sound convinced.

"Are you sure?" And I dug my key from my pocket, reached out and started to scrape at the earth in which Bairstowe's cobblestone was embedded.

"No," he cried in panic.

"Tell me where Hugh is."

"I can't!"

"Then ask your cronies!"

Silence. Then I heard a distant kind of whispering, very distant, almost below the level of hearing. Edward Bairstowe said sullenly: "On the Key. Near a boat called the *Berwick Boy*."

"Thank you," I said, pushing myself to my feet.

"This isn't the end of it," the spirit said, sullenly. "You'll not get the better of me. I'll get even, see if I don't."

I walked away, followed by the cat.

The *Berwick Boy* was an old grubby ship, covered in coal-dust and grime, and stinking of fish. She stood well downstream from the bridge, almost upon the Sandgate outside the town walls. No one was on deck, but I heard the raucous sound of drunken singing from some hidden cabin. A dog rushed up to the gangway and barked furiously; the cat trotted past in oblivious disdain.

At one of the mooring ropes, I stood and looked about. The most frequented part of the Key was further upstream; here it was almost deserted. Piles of coal stood next to a heap of old fishnets, apparently abandoned. The only light came from a lantern swaying from the *Berwick Boy's* mast; the flickering light cast confusing shadows across the coal and the nets, and a heap of ballast stones.

Hugh was not here. Damn Edward Bairstowe –

The cat mewed. It was balanced on top of a pile of coal, peering down the other side. It yowled again.

I clambered over the nets, scrabbled up the side of the pile of coal. The nuggets slid under my feet. I scrabbled for purchase, struggled to the top of the heap.

In a hollow between two piles of coal, lay Hugh's body, pale and naked.

25

We must never forget the greatest commandment of all.
We are not enjoined to love ourselves, nor our friends and family.
We are enjoined to love our neighbour, no matter who
they might be. And our Lord went further.
He enjoined us to love our enemies.
Not one man in ten strives to obey that commandment.
[Revd A. E., Sermon, St Nicholas's Church, Newcastle,
13 July 1735]

"Charles," Hugh said, still shivering. "It's hell's own mouth in there. God forbid I should ever go back."

I had stolen a blanket from the *Berwick Boy*, whipping it from a pile of goods on the deck while the guard dog was distracted by the cat. We must have made a ridiculous sight stumbling along the Key: Hugh dazed, half-drunk, and wrapped only in a blanket, me begrimed with coal-dust, and both of us followed by a mangy cat. The blanket stank of piss, and Hugh of gin. It was the devil of a job to get him up the flights of stairs to his attic room. My bruised knee began to ache again.

And all the time I'd been furious – furious at the men who'd done this, furious at my own stupidity, furious at my foolishness at allowing Hugh to get embroiled yet again in one of my misadventures.

Huddled on his bed with his own blankets wrapped around him, Hugh looked as if I had just dragged him from the river. His face was white as ice, eyes huge and dark and hollow. I had gone out again for the strongest brandy I could find, kicked the cat out of the door, lit a candle and settled down to coax the story out of Hugh.

The brandy was plainly restorative; as he sipped, his voice became louder and more indignant.

"I caught sight of the girl as I dashed out of that alley behind Holloway's shop. What the devil's her name?"

"Jennie McIntosh."

"She ran across the road into that chare and I went after her." He grimaced. "There were at least a dozen men waiting there." The blanket fell from one shoulder; he cursed and pulled it up again. Candlelight flickered across his face. "I'm no coward, Charles, but I know when it's wisest to make yourself scarce. I ran for it."

"But they caught you?"

"I fell over a damned child that crawled out of one of the hovels and they were on me at once. They bundled me into a house then all piled in. I yelled like fury and flailed at them, but one of 'em landed a blow to my head and I lost my senses. When I came round, I was bare as the day I came into the world, and shut up in the most stinking pit you can imagine. Charles," he said, with sudden indignation, "they took my coat! The dark blue one. My best coat!"

"It'll be sold secondhand tomorrow." I remembered the time. "Today, rather."

"And my breeches and shirt and stockings and shoes – "

"You were in a dark stinking pit," I reminded him, almost patiently.

"A cellar." He visibly shuddered and took a gulp of the brandy. "There were rats. And spirits – dozens of them! Nastiest lot I ever came across. Then all the men just rushed out!"

I was sitting in his one chair, at the table under the eaves; I toyed with the papers that lay neatly piled there, keeping my eye on the candle which was almost burnt down to a stub, and trying to control the anger that still threatened me. "Why?"

"Something was happening outside. God knows what!"

I knew what. "So how did you get out of the cellar?"

He showed me a grin. "Charles, they'd run off in haste!"

"Don't tell me they'd left the door unlocked!"

"Exactly. Though the place was in pitch darkness and I had to blunder around until I found the damn thing. And that wasn't fun in bare feet, I can tell you! When I got upstairs there was no getting into the street because everyone was out there, so I went up to the floors above. There were great holes knocked through the walls, joining all the houses in the row."

"Escape routes," I said, "in case they're pursued. They'll go in at one house and out at another."

"So," he said, "I climbed out of a window and dropped to the ground."

"From the second floor? Hugh!"

He grinned. "I'm a dancer, Charles. I know how to use my body. Only trouble was, it was an inside court. No way out to the street." He laughed and thrust the glass at me for more brandy. "So they caught me again and threw me back in the cellar. God, those spirits!"

"Where does the drink come in?" I asked. "You stank of it when I found you."

"Most of it went over my outside," he said. "They damn near choked me, trying to get it down my throat."

I mused on this. "They must have thought that if they killed you, there'd be too much fuss. But if they made you drunk, you'd probably be so confused you'd not remember anything. And when you came round, naked, on the Key you'd be worried about being a laughing stock, so you'd creep home and pretend nothing had happened."

I straightened the papers on the table. The behaviour of the men was logical enough; they had seized their chance when Hugh dashed into the chare after the girl. But the girl – Hugh had said she was running across the street when he came out of

Holloway's shop. Yet she had left the shop before we reached it and we had then spent time talking to Holloway. She should have been long gone. What had she been doing in the meantime?

"So many spirits," Hugh said, pulling the blankets closer. "I could hear them chattering all the time. Like in that fellow's shop. When was the last time you heard spirits talking to each other, Charles? You can't normally hear a thing. It was as if they didn't care."

The candle was on the verge of going out; I found another stub and lit one from the other. "Could you make out any specific words?"

"Nothing of significance. One said it had been fun."

That struck a chill into me.

"And I caught something about London. Someone was going there. From Shields, I think – there was talk of finding a ship there. And something about a fellow organising everything. Not a living man though, a spirit."

My heart near stopped; my voice sounded quite unlike my own. "A spirit? "Did they name it?"

He shook his head, took refuge in the brandy. "Said something about a stone. Yes, I know," he added before I could say anything. "Half the spirits in this world are on stones. But this was somewhere blue." He shook his head, puzzled. "Some painted house, do you think?" He glanced at me, stared. "That means something to you?'"

"Oh yes," I said, grimly. "It means a very great deal."

26

Brotherly love is a fine thing...
[Revd A. E., Sermon, St Nicholas's Church, Newcastle, 13 July 1735]

It was early morning when I walked back on to the bridge. I was so tired I could hardly think what day it was. Wednesday? Yes, it was Wednesday.

I felt I had hardly slept for days. I had huddled in Hugh's chair while he had fallen asleep like a baby and snored his way through what was left of the night. I had dozed, got up, walked about, sat down again, dozed, got up –

The blue stones. The stones that marked the division between Gateshead and Newcastle on the bridge. Edward Bairstowe was lodged barely a foot or two inside the boundary on the Newcastle side.

A family feud carried beyond death. Edward had resented and hated his brother and, even in death, was pursuing him still. He had had disreputable friends; no doubt some had followed him to the grave and were willing to play a trick or two on his behalf, frightening a sick, miserable man.

And the attacks on me, the first of which had taken place before I even met Edward Bairstowe? They must have been intended to frighten me off, to deprive William of his only ally.

So I came to the bridge in the grey early morning of a March Wednesday, shivering with cold and tiredness, and bitter with annoyance. I wanted to get this business over and done with, before anyone else got hurt. There were few people about: a brace of chapmen sauntered out across the bridge into the countryside; a few women came the other way with cheeses and eggs to sell. A wind beat down the river and rippled the water into wavelets flecked with white.

I stepped up to Edward Bairstowe's stone, stepped on him, stepped past. He howled in rage. I squatted down beside him. "Time for a reckoning, Bairstowe."

"Oh, very harsh," the spirit scoffed. "Some female crossed you, Patterson?"

"Not as much as you have."

"Me?" he mocked. "What can I have done? I'm anchored here when I shouldn't be. Just because my own hand did the fatal deed by accident!"

He sounded calm enough but I could see the agitation in the dull stain on the cobble.

"Spare me your whining," I snapped. "And if you're even now plotting to send a message to your former friends, telling them to lure me into another trap, don't even consider it."

"Mad," the spirit said. "Quite mad!"

"It's not a particularly efficient weapon," I pointed out. "Spirits can hardly seek out a man to beat him up, can they? They have to wait until he comes to them. And once warned, he can keep out of the most dangerous places."

"My dear fellow, I don't have the slightest…"

A horseman clattered past at speed, heading out of town. "Why attack William?"

He abandoned subterfuge. "A little entertainment brightens a dull death," he said, blandly.

"You must hate him beyond measure to carry the feud beyond death."

"He's alive," Bairstowe snarled. "That's enough."

"Ah," I said, shivering as the wind swept over me. "It's all about what happened that night, isn't it? The night you died."

The spirit was silent.

"Don't want to talk about it?"

"The inquest dealt with it."

"Talked to you, did they?"

"I told them the truth."

"Don't strain my credulity too far." Frustration with his obstinacy was making my palms sweat even in this chill. I balled my fists. I was going to punish Edward Bairstowe for his vicious tricks. "You argued over the deed, didn't you?" I said. "Where is it?"

"Go to the devil."

"Buried, you said. In your grave?"

He laughed at me. No, he was right – a foolish suggestion. How could a spirit have arranged that? He must have buried it before death. But where? Or had he buried it at all? Had he said that merely to mislead me?

"If William could sell the land," I pointed out, "he could leave the town. Wouldn't that suit you?"

"Off to London?" he snapped. "All the pleasures of the town while I'm trapped here! Never!"

So Edward shared the family's fascination with the metropolis.

I considered a moment. "He'll get – oh, perhaps two hundred guineas for the land?" (I had no idea what it was worth; I chose a figure at random.) "Consider, sir. First, all his creditors will be on his back, clamouring for payment – he'll not get away without paying some of them at least. Then there's the cost of the boat to London and lodgings there. He'll need fine new clothes..."

"I won't do it," the spirit said. But some of the anger was dying out of his voice. I talked on, listing all the expenses of London which I knew only too well. The spirit murmured, occasionally put in a word or two and began to sound almost cheerful. He was plainly plotting something. I didn't trust him one inch but if I could get the deed out of him, I'd think the beatings the spirits had given me at least half paid for.

The cat came up, sniffing at the spirit on its stone, with the curiosity all cats have for spirits – as if they have a particularly flavoursome smell. I owed it a debt for finding Hugh so I scratched behind its ears. Edward Bairstowe swore at it.

"Very well," he said, at last. "I'll tell you where the deed is."

I did not believe he acted from the goodness of his heart. "What do you want in exchange?"

"Company," he said. "Your time. An hour a day."

"Two hours a week."

He hummed and hawed. I didn't care what he decided, for I had no intention of keeping any promise made to him.

"And you'll make sure William goes off to London?" he demanded.

"I doubt I'll have to do more than drop the word into conversation."

"Oh very well," he said, irritably. "But you'll have to send William for the deed. Only he will be able to get it."

I had no intention of agreeing to that condition either; I needed to recover the deed myself in order to obtain Armstrong's payment.

"Of course," I said. "Where is it?"

Solomon Strolger called to me from the street as I reached the great west door of All Hallows. He was full of glee. "He's there – for the second day in a row!"

"He?" I asked blankly.

"Bairstowe!" Strolger hadn't an ounce of reticence in him – he didn't care if he broadcast his business (or anyone else's) to the respectable tradesmen walking along Silver Street. "He came up yesterday afternoon with his bag of tools and stomped inside as if it was the devil's own home. He swore at my second youngest who happened to get in his way," he added reflectively, "but he paid the price because the child still hasn't learnt not to bite."

I could not help laughing. "I warrant he was in a rage at that! So he's repairing the organ at last." I wondered why; I couldn't imagine that William had suddenly turned over a new leaf and resolved to work harder. Maybe he wanted the money.

"Repairing it?" Strolger said impishly. "He's dismantling it! He has taken away half a dozen ranks of pipes already and says we need a new soundboard. Well, I could have told him that years ago." His face changed – he had seen the cat which had followed me up from the Key. To my surprise, he crouched down and held out his hand to the animal. "Well, well, cat – life has been treating you hard, hasn't it?" There was almost a caress in his voice. The cat sniffed suspiciously at his fingertips. "Yours, Patterson?"

"God, no. It has been following me for days."

"You need some good food and a warm blanket," Strolger crooned. He dived forward, scooped up the cat. It did not struggle. "Something to keep the children amused, eh, Patterson? Go on in – I daresay William will be glad of an excuse to stop work."

The church was still as I walked up the nave. At the foot of the loft stairs, I glanced back to the gallery above the west door where the organ stood. If Bairstowe was working there, he was remarkably quiet. No doubt he was behind the curtain, in the bowels of the organ. Or helping himself to Strolger's ale.

I climbed up the stairs and walked along the Sailors' Gallery, my footsteps echoing. I could hear Strolger's voice below and the excited chatter of children. The charity pews were closed and locked; behind them the curtain hung slightly askew. Bairstowe's tools were spread out across the organ stool and across the floor in front of the console.

I called his name but heard no answer. No sound of movement. I began to think that he had fooled Strolger; he must have crept out of the vestry when Strolger wasn't looking. I lifted the curtain.

The organ looked in greater chaos than before. The rank of pipes I had seen before still stood against the wall, but more pipes had been moved and lay haphazardly in another corner. Pallets, sliders and other more mysterious pieces of wood lay scattered about the floor.

William Bairstowe lay on the floor by the bellows blower's chair.

27

Set not your mind on earthly things for all may feel
the dread touch of eternity when least expected.
[Revd Righteous Graham, Sermon preached on the Sandgate,
Newcastle, May 1642]

Bairstowe lay with his hand on one of the pallets, as if he had been in the act of putting it down when he fell. His right arm was extended, his legs crumpled up, his head turned away from me.

I stood very still, taking in the scene. I was shocked, but a part of my mind was curiously detached and businesslike. I noted the dusty floor, patterned with footprints, some old and half-covered with dust, others newer. One set, by the shelf that held the ale jug, were plainly mine from yesterday. A confused mess by the bellows handle was made by big patched boots, no doubt belonging to the blower. A smaller foot was probably Strolger's. The vast majority were certainly Bairstowe's, made as he came and went about his work. I could not see any marks that were inexplicable.

I noted also that there was no blood.

I stepped carefully across Bairstowe's body – and at the same moment he gave a great snort. Startled to realise he was still alive, I looked down, and saw that his eyes were open and moving. The left side of his face seemed oddly slack, dragged down.

I went swiftly back along the Sailors' Gallery, leant over the railing to peer down at the open west door under the organ. Just outside, I could see half a dozen children playing with the complacent cat; Solomon Strolger was approaching with a dishful of meat.

"Bairstowe's had a seizure!" I called. "Fetch a surgeon!"

Strolger calmly put the dish down and said something to the oldest boy who ran off; Strolger himself turned into the nave. I went quickly back to the organ. I had something to find and I wanted no witnesses, least of all Strolger – he was a notorious gossip.

I ducked under the curtain again, stepped across Bairstowe and reached for the rank of pipes that stood against the wall – the ones I had seen on my first visit. The deed was in the largest of the rank, Edward Bairstowe had said; I upended the pipe.

Nothing fell out but dust.

I could hear Strolger's steps in the Sailors' Gallery. Curbing my impatience, I went methodically through each pipe against the wall. Behind me, Bairstowe was making odd noises, guttural sounds. I glanced back – his frantic eyes darted this way and that. I went back to my search.

The deed was not there. Edward Bairstowe had lied to me.

Strolger lifted the curtain, clicking his tongue as he saw Bairstowe. He was followed by the cat, which stepped delicately round Bairstowe and went to sniff at corners here and there. Behind both of them came a burly man who looked like a labourer.

Strolger walked carefully round Bairstowe's feet then astonished me by bending down and put his hand consolingly on Bairstowe's shoulder. "Don't fret yourself, William," he said kindly. "We'll get you home."

Another noise from Bairstowe's tortured throat, a dreadful hacking sound. After an appalled moment, I recognised it for what it was – Bairstowe was racked with vicious, bitter laughter.

Gale the barber surgeon came at last, a man of slight stature and quick movements. Strolger came to my side as Gale looked

Bairstowe over, and said in a low voice: "This was how old William died." He shook his head. "These things run in families."

An apoplexy, he meant. After all these threats, had William been struck down not by man, but by God?

We waited an age for Gale to be done. Strolger held up the curtain to let light in and I fidgeted; the labourer looked placidly on. The cat roamed round the loft, sniffing delicately at holes in the floorboards, at the pipes standing against the wall, glancing sideways as if a mouse or spider had caught its attention. The dust on the pipes, I saw to my horror, showed the imprint of my fingers.

At last Gale straightened and looked about him. "That door." He was pointing in fact to part of the organ case which had been propped, years ago to judge by the dust, against the wall. "We need it to carry him back to his house."

Strolger used the curtain to wipe the dust from the wood while the labourer fetched another labourer; Gale supervised the lifting of Bairstowe, groaning wretchedly, on to the door. The labourers bore him past the scholars' pews, and along the Sailors' Gallery. At the stair down, they realised they could not manoeuvre their burden round its tight curves and after a great fuss, took Bairstowe by the head and feet and manhandled him down the stairs. Gale hurried down after them. I watched from the Sailors' Gallery as they disappeared into the street. Gale would bleed Bairstowe but I doubted it would do much good.

Strolger was peering into the innards of the organ. He gestured melodramatically. "Look at what he has done!"

I contemplated the removed pipes, the split soundboard, the scatter of pallets and sliders.

"It was a cipher," Strolger moaned. "Just dust causing the mechanism to stick. And now look."

"You'll have to get Bridges from London in to fix it."

"But that could take months!" Strolger seized my arm.

"Patterson, take the bellows, will you? I won't keep you long, I promise. I just want to see what he's left me." He scrambled on to the organ stool, pulled out a few stops.

I might as well stay, I supposed. I could think over the situation here as well as anywhere else. I pulled up the chair and pumped the bellows handle up and down while Strolger ran his hands over the manuals, playing a few psalm tunes with, for once, relative simplicity. There were strange gaps in the harmony where pipes must be missing. I heard Strolger groaning, but was preoccupied with my own thoughts.

Edward Bairstowe had told me he had rolled the deed into the largest of the pipes against the wall. I stared at the pipes propped against the rough stones of the organ loft. I had admired Edward's ingenuity; it was clever to hide the deed where William might discover it, if only he did his work. But Edward had been certain he would not do the work, in order to disoblige Strolger, and the vestry were known to be too mean to call in a London builder. Yes, it had been a good place to hide the deed.

Except that it was not here. Edward had lied.

Unless –

I stopped pumping and the organ whined down. Strolger hardly noticed; I heard him muttering to himself. "No four-foot principal – how can I manage without a four-foot on the Great? Though he has repaired the eight-foot on the Swell... Do you go, Patterson? Yes, yes, pray do. I have heard enough." As I started down the stairs, I heard him say despairingly: "Far too much."

Unless, I thought, William Bairstowe had himself found the deed this afternoon. Perhaps that was what he had been trying to tell me. Perhaps it was even now in one of his pockets.

I ran for the organ manufactory.

It was impossible. It was like the day Tom Eade had died – the neighbours crowded into the alley and passers by crammed behind them. I pushed my way through the mob, heard the spirit calling. "Such a fuss," she said happily.

In the yard, the labourers who had carried William Bairstowe home were enjoying a gossip with a neighbour. Gale, the barber surgeon, could be heard behind an open window on the first floor, murmuring confidentially. No sign of Tom Eade's spirit, nor of the other world. Too many people about, no doubt.

I accosted one of the labourers. "Is Bairstowe dead?"

He shrugged. There was no help for it – I had to walk in as if I was a welcome guest and demand news.

I'd set one foot inside the house when I came face to face with Jennie McIntosh, bearing a bowl full of blood, watching carefully to make sure it did not spill. She glanced up then looked down again quickly when she recognised me.

"I heard what had happened," she said, in a low tone. "The spirits were gossiping about it. I had to come back. It's my duty."

Duty, I reflected, was an important word in the Bairstowe household.

"Are you safe here?"

"She's not a bad mistress," she said. "And she needs help."

"Are you sure?"

"Certain, sir."

"If you change your mind, there is always a refuge for you at Mrs Jerdoun's."

Now, what did that look mean? That darting glance, half-veiled? In God's name, had she conceived entirely the wrong view of my relations with Mrs Jerdoun? I opened my mouth to disabuse her, closed it again. She would not believe any protestations.

"Is your mistress here?"

"Upstairs, sir."

I walked into the house as the maid went out with the bowl of blood. And there stood Mary Bairstowe herself, regarding me from the far door of the kitchen with a face grim as death. Gale the barber surgeon was directly behind her; he murmured farewell and she saw him out civilly enough, then swung back to me.

"What the devil are you doing here?"

I started to point out that I was the one who had found her husband and sent him back home to her, but she was not to be silenced.

"You'll not get any money from me! And you'll certainly get nothing out of him. Neither dead nor alive, he is. What good d'you think that's to me? And I'll thank you not to interfere with the girl. Encouraging her to run away." Her lip curled. "I know what you're after."

"Mrs Bairstowe," I said, goaded. "I am after the truth."

She snorted in derision. I lost my temper.

"Your husband asked me to look after his interests, Mrs Bairstowe," I snapped, "and I will, money or no! And I warn you, madam, that if I hear that your husband has died and that your neglect has anything to do with it, you will answer to me."

And on this fine sentiment I slammed the door and strode out into the yard.

The labourers and neighbours had disappeared, but halfway across the yard, Gale the barber surgeon was conversing with – to my surprise – Claudius Heron. Even as I watched, Gale bobbed (a little obsequiously, I thought) and walked off.

Heron had seen me; we met at the heart of the yard, with the shut-up workshop on one side and the house standing open behind me, both equally silent. Now most of the bystanders had disappeared, the soft singing of the spirit could be distinctly heard. Tom Eade's spirit remained silent.

"You found Bairstowe, I hear," Heron said, without preamble.

I nodded. "In the organ loft of All Hallows."

"Fate sometimes takes matters out of our hands." Heron was cool and unapproachable as always but there was a touch of annoyance there too, as if he wasn't used to anyone or anything, even the hand of God, thwarting him. He was dressed in a dark coat whose colour emphasised his pale colouring and whose fine cloth emphasised his wealth.

"I came to demand another word with him," he said. "And found this mess. There is no doubt that it was illness that struck him down?"

"No doubt whatsoever."

"Just like his father," he commented.

"Another word?" I said, having just registered his previous comment.

"I spoke with him yesterday, early in the afternoon." He set his face hard. "I told him it was plain he had vandalised his own workshop and that no one could mistake his intentions. I was not, I said, prepared for him to disrupt the lives of others for his own ends."

"The lives of others." I had an uneasy feeling that Heron was referring to me.

"I told him that I would not let the matter rest if he neglected to pay what he owed."

It was plain that he had decided to take charge of the matter, and order both my affairs and Bairstowe's as he saw fit. Which is not untypical of the gentry. The world, they think, should be as they wish, and they will take whatever steps are necessary to ensure their preferred outcome. At least Bairstowe's attendance at All Hallows was explained. Heron had told him to do the work and had been obeyed; Bairstowe must have decided it was easier to give way than to fight.

I heard a noise behind me and turned to see Mary Bairstowe glowering at us from her doorstep. She was staring with undisguised hostility.

"Be away with you!"

No gentleman could be expected to accept such language from his social inferiors. Heron stiffened, then walked towards her. He did not raise his voice, or contort his face, but she retreated before him into the house, leaving the door open for him to follow. I heard him say: "Your husband is upstairs, I believe," and heard her reply, with shaken composure, "Yes, sir." Then he walked past her into the house as if it was his own.

I was left in the deserted yard. There was plainly nothing more to be gained here. I could not talk my way into the house as Heron had, and, even if I had followed him in, I would have no opportunity to search Bairstowe's pockets for the deed. In any case, how could I justify taking the deed from the man whose property it rightfully was, merely to pretend that I myself had found it, and thus be able to claim a reward?

I was staring at financial ruin. No money would be forthcoming from William Bairstowe now nor from Armstrong, even though the deed was found. And I had barely three shillings of Bairstowe's guinea left.

What in heaven's name was I to do?

28

There is nothing to be gained from revenge; it is the lowest of emotions. I beg you to ignore all such ignoble promptings.
[AMOR PACIS, Letter to his Son, printed for the Author, Newcastle, 1735]

I went back out into the street. The wind swirled along the road, dragging the dust with it and I wished I had dressed more warmly. A few bystanders still lingered; they looked as aimless as I felt. Strolger's children were playing in the street with the cat.

"Mr Patterson."

The voice was sharp, even annoyed. Startled, I glanced round and saw Esther Jerdoun, wrapped in a dark cloak against the chill.

"That girl you brought me," she said. "She has left the house."

I gathered my thoughts with difficulty. "She has returned to her place."

"William Bairstowe has been taken ill, I'm told."

"An apoplexy."

"He is like to die?"

How these few words brought my failure home to me, bitterly. Yet what can a man do against the will of God? "I think it likely, yes. Men so stricken rarely survive. His father did not. And such things often run in families."

I was talking for the sake of it, in the face of her forbidding displeasure. Surely she could not still believe the girl was my mistress?

"I do not shirk my responsibilities," she said, at last. She was silent for a moment as an elderly man shuffled past. "You gave the girl into my care and I undertook to protect her."

"It was her own wish to remove herself from your house."

"She's a fool," she said, surprising me with the scorn in her voice. "I can not abide such humble submissive girls!" The sarcasm with which she spoke these last words almost suggested she thought the girl's humility assumed.

"I think you are a little harsh," I said. "Maids must be submissive to their employers."

"They do not have to be sly," she retorted.

"I have never found her so."

"No," she snapped. "So I perceive."

We stood in the street, with a cart rattling past and the children shrieking with glee, and looked at each other with some hostility. I thought she was not in the best position to understand the lot of those who must rely on the goodwill of others for their well-being. She thought – well, I did not know what she thought. There were times when she bewildered me.

Something had to be said. I began, "She has been much abused – "

"So," Mrs Jerdoun said, with bite. "Now she has found a champion. And you, I daresay, will ensure her welfare. I wish you good luck of her. Good day, sir."

"Mrs Jerdoun – "

But she was already striding off up the street.

Annoyed and despondent, I went to Mrs Hill's tavern in the Fleshmarket to get drunk on the best ale in town. But fingering the few coins left in my pocket after I had bought the first tankard, I knew it would be the height of folly to spend money on indulgences – there were still three weeks left until the end of the quarter. I made my calculations yet again. Claudius Heron and Mrs Jerdoun at least would pay me promptly – that income, spent cautiously, would keep me a month or two. If I could persuade another pupil or two to pay, I might reach Race Week without going hungry.

And then I would have no choice but to challenge the attractions of Signora Mazzanti by putting on a concert of my own. A risky business: the expenses of running a concert – hiring the room, heating and lighting it, printing the tickets and so on – could easily run to as much as eight pounds. And if no one bought tickets, I might make no profit and end up deep in debt.

I pushed the ale away morosely. I had another reason not to get drunk. Mrs Jerdoun's daily lesson was in an hour or so and it would be the height of folly to turn up inebriated. But would the lady even attend?

A boy came into the tavern, hesitating at the door and glancing about the assembled company. I recognised the boy before he saw me, although I did not know his name. He was the eldest child of the widow that lives below Demsey, a serious-looking lad of about ten years old. He saw me and came across.

"Mr Patterson, sir? Mr Demsey sent me with a message." He had been taught to speak nicely, with not a trace of the local accent. He presented me with a screw of paper; I smiled on him but he stared impassively back.

"What's your name?"

"Thomas, sir."

"Tom for short?"

He did not respond to my friendly overtures. "No, sir. Just Thomas, sir."

Sighing, I unscrewed the paper. The message was short.

Holloway's off to Shields. Following him. I've paid the boy. HD

I stared at the scrawl in bewilderment. Why the devil was Hugh following Holloway to Shields? The fellow was probably just off on a business trip. Well, at least Hugh had had the sense to send a note, rather than entrusting the message to a spirit.

Even as I thought that, I saw a gleam of light on a wall nearby.

I crumpled the note, and fished in my pocket for a penny. The boy took a step back.

"Mr Demsey has paid me, sir."

"For sending the note. I'm paying you for delivering it."

He shook his head. "That was not the agreement I made, sir. Good day."

And with the dignity of a man three or four times his age, he turned and walked away. I admired his probity but feared that in another ten years he would be a pedantic sour-faced fellow. He looked very like what I had seen of his mother.

The spirit slid on to the bench next to me and manoeuvred round a spill of beer. "Mr Patterson, sir."

"Who the devil are you?"

"Just a fellow out for a good time." The spirit's voice took on a sly tone. "Billet-doux from a young lady, eh?"

I stuffed Hugh's note into my pocket. "None of your business."

"Oh come, sir," said the spirit. "I like a good tale. Particularly when it involves a lady, eh? Or rather, a female who ain't a lady. Eh?"

If he had been alive, he would have been winking and nudging me in the ribs. I drained my ale and walked out. Never trust a spirit, I said to myself; I'll never trust a spirit again.

The lesson with Mrs Jerdoun did not go well. She was stiff and polite, to the extent that the maid, sewing in the corner, glanced across with a puzzled frown. I was stiff and polite in return, still annoyed by the fact she believed Jennie to be my mistress. I had said she was not. I felt that she should have believed me.

Yet I was secretly glad she did not.

At the lesson's end, Mrs Jerdoun swept out of the Assembly Rooms with a curt farewell, leaving me only with a faint reminder of her perfume. I wandered out into a thin drizzle on Westgate, trying to talk myself out of a depression. I had no money and had lost the trust of the woman I admired. I told myself I was still alive and still had my musical skills; moreover, I knew how to live frugally. But I was not cheered.

I had walked as far as St John's church when I heard my name called; I turned to see a muffled figure hurrying towards me through the thickening rain. He was so wrapped up in clothes that I did not recognise him at first. Richard Softly.

He was out of breath and dishevelled, his eyes dark-rimmed and bloodshot. In heaven's name, had he been crying? He had gone beyond that now. He was filled with anger, incoherent and stuttering, hardly able to get words out between his clenched teeth. He thrust a note at me, so fiercely that I took a step back against the wall of the church porch.

"You had a hand in it," he said, as I clutched at the paper. "You had a share in it. You and those Bairstowes."

"A hand in what?" The paper was damp and warm in my hand. He must have been clutching it all the way up the street.

"It's thanks to all of you," he said, his voice breaking. An elderly labourer hurrying across the road looked curiously at him. Rain splattered against us.

"Your sister," I said, with sudden fear. "Is this to do with her? Something has happened?"

"She's dead," he burst out. "Pushed into the river last night."

Last night I had been on the bridge talking to Edward Bairstowe. I remembered hearing screams and a splash. God, could that have been the girl falling in? I had taken it for revellers. "Pushed?" I echoed. "Are you saying she was deliberately killed?"

"They're saying she jumped," he said fiercely. "Distressed about *him*."

"Tom Eade?"

I remembered the girl as I had last seen her, the determination in her face. And there had been something secret there too – she'd had plans. I couldn't believe they had included suicide.

"She would not have jumped into the river," I said, with certainty. "If she had intended to kill herself, she would have done it in the yard, so she could be with Eade."

He nodded again. He seemed visibly to become calmer; perhaps he had anticipated that I would not believe him.

"Read the note," he said. "Two days ago she gave me it. She said if something happened to her, I should bring it to you."

I hesitated before opening the paper. "She believed Tom Eade had been murdered."

"He was murdered," he said. "I don't know what they were planning, the two of them, but William Bairstowe was at the heart of it."

I drew him out of the rain into the church porch, and sat him down on the stone bench against the wall; it was chill but tolerably dry. A brewer's dray clattered past outside. I was beginning to suspect I knew what Tom Eade and his fisher girl had been doing.

"Your sister told me that she and Eade were planning to set up a food stall."

"That was why he was so close with money," Softly said, with a mixture of contempt and envy. "Saving every penny, the pair of them."

"And not above taking what wasn't theirs?"

He reddened. The rain blew in around our feet.

I said, "Come, come, we both know that John Holloway's none too canny with money and doesn't miss the odd shilling or two from his receipts."

"I have no part in that," he said sharply. I reflected wryly that he was indeed probably honest, yet Holloway valued him less than Tom Eade, who had been quite the opposite.

"You didn't tell Holloway that Eade was stealing from him?"

"How could I?" he burst out. "If I'd told him, he'd have fired Tom, handed him over to the Assizes even! She'd never have forgiven me. Perhaps she'd have been taken as well!"

I nodded. "So your sister and Eade were saving, and didn't mind too much what they did to get money. Would that include blackmailing William Bairstowe?"

"There's something wrong in that house," he said sullenly.

I didn't disagree with that. I contemplated the possibilities; William Bairstowe was careless with money himself – perhaps there had been dubious activities that had come to the ears of Eade and his lover. Maybe Holloway had let something slip in Eade's hearing. Or had it been something about William's relationship with the maid? She had, after all, been the one Tom Eade had 'courted'. Or had that just been a ruse to get inside the house?

Was it something to do with the death of Edward Bairstowe? There was something not yet told about that.

Shivering in the chill of the porch, I unfolded the note from the fisher girl. The rain spotted it at once. Holloway's name decorated the top of the page with extravagant curls and loops; the words below were carefully and neatly written. In no way could they be described as a childish scrawl; it seemed unlikely, on this evidence, that the girl had been the originator of the threatening notes William Bairstowe had received.

The note read: *Look inside that house. Look at the pair of them and you'll see what they want to keep quiet.*

I had hoped for something more informative.

Look inside that house. She must mean Bairstowe's house. What could there be that was so significant? Others had been in there – Gale, the barber surgeon, Claudius Heron. Whatever the girl referred to could not be on open display, or it would have been remarked upon. A casual social visit would clearly not reveal it.

I chewed on that fact, while the daylight lengthened and evening came on. I went back to the Assembly Rooms, was fortunate enough to find the Steward distracted by a gentleman who wanted to use the Rooms for card assemblies, and went upstairs to open the harpsichord. I was in sore need of a practice – at least the present lull in my teaching gave me time for that.

I played through some of Scarlatti's sonatas, preoccupied at first by thoughts of the Bairstowe household. Slowly the music took hold of me. The difficulties of a piece have always engrossed me; I practised several challenging passages with increasing determination.

And all the time, the puzzle revolved in the back of my mind. I had known the fisher girl only slightly but I was convinced she would not have killed herself. Not, at least, before she had had the opportunity to avenge her lover. Two deaths now. One called accident, the other called self-destruction. Two young people rubbed out of life. They deserved justice. William Bairstowe too had asked for help – did my commitment to that end, now he was cast down by fate?

Money was one thing, and I sorely needed it. But I had made promises too and I would not back out of them while there was something left that I could do.

Look inside that house, the fisher girl had said. And look I would.

29

Duty and obedience are a wife's glory.
[Sermon preached by Revd Mr Ellison,
afternoon lecturer at St Nicholas's Church, 17 August 1735]

The alley was dark. I tiptoed along it, trailing my fingers across the wall to keep my balance. By some miracle I avoided treading in any dog shit. I could hear the spirit singing faintly, her voice ebbing and flowing like the sea. She was very close now, I thought, to that final dissolution which we all must face, that final fading into the night air.

A blur of light illuminated the end of the alley. I peered into the yard and saw a light burning behind curtains at the top of the house, in the attics. A bright light that suggested many candles flickering. I thought too that I saw a light in a room on the floor below but it was so faint I wondered if I was imagining it.

I stood for a long moment, to be sure no one was moving about the house or yard. What I was proposing to do was foolish in the extreme; if Mary Bairstowe discovered me in her house, she would be entitled to call out the constable and hand me over for trial. And she would certainly do so. I could hear Hugh's voice in my ear, demanding what the devil I was doing. But Hugh was in Shields and I must act on my own. And act I would; Tom Eade and his lover demanded it. Even William Bairstowe, rude as he was, was entitled to justice.

There was something wrong about the workshop. The door was ajar. Was someone inside? There was no light. I crept across the yard and slid to one side of the door. Looking down at the new lock, I could see that the key had been turned – indeed it was still in the lock – but the catch had not engaged, and the door had swung open.

I nudged it further open. Light seeping from the attic window of the house showed me a dark hump just inside the workshop. I sank on to hands and knees, crawled to the mysterious bundle.

As soon as my hand touched it, I knew what it was – Bairstowe's bag of tools, presumably dumped here out of the way. I fumbled for the opening, pushed my hand inside and felt cautiously for an edge of parchment, taking care not to let any of the tools clink against each other.

The deed was not in the bag.

I retreated and pushed the door to, leaving it as I had found it. I was gathering myself up to run across the yard to the house when a voice spoke above my head. The spirit of Tom Eade said: "Is it true she's dead?"

I shifted back into the shadows around the workshop. "Your lover? Yes."

"In the river, they say."

"Yes."

I looked for the spirit but saw nothing. Not a gleam on the door, or the window. Not the slightest suspicion of brightness. For a moment I wondered if he might have slipped through into that other world. Then he spoke once more.

"I'll never talk to her again," he said. "Never kiss her, never caress her hair, never hear a word from her." A silence. "They couldn't even let her die here, with me."

"If she'd lived, she'd have told everything she knew, sooner or later," I said.

"All we wanted was enough money to set ourselves up in business," the spirit said. "Why shouldn't we have something of our own? We'd have done well for ourselves."

They would have, too. They had clearly both been determined people.

"Was that too much to ask?" he said. "Why should they have it all?"

"No reason."

"Anyway," he said. "Folks who don't want to be blackmailed shouldn't have secrets."

"Big secrets?" I asked, cautiously.

"*He'd* have thought so," the spirit said.

"William Bairstowe?"

"Go see," said the spirit. "Thought I'd never tell, didn't they? Go in," he said again. "Have a look. I make you a gift of it. Tell everyone. They killed her and by God, I'll ruin them."

He fell silent, and no manner of cajoling would get more out of him.

I looked at the house, at the bright light in the attics and the pale light on the floor below. Bairstowe would have thought the secret significant, Eade said. So it was not Bairstowe being blackmailed; on the contrary, he was the threat Tom Eade had held over his victim's head. His victims' heads – he had talked of *them.*

I tried the house door; to my surprise, it was unlocked and unbolted. They must have been confident they would not be discovered. I pushed the door open and walked in. The kitchen was cold and dark. No smells of cooking; the grate might have been unused a year or more. I felt my way along the wall, trying to remember the places where furniture stood. The door to the rest of the house was here somewhere – I found it, pushed it open.

A nightlight stood at the foot of stairs. I went cautiously up. It was not an old house and the stairs did not creak. At the first floor, I stood listening for a moment. I could heard women's voices at a distance. They must be in the attics, in the maid's room.

I walked through the rooms on the first floor. They were small and ill-furnished. A few threadbare rugs had been tossed over the floor boards; chairs were of good quality but their coverings worn into holes. Curtains were dusty, windows grimy.

In the largest room, heavy curtains had been drawn. A candle on a table guttered, and tossed wild shadows over the walls. Bairstowe lay naked on his back in a crumpled bed, with nothing but a blanket thrown over him. His shoulders were bare, uncovered, blue with cold. The seizure had drawn down the left side of his face and spittle dribbled from that side of his mouth; his left hand lay heavy on the blanket, but his right plucked at the cloth again, again, again. That slight touch of life was almost too dreadful to look upon.

I bent over him and saw that his eyes were open. His gaze slid to me. A grunt rose in this throat, a helpless attempt to speak. I felt a desperate urge to say something consoling.

"It was an act of God," I said. "His will, not that of mortal man."

More grunting. Sweat stood on his forehead. I looked about for water to give him but there was none. The right hand clutched feebly at my sleeve as he struggled to speak, and I struggled to comprehend. He could not form the words. He dropped my sleeve and showed me his right hand, fingers wide outstretched. Six times more, he fought to do the same, closing and opening his hand convulsively. Thirty fingers he showed me.

I bent over him again. "You want me to go on looking for the man threatening you?"

Tears were coursing down his face.

"You know," I said. "You know now who has been threatening you."

He stared at me mutely, his hand plucking convulsively at the blanket. And those pleading eyes tore at me – I could not begin to fathom what he was trying to say, or what he wanted me to do.

"I have been trying to find the deed," I said. "The deed to this land, the one your brother hid. So you can sell the manufactory." Somehow, all this seemed unspeakably pointless, even sordid. The man probably had only hours to live and I was talking of money. But again he made a tremendous effort to say something.

"You know where it is?"

More grunting.

It was impossible to understand him. In the end, I covered his shoulders with the blanket, fetched water from the kitchen and moistened his lips. Then I searched the room for the deed but there was hardly any place it could be hidden – only a press with some linen in it, and Bairstowe's clothes tossed casually on to a chair. He stared at the ceiling unseeingly while I searched. I had the impression he did not know when I left.

I went back to the stairs. Halfway up the flight to the attics, I could hear the women's voices more loudly. Mrs Bairstowe's I recognised at once. But did the other belong to Jennie McIntosh? It was not the quiet, timid voice she usually employed but a clear ringing tone with a hint of a pleasant Scotch burr. The women were laughing, swapping gossip about someone evidently known to them both.

I went up another step, another, and glimpsed them sitting in a bright room, with sweetmeats in a dish between them and wine in sparkling glasses. The maid had taken off her cap; her dark hair hung loose below her shoulders and her bodice was loosened and her breast exposed. And I saw Mrs Bairstowe lean towards her…

I went down again quickly, quietly, before I was seen, and let myself out into the yard.

In the alley, I turned back to look at the house. Close by me came the faintest of whispers, and I saw, in the light seeping from the attic window, a faint curl of smoke, as from a candle that had just been extinguished. The smoke dissipated, dissolved into the air.

The alley was silent. The spirit had gone.

I crawled into my bed exhausted and fell asleep at once, without dreaming. When I woke, I lay staring into darkness, somewhat disorientated. There were noises in the street below, cautious noises. Perhaps some of the miners were coming home very late, or very early, and were anxious not to disturb the landlady. It was still dark, I must hardly have slept at all.

I remembered William Bairstowe alone in his bed, in the darkness, while his wife and maid laughed in the bright room above…

The noise outside came again. A shuffling and a soft clattering, as if something knocked against the wall just beneath my window. Annoyed, I crawled across the bed and lifted the curtain. A shadowy figure moved in the street below, bending to pick something up from the ground. A woman with full dark skirts and a darker cloak drawn about her. She straightened and looked up, and her face caught a streak of moonlight.

Catherine, Esther Jerdoun's maid.

30

We hear that the Rose of Greenwich, commanded by Captain James, has lately arrived at Shields. [Newcastle Courant, 6 March 1736]

I was dressed and halfway down the stairs before the next handful of pebbles clattered against my window. Panicking. Outside, the maid started in surprise as I seized her arm.

"Oh, thank God," she whispered. She was trembling but took a deep breath. "She's gone."

"Mrs Jerdoun?" I hardly recognised my own voice.

"Within this last hour."

"What time is it?"

"The hall clock said two when I left the house."

I bit back my fear. The woman was distressed enough. And I needed her calm and sensible, to tell me everything that had happened. And quickly.

I rubbed at her hands; they were cold to freezing – the night was chill and she had clearly thrown on the first clothing she had found, a thin gown. But her trembling eased, as did her ragged breathing. She gave me a tiny tight smile. "Can we walk?" she whispered.

She took my arm, and we walked down the moonlit street, conversing in quiet murmurs to minimise the danger of being overheard by man or spirit. Blood was pounding in my head. Esther, Esther…

"What happened?"

"It was a trap," Catherine said, vehemently. "I'm sure of it! The boy's spirit alerted me." (The boy whose spirit inhabited Mrs Jerdoun's house had formerly been my apprentice, George.)

"He came to wake me. Evidently he heard a noise at the front door and went down to investigate, only to realise that a spirit from outside the house was talking to Mrs Jerdoun at her bedroom window."

It sounded like a deliberate plot to get George out of the way. He had apparently been indignant, feeling proprietorial about the house, as the only spirit who inhabited it. But the unknown spirit had been there only moments, and George had not been quick enough to reach him and hear what was being said.

"And while he was wandering about the house trying to find the interloper," Catherine said, "someone pushed a note under the door, and Mrs Jerdoun went down to fetch it. I think the unknown spirit must have warned her it would be there. According to George, she picked up the note, read it, went back upstairs, dressed and went out. He thinks there was someone waiting outside but naturally he could not go out to check."

That, of course, is the worst of being confined to the place of one's death.

"Did he not speak to Mrs Jerdoun? Ask her what was happening?"

Catherine looked at me with a rueful smile. She was not a particularly attractive woman, in her thirties perhaps, short and undistinguished in person, with mousy brown hair. But the smile transformed her face.

"He died as a boy, Mr Patterson, at that age when women are a source of growing fascination but extreme embarrassment. He would not dream of going anywhere near Mrs Jerdoun's rooms. He can hardly bring himself to utter a word to her, he adores her so much. But he had the sense to come and wake me. Though I wish he had done it sooner." She drew her cloak closer about her against the chill night. "She was gone long before I worked out what had happened."

We had walked up into the Bigg Market in the thin moonlight

and now turned down towards St Nicholas's church. Even at this late – or early – hour, lights burned in some of the taverns. The sound of laughter and of singing drifted through ill-fitting windows and doors.

"I found the note," Catherine said, dragging a piece of paper from the folds of her cloak. "She must have thrown it on the bed when she went back to dress. Her nightrobe was on top of it."

The moonlight was not bright enough to allow me to read the note so I moved to the pool of light cast by a lantern above a shop. The top of the paper had been torn off unevenly and the superscription had been misspelled: *Mrs Jerdoon*, it said, in an untidy childish scrawl.

I stood looking at the note for a moment without taking in what it said. A childish scrawl. Had the writer of this note also written the threatening notes to William Bairstowe? At any rate, the scrawl surely made it clear that Mrs Jerdoun's disappearance was connected to William Bairstowe's affairs. Catherine was hovering at my elbow in increasing anxiety. I read the note.

We have the musicl gentlman, it read. *If you want to see him agen, bring 20 ginease.*

They had trapped her. They had led her to believe they held me prisoner but were willing to ransom me. But in heaven's name, why?

And then the full force of the plan burst on me. They now had a weapon to use against me. They could threaten to harm Esther if I did not do as they wanted. But what was that? Did they merely want me to abandon my interference or did they want something more specific? The deed, for instance?

I stood there in the cold street, torn between desperate anxiety for Esther and a strange kind of pleasure that she had rushed straight off to try and rescue me, despite the risk to herself. But how had they known that Mrs Jerdoun's safety was so important to me? And who were they? God, Esther's well-being depended on my help and I had not the slightest idea where she might be or who was holding her!

A shout came from the nearest tavern, the sound of men brawling. Catherine was looking at me steadily, calmer now. "Mrs Jerdoun is no swooning weakling, sir. They'll not find her easy to deal with."

"I know that," I said, with a ghost of a laugh. "Do you know if she took any money with her?"

"She might have," she said. "She had some left over from her travelling but I don't know where she kept it."

"Or jewellery?"

"No, sir. That was my first thought. I checked it before I came out. There is not a piece missing." She looked at me anxiously. "What are you going to do, sir?"

"Go after her."

"But where?" She leant forward, her face reddened by the lamplight. "I questioned George, sir, to find whether any place was mentioned. But he heard nothing."

I was looking again at the note, as if it might somehow inspire me. My attention was caught by the top of the sheet. The paper had been folded over, then torn along the fold. But at the right side, it had torn unevenly, leaving a small triangle of the piece that had been removed. And on that tiny triangle seemed to be a mark –

I angled the paper this way and that under the uncertain light of the lantern. Yes, it was a printed line, a fragment of a curlicue of extravagant decoration.

Like an ornamental decoration to the letter Y, perhaps.

"Sir?" Catherine pressed.

"I saw a paper very like this earlier today." After seeing Richard Softly, I had thrust the fisher girl's note into a coat pocket; I fished it out, crumpled and faintly grubby. Catherine peered over my arm, as I held the two papers close together.

"They are very similar," she said. "If that piece had not been torn away, they could have been much the same size. Oh!"

I had shown her the outside of the fisher girl's note at first; now I turned it over and she saw the letterheading, the name of John Holloway in beautiful elaborate swirls, with a curl or six under the Y.

I stood at the foot of the Side in shadow, staring at Holloway's shop which caught the full glare of the moonlight. It stood closed and silent, the light lining its ancient timbers and leaning windows. The street was utterly deserted; I heard only the faint hoot of an owl, the sharp bark of a fox.

The note had to be from Holloway. He had torn off his letterhead to hide his identity, not knowing that Softly had stolen a sheet for his sister and that I would recognise it. He must have spent the day in Shields, as Hugh's note had told me, then returned to hear the news of what had happened to his brother-in-law. That had spurred him to capture Esther to use as a weapon against me. Did that mean there was something untoward about Bairstowe's apoplexy after all? Holloway must think I knew something he wanted kept secret. But in heaven's name, what?

I bit hard on fear, and tried to think logically. Holloway had kidnapped Esther. Would he have hidden her in the shop? Surely not – suppose she shouted for help? Of course, to prevent such an eventuality, she could have been tied up, a cloth tied about her mouth. Even the possibility filled me with rage.

I crossed the road and walked purposefully for Holloway's shop. As I came up to the door, I could hear whispering – the never-ending conversations of the multitude of spirits who inhabited the place. Then one of the spirits said distinctly: "Quiet!" A silence began like a pool at my feet, spread out like ripples, eddied and finally settled on the entire building.

I walked down the alley to the back of the house. There was not a light anywhere. If Holloway was here, he was hiding from me. I was inclined to think I was wrong; he had taken Esther somewhere else. But in God's name, where?

I could at least leave a message for him.

"Spirits!" I called. My voice echoed oddly in the emptiness of the confined yard, startling me with its harshness. "Tell Holloway I want the lady. If any harm comes to her, I'll make sure he hangs for it."

Silence. I snapped: "Is that understood?"

A faint whisper – like an echo. "Understood..."

And, as I started back down the alley towards the street, a second murmur: "Do *you* understand?"

At the last moment, I did understand. I swung round but it was already too late. A flurry of footsteps, a snatch of heavy breathing, the heavy reek of gin –

Then pain and darkness.

31

There is a strong case to be made for demolishing these noisome chares; they are the haunts of the very lowest kinds of rogues.
[ANON, Letter to Newcastle Courant, 6 March 1736]

After a time, I seemed to dream of floating, of rocking as in a ship or a carriage. Of sliding across a floor. Of being smothered in stinking blankets.

And woke to a worse reality: I lay in darkness, on cold stone. I could smell vomit, and the reek of damp rot. My head felt as if it would burst with pain.

A rat squealed.

I tried to turn over, gasped in pain, had to wait until dizziness subsided. I put out a hand into the darkness, felt the cold rough stone of a wall. Pulling against it, I dragged myself to my feet. Dizziness almost overwhelmed me; I leant back thankfully.

Men's voices in the distance. A rustle closer by – the rats, no doubt.

At least I was still fully clothed. I felt in my pockets. My few coins had gone as had the two notes.

I felt my way about the room. The walls were slick with damp and mould, and stank of the sewer. My fingers touched wood. A door, rotting but still firm where it needed to be, about the hinges and the lock. There was no window. I must be in the cellar of one of the houses in Ratten Row – perhaps even the one Hugh had been locked in.

I battered on the door, shouted. No answer. I considered kicking the door out, then realised it opened inwards. I battered again. And heard a bolt being drawn.

I jerked back just in time to prevent myself being bowled over by the door. The newcomer was outlined against a candle on a stair behind him. A tall man, cadaverous in ragged clothes. "Shut your noise!" His temple, I noticed, was bleeding from a wound high on the hairline; dried blood streaked the left side of his face.

"Did she do that to you?" I said, savagely, and launched myself at him.

He was taken by surprise, toppled backwards, but struck out all the same. His fist landed on my side. I gasped for breath, kicked back. He grunted, fell, and his head struck the bottom stair. Bone cracked. He lay still.

I vaulted over him, scrambled up the stairs in the poor light of the flaring candle. There was no door at the top of the stair – I found myself in another stinking room, lit through an open doorway on its far side. Moonlight flooded in from a narrow yard. A means of escape lay before me.

Not without Esther.

I turned on my heels. A rickety stair led up from one corner of the room; I could hear drunken voices singing above. No one seemed to have heard my scuffle with the ruffian.

A soft voice called: "Charles? Charles!"

My heart leapt. I glanced about the room. The moonlight slanting in from the yard showed me a door on the far side of the room. I leant close to it and whispered: "Esther?"

She must be close behind the door. She said, prosaically: "I heard you shouting. The door is locked."

It was not. A stout bar had been wedged across it; the bar was tight and would not shift. I battered at it with the palm of my hand, felt it move slightly. Then it gave way with a clatter; breathlessly, I stared over my shoulder at the stairs.

No sound but the drunken singing. They could not have heard. I lifted the bar from its sockets and dragged the door open. Moonlight gleamed through a small window high in one wall of the bare room and showed me Esther Jerdoun; her pale hair was loose about her shoulders, her breeches covered by a long coat. She was holding a pistol. And smiling.

"I anticipated rescuing you, and now you are rescuing me."

"I wish we were both safe at home," I said dryly.

"Amen to that."

I was keeping my distance, not for fear of the pistol but for fear of seizing her and embracing her in sheer relief. I stared at the weapon. "Have you used that thing?"

"Alas, yes," she said. "It is empty. But it makes a useful club. I hit one fellow over the head with it and none of them have come near me since."

"I think I met your victim just now."

We stood looking at each other in the glow of moonlight, both of us smiling. Then she murmured: "Do we stand here talking for an hour or two then?"

I seized her hand. "No. Let's be out of here!"

We had reached the door to the yard when we heard shouting upstairs and the thud of footsteps on the stairs. What had alarmed them I didn't know and I didn't want to stay and find out. We ran outside. Damn it, Hugh was right – the yard was enclosed. There was no way out except back into the house.

Except –

In front of us was a wall, perhaps ten feet high. In the deep shadow cast by the moonlight, I held out my hands; without hesitation, Esther stepped into them and clambered up on to the wall. From the top, she reached down for me. I took hold of her hand, scrabbled at the rough stones. The men burst screaming and shouting into the yard as I dropped down the other side.

Another yard, another house. I flung myself against the back door. It burst open.

We were precipitated into a room crowded with sleeping bodies – seven or eight men bundled in grimy blankets on the floor. Esther leapt over them and flung open a door on the far side of the room. We glimpsed a window giving on to the street, and saw men rushing along to burst in the front door.

"Up!" I said breathlessly, thinking of what Hugh had told me. "Go up!"

The stairs were narrow, uneven and rotten. Following Esther in a rush, I stubbed my toe on every step, fell twice, came out into a room where an old woman sat rocking and moaning over a young girl wrapped in an old shawl. The room stank of death. Men were shouting below, footsteps clattered on the floorboards on the stairs behind us.

We scrambled up to the next floor, struggling for breath. "Where are we going?" Esther gasped.

"These houses all connect with each other, probably in the attics."

Up to another floor, crowded with sleeping bodies who mumbled as we accidentally kicked them. The windows were squares of old newspaper pasted on to rotting frames letting in bright moonlight. The stench of urine was appalling. I clambered up again to the attics, Esther close behind me. Half the stairs were missing – I put my foot in a gap and pitched forward. Men burst into the room behind us. I dragged my foot out of the hole, crawled on and up.

Behind me, Esther cried out. I glanced back. A man below her on the stairs had hold of her ankle.

She kicked out at him but he held on. I started back to her but she called: "Go on, go on!" Her hands were at her throat; a second later, she swung her cloak in a great arc. Its folds enveloped her attacker. He yelped, fell back on top of his fellows.

We crawled up the last steep stairs. The attic was as full of sleepers as the rooms below. I ran the length of it, seeing a dark gap in the wall on the far side. A hole had been knocked through the bricks beside the chimney stack and the gap shored up by beams that looked like old ship's timbers. As Esther raced past me, into the attic of the next house, I threw my weight against one of the timbers, felt it shift, tried again. It toppled and I ducked through the hole just as the makeshift lintel gave way. There was a rumbling and a roar, and the wall caved in. The roof above cracked; slates started to slide and crashed down into the attic.

We stumbled to a halt, stone dust rising around us; I jumped as a slate crashed to the floor behind me. Moonlight gleamed through the new hole in the roof and showed us the contents of the attic.

It was a treasure trove. Boxes of candles, casks of beer, coils of rope, bolts of cloth. Clothes were heaped in one corner – I spotted Hugh's coat, recognising it by the gleam of the huge buttons.

"Stolen goods," I said. Bedwalters would be delighted to hear of this – if he could get together a band of men audacious enough to raid the house.

"Men on the stairs!" Esther said breathlessly. Voices. We were cut off from our original pursuers by the debris, but the men in this new house were coming to see what was happening. And the holes in the roof were still tearing apart, albeit more slowly; rafters hung loose, and the lime and horsehair plaster that rendered the roof watertight peeled away and dropped down around us. Stone dust trickled down the wall.

I seized a coil of rope. "Knock out that window!"

The frame was covered only by paper. Esther seized a slate from the floor and threw it at the window. Remnants of glass behind the paper shattered and fell tinkling into the alley below. I tied the rope to a full cask in the centre of the attic, dropped the end of the rope out of the window. "Can you climb down?"

"Of course."

She swung herself out of the window even as the first of the men from below burst in. His way was blocked by fallen rubble from the roof. I saw him snarl and lift his hand. I ducked. A pistol shot whined over my head. I groped around for something to throw at him, found nothing better than a sackful of candles, tossed them one after another in his direction.

"Charles!" Esther called. "Quickly! Come down now!"

I scrambled to the window, tossed down Hugh's coat to her. Another pistol ball whistled past my ear, smacked into the stone of the wall and fell flattened to the ground outside. Then I was over the sill and sliding down the rope, heedless of burns to my hands.

Halfway down, I felt the cask shift. The rope went slack. I fell – but it was barely four feet to the ground and Esther steadied me.

"Run!" I gasped.

We ran. Along the chare. It was so narrow that the moon hardly penetrated it; we stumbled from one wall to another. The cobbles were filthy, littered with shit, human and animal, scattered with debris that tripped us. But there was the end of the chare, framing a sliver of moonlit Key –

And there was Mary Bairstowe.

32

There are certain things, sir, that should never go outside the family. These things are not the business of strangers.
[AMOR PACIS, Letter to his Son, printed for the Author, Newcastle, 1735]

She stood in the moonlight like a sour-faced Gorgon. "Take hold of them," she said. I glanced back, saw men advancing from the houses.

"No," Esther said, and lifted her pistol. If she thought she could intimidate Mrs Bairstowe with an empty pistol, I knew her to be wrong. But she simply said: "Go to the devil," and *fired.*

Mrs Bairstowe did not so much as flinch as the shot whistled past. A man took the pistol out of Esther's hand. "Thank you kindly, lady, but I'll take my own back."

Esther met my gaze and smiled ruefully. "I took the weapon off one of the sleepers in the attic."

Two or three of the men were laughing. "You've led us a fine dance, I'll say that," said the keelman who'd taken the pistol. "Best night's pleasure I've had in a long time."

"There'll be more," someone else said, coarsely.

I turned back at Mary Bairstowe and saw Jennie McIntosh dancing at her heels. Demure, submissive little Jennie, with a smile of pure vindictive pleasure on her face. Esther had been right. She was sly.

"You saw me earlier," I said, realising how clumsy I had been. "When I crept into your house to find out what was going on."

"You should be lighter on your feet," Jennie said.

"I'll remember that for next time."

Esther was close beside me, so close I could feel her warmth, and see the fearless look of calculation on her face. God help us, she had something else in mind; I must deter her from doing anything rash. We were grossly outnumbered and could not hope to win a fight. Talking, that's what we needed. I clenched my fist, slowly unclenched it, willing myself to be calm.

"You can go now," Mary Bairstowe said to the men. They did not move. Except for one lean man, who came forward insolently, sneering at me. He still reeked of gin.

"Nay," he said, pointing at me. "Not till I've had my own back on him."

"You might not win," I said, coolly. "Any more than you did the last time." The men laughed, which clearly enraged the fellow.

"And I'll have the breeches off the lady!"

Esther caught my arm as I started towards him. "If you think I am easy pickings," she said to him, "think again!" She leant towards him and said softly, "I do not fight fair."

More laughter. Mrs Bairstowe was shouting in fury, trying to subdue them. "Be gone with the lot of you!"

"Nay, lady," said the man. "We've done your bidding. We've caught them for you. Now we want our payment."

They stood face to face, equally belligerent, equally determined not to give way. I was happy to encourage them; if I could engineer a fight between them, we might have a chance to escape. What might annoy the hard-faced man further? Money, that's what.

"I knew the plot but not the plotter," I said to Mary Bairstowe. "You were the one threatening your husband. You want him dead so you can sell the manufactory and go off with the proceeds. If you can find the deed of course."

There was silence. The men shifted restlessly.

"What deed?" said the hard-faced man.

"There's money in deeds," one of his followers said.

"If you can read 'em," said another, with a roar of laughter.

"Lots of money," I said. "That's why she wants it. And I know where it is."

"I might want it myself," said the hard-faced man, softly. I shivered when I heard that tone of voice. Mary Bairstowe did not move; she stood four-square, defying the lot of them.

I leant towards Esther. "Be ready to run – "

But at that moment, another figure appeared from the Keyside. Holloway, with a pistol in his hand. The men growled when they saw him; he looked taken aback by their hostility. My heart leapt. If Holloway was here, then Hugh might not be far away. I knew Hugh's tenacity; he would not have simply gone home after Holloway got back to town. He would have continued to follow Holloway. Unless, God forbid, Holloway had got rid of him.

Uneasy and skittish, Holloway bent close to his sister: "The ship leaves tomorrow."

A ship? Hugh had said the spirits in the house had talked of a ship, and London too. And Shields, where Holloway had spent the day, was the best place to find such a ship. Damn it if Hugh hadn't been on to something after all. I said brightly: "You mean the ship from Shields? To London, I take it?"

There were more angry rumbles from behind us; Mary Bairstowe yelled. "I said ye can go! We've done with ye."

"Mebbe we haven't done with ye," someone said quietly.

Demure little Jennie McIntosh sauntered forward. I had to admire her – a few short sentences in an unintelligible patois, an argument or two, and she had them turning, albeit reluctantly, for their chares. Of course she was of their stock; she knew what they wanted. She gave me a saucy look, took Hugh's coat out of my hands, gave it back to the men. No doubt she had also promised them our clothes in due course.

Only the hard-faced man lingered to give me a sour look.

"I'll see ye agen," he said.

"And I'll beat you again," I said, cordially.

He snarled at me.

"Now," Mrs Bairstowe said, when we were alone on the lantern-lit Key. "Where's this deed?"

"He knows where the deed is?" Holloway said eagerly.

"So he says."

"I do," I agreed. "And I'll show you. On one condition."

"No," Jennie McIntosh said. She laughed. "We're not letting you go. You know too much."

"Then why should I tell you where the deed is?"

Holloway and the maid exchanged glances at that; Mrs Bairstowe remained stolidly impassive. "Reckon you could keep quiet for thirty guineas?"

I was ready to agree to anything that would get us out of there alive. "Easily," I said.

"He's lying." Holloway threatened us with the pistol. "He'll go straight to the constable."

An owl swooped overhead, a great white shape in the darkness. I didn't want owls; I wanted people – drunks, thieves, whores – anyone to distract our captors and give us a chance to run off. There was no one. No one but Esther and myself and our own quick wits to get us out of this mess.

"It was a nice trick you pulled on Demsey and myself," I said, to flatter Holloway. "You and Jennie here staged that scene in your house, didn't you? Jennie even lingered outside until Hugh could catch up with her, so she could lead us into the chares. Her friends were supposed to oblige you by beating us up and thereby frightening us so much we would give up our pursuit of you. In return, they'd get our clothes. A pity the spirits intervened."

"Lord," Jennie McIntosh said, with a yawn. "How you can talk!"

"And since that didn't work, you've engineered this plot. I admire your persistence."

Where the devil was Hugh?

"Of course, something did come of that first plot," I said, reflectively. "Jennie was supposed to gain my confidence. Which she did. And I bore her off to Mrs Jerdoun, which gave you the idea to play this second trick."

"Aye," Mary Bairstowe said. "And just think on this. If ye give us away, we've no reason not to tell the world about your lady friend." Her gaze flickered up and down Esther's slim breeched figure. "If ye can call her a lady."

Esther stood silently beside me, her face calm, her breathing untroubled. But I knew her well enough to recognise the alert readiness in her; she would act the moment I gave the word. My admiration for her was boundless.

My hands hurt like the very devil from the rope burns and my eyes ached with the strain of seeing in the flickering lantern light as I tried to stare Mrs Bairstowe out of composure. "We can come to an arrangement that will suit us all, surely?"

"Keep talking," Mary Bairstowe said grimly.

"You want the deed so you can sell the property and take yourself off somewhere on the proceeds."

"London," Jennie said, with relish. Holloway grinned widely. That obsession again!

"But for you to inherit the money, William must die. And, unfortunately, he lingers between life and death."

"He'll die," Mary Bairstowe said, contemptuously. "Like his father before him."

"You'll have to be careful," I said. "If you're suspected of having a hand in his death, you'll inherit nothing. And Edward Bairstowe is doing his best to thwart you by refusing to reveal the whereabouts of the deed."

"Edward is a rogue and a cheat," she said.

"Kindred spirits," I said. "Lawyer Armstrong told me you were as thick as thieves once." She said nothing yet I sensed indecision in her. Perhaps she was as puzzled as I was about how to come off safe from this situation. One thing was certain: she was the leader of the conspirators. Where she led, the others would follow. "You and Edward were going to kill William, weren't you?" I pressed. "Five years ago."

Jennie McIntosh began to protest impatiently but I thought I had the whole of it now and wanted Mary Bairstowe's confirmation. "Edward's threat to jump from the bridge was a trap. He never got up on that parapet, although he threatened to do so. He was simply trying to lure William within reach of the knife. When William tried to take the knife off him, there would have been a terrible accident and William would have been killed."

"Ye can talk," the woman said. "I'll give you that."

"You had to play the farce out," I said, "because William had to believe it. When the coroner questioned his spirit later, you had to be certain William would say it had been an accident. Only it had been sleeting and the cobbles were slick. Edward fell and the knife cut into his throat." She still said nothing. "Why did you wait another five years before trying a second time?"

"The deed, man," Holloway said, impatiently. "We had to have the deed."

I laughed; Esther murmured a warning.

"Of course," I agreed. "Not much point in going to all this trouble if you can't prove ownership of the land. And Edward wouldn't tell you where the deed is. What was the matter? Argued, did you?"

"He thought we'd tried to cheat him," Holloway said, indignantly. Mary Bairstowe stood impassive in the moonlight, as if she didn't care what we did and didn't know.

"Edward thought that you and William had plotted against him, and intended that he should die?"

Mary Bairstowe said nothing.

"A tangled web," I said. "You plotted with Edward against

William, Edward thinks you plotted with William against him, and in reality you were plotting with your brother to kill them both and take the money."

Mary Bairstowe said heavily: "The only folks you can trust are your own." I saw Holloway flush with pleasure.

"Which of course," I said, "is why you chose Holloway to stage that scene in the yard and hit you over the head. One more piece of evidence to convince everyone that William really was under threat and from an unknown outsider. And he himself was helping by muttering about persecution, and spirits being after him, and generally becoming more and more unstable. Wasn't John panicked when he realised how hard he had hit you!"

"I didn't mean – " Holloway began but Mrs Bairstowe put a hand on his arm.

"Aye," she said, "I know."

Esther was murmuring uneasily in my ear. "This will only make them more anxious to kill us!"

"Trust me," I said.

She hesitated, then nodded. That meant more to me than almost anything else that night. Now all I had to do was to justify her faith in me.

"But you have tried again even though you don't have the deed," I said. "You sent William those notes written by our friend Jennie here."

The girl curtseyed mockingly to me.

"And when he, and I, didn't seem to take much notice of them, you wrecked his workshop to make the point."

"Well, he doesn't use it much," she said.

"And I thought he'd done it. No wonder he was so indignant. Next time don't break the lock from inside. But why try to kill William even though the deed is still missing?"

"The organ in the Cordwainers' Hall?" Esther suggested.

"They'll use the proceeds of the sale to take them to London."

"Fifty guineas," I mused. "That won't get you far in London, especially not with three of you."

"We're going," Jennie McIntosh said with a pout of determination, flaunting her moonlit curls. "I'm not staying in this hole any longer."

We all looked at her. Holloway was nodding in agreement; I swear I even saw Mary Bairstowe's face soften. So the girl was leading them all by the nose, was she? Seizing her chance of bliss come what may, while Mary Bairstowe and John Holloway were both besotted with her. I wondered just how much she cared for the pair of them, and how soon they would find their demure maid dancing attendance on the first handsome man who dangled a few guineas in front of her eyes.

"I know where the deed is," I said, determinedly bringing the conversation back to the point. If no one was going to break in on our *tête à tête* and distract our captors, our best chance was to get out of this damn chare and into the wide streets where we might have a chance of running. If we could evade that pistol of Holloway's.

I thought I heard the sound of footsteps down the Key and risked a quick glance in that direction. I saw no one, though the erratic light of the lanterns, which were burning low, was confusing.

"Let's make a deal," I said. "We give you the deed. You ride off to Shields and take that ship for London. Whatever business you need to do in selling the property when your husband dies can be done through lawyers. After all, as yet no crime has been committed. Edward died by his own hand, William was struck down by God. And meanwhile, we'll forget all about it."

Mary Bairstowe was laughing softly. "You're forgetting a pair of love-birds."

I had been hoping that she would not think of Tom Eade and

his lover. I sighed with resignation. "That's a tale easily told. Tom and his girl found out about you and Jennie here, and threatened to tell your husband unless you paid them not to. So you killed first him and then her."

"Easy meat," she said contemptuously.

"Did you push her into the river yourself? That was unkind of you." She was plainly unmoved. "But did you not think that Tom Eade would talk once he knew his lover was dead?"

"Of course!" said Esther, beside me. "That's why they are in such a rush to go tonight. Because tomorrow Tom Eade will talk his heart out to the constable."

I nodded, smiling at Mary Bairstowe. "You miscalculated. He talked to me tonight."

"That's your bad luck," Jennie McIntosh said.

"It must have been a difficult decision to make," I mused. "Alive, the girl would have bled you dry. Dead, her lover will betray you. All you can do is act and act quickly. Hence your need to kill William now. Hence Holloway's trip to North Shields to book passage on a ship. And your eagerness to be rid of me."

"I'm not afraid of you," Mary Bairstowe said contemptuously. "But there are folks who'll listen to you. That gentleman William was supposed to be building an organ for – he'll have friends in London. He'll send them after us."

Holloway was restless, casting anxious glances up and down the Key. "Let's be done with it. Get the deed and be gone from this pestilential town."

"Kill them," Jennie McIntosh said. "There's no need to take risks."

Mary Bairstowe spoke heavily. "I want that deed." She glanced at the maid. "Ye want the money, don't you? We can't sell the land without the deed." A steady look back at me. "We'll buy it from you. You give us the deed and we give you your lives."

Holloway burst into anger. "Jennie's right. They'll talk! We can't leave them alive!"

"We won't talk," I said. "Leave William alive, and leave us alive, and we'll keep quiet."

Mary Bairstowe considered. "Aye," she said at last, and silenced the other two with a look.

33

Never count on the good will of Fate…
[AMOR PACIS, Letter to his Son, printed for the Author, Newcastle, 1735]

We walked back through the narrow chare and up the silent stinking moonlit stretch of Butcher Bank. Esther and I walked first, arm in arm, like a married couple; she cast me an occasional watchful look, as if to say 'I know you're planning something – I'm ready to aid you'. She seemed confident in my ingenuity. I wished I felt the same.

Holloway came behind us, with the pistol poking in my back. Then Mrs Bairstowe, breathing heavily on the hill, behind him. The maid was on Mary Bairstowe's arm; I heard her murmur, thought I caught the word London.

And somewhere behind all of us, I hoped, came Hugh.

As we walked, Esther said pensively, "Why did William Bairstowe never suspect any threat against him till now?"

"Because he's a fool," Holloway said, behind us.

"He's a man who can't see further than his own business," I said. "He noticed nothing amiss in the matter of Edward's death. Remember, he was accustomed to Edward's wildness. He didn't even worry when the notes arrived – he thought them some foolish prank. It was the attacks by the spirits that alarmed him."

Deliberately I raised my voice so that Mary Bairstowe could hear me. "Edward knew William did not take the notes seriously so he organised the spirits' attacks to alert William to his wife's plans."

"But why?" Esther asked, with a puzzled frown.

"To thwart those plans. Edward, you see, believes Mary Bairstowe caused his death. And he was right, wasn't he?"

"You're talking nonsense," Mary Bairstowe said implacably. It was irritating not to be able to see her. "No one knew what John and I were planning for Edward's death. No one knew Jennie and I were sending those notes, neither. Edward cannot have taken a hand in the business."

"John knew," I pointed out, casting Holloway a mocking backwards glance. "And John – " I teased them with a moment's silence, as we walked up the moonlit street. "John tells the spirits everything."

"No," Holloway protested, with sudden vehemence. "They wouldn't tell anyone. They're my friends."

"Spirits are no one's friends," I said bitterly, and saw Esther Jerdoun look at me sharply. "They know everything, or can know everything if they take the trouble, and there is nothing anyone can do to punish them. They may do as they please. Edward wants his revenge, on his brother and on you, doesn't he, madam? That's why he used the spirit attacks to alert William to your plans. He achieves two objects with one action. On the one hand he thwarts your plans, on the other he frightens his brother almost beyond endurance."

We walked on in silence, turning into Silver Street. Three lanterns burned in the street, one at the gate of All Hallows. I said to Esther: "William suspected neither his brother nor his wife. He merely supposed he had offended someone with his manner or his unscrupulous business dealings. He didn't mention the deed to me because he didn't think it had anything to do with the attacks on him."

All Hallows loomed before us; the moon, nearly full, slid behind the tower. "The deed's in the church," I said.

Holloway seized his sister's arm. He seemed unnerved by my accusations against the spirits. "It's a trap!"

"Go in," Mrs Bairstowe said.

"It's dark," I pointed out. "We won't be able to see in there."

The maid swore and darted to the nearest lantern. She unhooked it from its bracket and brought it back, flaring and spluttering.

We went into the church.

The great building, dilapidated as it was, had a solemn grandeur in the darkness. Shadowy pillars rose up to the vaulted roof. I thought I heard a faint whistle and chatter; a tiny bird swooped in the recesses of the chancel, flittered and was gone. We stood for a moment to adjust our vision in the lantern light; Holloway dug the pistol into my back.

"Where is it?"

I went down the aisle slowly, arm in arm with Esther; she glanced at me as if trying to judge when I would make a move. I wished I knew what to do. I was praying that Hugh was here, slipping through the west door after us, hiding amongst the dark, locked pews. In the name of all that was holy, I didn't want to go up the narrow stairs to the organ loft with Holloway's pistol in my back. Not in his present nervous state. Nor did I want to cross the organ loft in the darkness – I had an unfortunate encounter in an organ loft not so long ago and damn near lost my life. I suppose there are worse places for a musician to die but I would rather not die at all. Not for a good few years yet.

The lantern light was fitful and the maid walked with it behind us. The light cast dancing shadows before us and hid obstacles in our way. Esther walked into the edge of a pew and stifled a curse. Mrs Bairstowe said again: "Where's the deed?"

"In the organ loft," I said, reluctantly.

"Stop!" We halted while she walked round to stand in front of us. Holloway's pistol was still at my back. The maid leant against the side of a pew on the other side of the aisle. In the flickering light cast by the lantern, I saw that the door of the pew next to us stood unlocked and ajar. But even if we dashed inside, where could we go from there?

"Now," Mrs Bairstowe said. "I'm going to keep my hands on her ladyship and you are going to go with John to get the deed. So if there's mischief planned, the lady will suffer. Understand me?"

I did not want to be separated from Esther. Together we might surprise them; separately we could not. And Jennie McIntosh and Mary Bairstowe were no weaklings, in body or in mind – they would not hesitate to injure Esther.

I heard myself laughing, as if hysterically, allowed my voice to rise in volume. Inwardly, I was praying, and praying that I had guessed correctly. "What the devil do you think I plan to do? Create some diversion?"

On the words, the great west door slammed shut.

Jennie McIntosh jumped and dropped the lantern. I heard it smash on the floor. The light flared and went out. In the darkness, I threw myself against Esther and she pitched sideways; we crashed to the floor of the open pew. And in the same moment, I heard a shot, a grunt, and a heavy thud.

Then silence.

34

… never believe that you will wake to another day.
[AMOR PACIS, Letter to his Son, printed for the Author, Newcastle, 1735]

In the silence, I heard a faint singing, as if the dissolved spirit in the alley had returned. But this was a male spirit, unharmonious, its voice cracked, singing, very solemnly, Purcell's music for the funeral sentences. *Man that is born of woman hath but a short time to live.* The voice echoed in the pitch-black church.

"Charles?" Esther whispered.

She was visible only as a sense of movement, against the wall of the pew.

"I'm safe," I whispered. "Are you hurt?"

"Bruised. Nothing more."

No other sound but the swift patter of running feet.

Holloway said uncertainly, "Mary?"

I heard the west door swing open. Peering from the end of the pew, I saw a sliver of the moonlit street and Jennie McIntosh's slim figure, squeezing through the narrow gap.

"Hugh!" I called. "Do you have a lantern?"

His voice came back from somewhere at the west end, under the organ gallery. "Can't get the damn flint to strike."

A moment later, light flared, then settled. The light advanced up the nave, held by a shadowy half-lit figure. I could see Holloway, standing very still; I reached out and took the pistol from his nerveless hand.

We looked down on Mary Bairstowe's slumped figure. Esther was rubbing her right arm as if it hurt; Hugh was dishevelled, covered with dust from travelling, and bleary-eyed. Holloway, stricken, stood with tears coursing down his cheeks. And I – I was wondering how we were going to get out of this mess.

I gave Holloway back the pistol. "Throw it in the river. Then go home and be surprised when they come to tell you your sister's dead."

"Charles!" Hugh protested. "You cannot let the fellow go! He killed her."

"He was aiming at me."

"He's a villain. They were plotting to kill Bairstowe!"

"He's already been punished," I said. I held out the pistol to Holloway; he seemed hardly to notice.

"Forget the trip to London. Sit quiet a few years and pretend you know nothing. Better still, sit quiet for the rest of your life."

He gave me a helpless look. "There is nothing left in life."

"For God's sake!" Esther said impatiently. "Stop whining and thank your maker no one will bring you to book for this stupid business."

He stared at her unseeingly, then looked at me, looked down at the pistol. With a convulsive gesture, he knocked my hand aside; the pistol slipped from my grasp and went clattering amongst the pews. Then Holloway swung round and was off at a halting, panicked run. And we three were left, silently looking down at the crumpled body of Mary Bairstowe, while the unseen spirit intoned the funeral sentences into the darkness around us.

35

We hear that Mr William Bairstowe, organ-builder, dropped down dead in the organ loft in All Hallows' Church last Wednesday.
[Newcastle Courant 13 March 1736]

We argued about whether to call out Bedwalters, and tell him frankly what had happened, but it was such an unlikely tale we thought he would not believe us. After all, we still had the fatal pistol in our possession. Moreover, I was unhappy that Esther – Mrs Jerdoun – should be involved at all. Yet there would be no escaping should the spirit choose to accuse us. In the end, Hugh pointed out that if we were not seen near the body, we might be able to claim that Mary Bairstowe's spirit was being vindictive in any accusations against us, and we decided to leave the body for someone else to discover.

So Hugh and Esther went off together for safety's sake, in case the ruffians from the chares still roamed the streets; I gave Hugh the pistol to throw into the river.

I waited until they were gone, then took the lantern up the stairs in the middle of the church. As I walked down the Sailors' Gallery towards the organ, my footsteps echoed in the great empty church; leaning over the balustrade, I saw the huddled dark shape on the nave floor below, and shuddered. We all came to an end sooner or later but to meet one's fate at the hands of the only person one trusts is dreadful irony.

The organ loft swam with shadows, cast by the huge case, the organ stool, the charity children's pews. I ducked under the curtain and stood looking for a moment at the debris before me: the ranks of pipes Bairstowe had laid on the floor, the discarded pallets, a rag or two and a missed tool.

Bairstowe, in his short time in the church, had dismantled parts of the mechanism but yesterday Strolger had also said that he had repaired one of the ranks of pipes. Perhaps William had guessed what I was looking for when he saw me searching – perhaps that was what he had been trying to tell me as he lay stricken on the floor.

I shone the lantern into the cobwebby interior of the organ. Bairstowe had swept most of the mouse-droppings into a heap; a mummified mouse lay dead in a corner. Bairstowe had repaired one of the ranks on the Swell, Strolger had said. The work was easily recognisable – the pipes were the only clean things in the entire interior. Five gleaming pewter-grey pipes had been restored to their places – I shone the lantern at the largest.

Edward had not lied after all.

The parchment crackled in my hands as I eased it from the pipe. It was curved into a tube beyond remedy and I struggled to unroll it. I glimpsed a date fifty years before and the words *Whereas this deed witnesseth that the Vestry of All Hallows Church...*

It was what I had been looking for.

There was one more thing to be done before I could go home. William Bairstowe could not be left in his house, to die alone. I left the church, walked down Silver Street towards the manufactory. The alley was oddly quiet, being now unspirited, but when I came into the yard, I saw lights burning in the house, on the second floor where I knew William Bairstowe's room to be. There was a light in the attic too. Surely Jennie McIntosh could not have returned?

As I approached the door, she burst out of it, coming to an abrupt halt as she saw me. She wore travelling clothes, a thick cloak over her shoulders, a demure cap on her head. A heavy bag hung in her hands. As she jerked back, startled, I heard coins jingle in the bag.

"Off to London?" I said.

She sneered at me. "No business of yours, sir."

"It's William Bairstowe's business if you're making off with his savings."

"His savings!" she spat. "I've taken nothing of his. It's all hers. What we were going to live on in London until the house was sold." She stood looking at me. "Well, and are you going to stop me?"

"What would you do if I did?"

"Tell a round tale." She laughed. "Say you shot her. Say she came upon you and your whore playing together in the church and threatened to tell the world so you shot her to prevent it. Couldn't have your reputation tarnished, could you? Not that you're too concerned about the lady's reputation, eh?" Her face twisted in contempt. "You men never worry about us. We're only here for one thing, aren't we? For your service or your pleasure – and oftentimes they're the same thing."

I could hardly try and persuade her she was wrong; the whole of her experience said otherwise. I stood back.

"I'm not preventing you going. Take your ship to London and spend your mistress's money."

"It's mine," she said sharply. "She wanted me to share it."

I merely nodded and she was gone, slipping out of the bright light cast by the candles in the house, into the dark alley. I did not know what she would do in London but I did know that even the greatest amount of money lasts only a short time there. Once it was gone, she would have to become a servant again, or worse. And I did not doubt that in a few years time, I would be reading her name in the *Courant* as condemned to transportation or to the gallows.

"Good riddance," Tom Eade's spirit said bitterly out of the darkness.

"Pity her," I said. "At least you had your love, for however short a time. I don't think she knows the meaning of the word."

"She didn't pity my lass," he said.

The kitchen was cold, the fire long since gone out. Plates still stood in ranks upon the dresser, although I saw a gap in the rank of knives – the girl had taken some defence against the world. I went into the back of the house; as I mounted the stairs, a faint snoring came from upstairs, a rattle of breath, a pause, more snoring. William Bairstowe plainly still lived. I went through the door into his room, and saw, to my amazement, Claudius Heron, looking up from a chair at the side of the bed.

He had a book upon his knee and a pistol in his hand. As he looked up, he half-raised the pistol, recognised me, lowered the weapon again. "Caught her, have you?"

I laughed unwillingly. "Have I been running about the town in a mad confusion for days, while you have known all along?"

He shook his head, indicated at another chair that stood against the wall. I dragged it forward, and he reached for wine that stood on a small table beside the bed. There were, I noted, two glasses, one unused. Candlelight gleamed off Heron's pale hair, glittered in his eyes.

"I have had plenty of time to consider the matter, sitting here tonight."

I looked on William Bairstowe in the neatly-ordered bed, with his slack mouth and stentorian breathing. His colour seemed better.

"Even then," Heron said, "I had not fully resolved the matter until the maid came running back." He filled a glass and held it out to me. I downed the wine eagerly, not knowing till then how thirsty I was; I had taken neither drink nor food for half a day.

"I heard a shot," Heron said. "Then the maid came home without the mistress, ransacked the place and made off again." He smiled thinly, his eyes on my face. "I overheard your conversation below. Is the woman dead?"

"Yes, and unfortunately – "

"Yes?"

"In the church."

He grimaced. "That will cause a stir. We will have the bishop, the archbishop and half a hundred other clerics descend on us."

"We did think of dragging her into the churchyard," I said. "But we thought better of it. We can't drag her spirit out of the church."

"We?"

I told him the story. His face tightened when I told him how I had been knocked out, and lengthened in unmistakeable disapproval when I told him of Esther's exploits, and I told him as little of that as I could. He sat in the flickering candlelight, his long thin fingers clasped around the stem of his wineglass, leaning across to refill my glass from time to time, only speaking at the end.

"The spirit will be malicious. When she disembodies in two or three days from now, she will be eager to talk, and you can be certain she will not be complimentary to any of you."

I sighed. "Esther – Mrs Jerdoun – has gone home and her servants will say she has been in bed with a slight fever. Her maid will swear she has sat with her all the time. Hugh and I will say we were in our respective beds. What more can we do?"

Heron considered, staring at William Bairstowe's restless figure.

"Go downstairs and find some water," he said. "Clean yourself. There are cold meats on a platter and some stale bread in the kitchen. Bring them back up with you."

I stared at him in confusion.

"You have been here with me all night," he said, drinking wine. "Looking after Bairstowe in the unaccountable absence of his wife. We dismissed the nurse together. She was so abominably drunk she probably saw three of me in any case. And we have been talking ever since." His thin lips curved into a cynical smile. "No one will doubt my word."

I hesitated but got up to do as he directed. "They will ask why the spirit should lie," I pointed out.

"You were hired to find the deed and did not. She thought you were cheating her husband and is therefore intent on revenge."

"There is a problem with that story," I said, and showed him what was in the pocket of my coat. "I have found the deed."

He stared at the stiff parchment now for ever curled into a cylinder then took it from me, unrolling it with difficulty and angling the parchment to catch the candlelight. "I'm no expert in these matters but it looks in order." He examined the seal. "Gale says Bairstowe may well recover. With this, he can sell the land and live in tolerable comfort."

"Half paralysed," I said. "I'd not choose that kind of life."

"I daresay," Heron said, "he will derive much enjoyment from raging about his lot." He rolled up the deed and handed it back to me. "Thank God this matter is finished."

"No," I said. "It is not quite finished yet."

36

Any civilised man or woman must shudder at the desecration of one of our churches this week. Can anyone understand the depths of depravity that led to this horror, or the wickedness that can hide behind the most innocent and fair of facades?
[Revd A. E., Letter to Newcastle Courant, 13 March 1736]

I waited, through the shrieking of the churchwarden who discovered the body in the morning, through the sending for the surgeon and through his pronouncement that the woman was dead. Through the confusion and the urgent discussion as to whether the church could still be used as a place of worship or whether it had been desecrated, whether the bishop should be sent for or the archbishop, whether the church should be closed up, and if so, for how long. Solomon Strolger began to look hopeful at this and talked of taking his family off to London to visit his mother. He asked if I would look after the cat while they were away. I was feeling favourably disposed towards it for finding Hugh on the Key, and said I would.

I occupied some of this time by going back to Thomas Saint's printing office and reading through his archives once more. The account of Edward Bairstowe's death made more sense now, though I wondered how Mary and Edward had ever thought they could succeed in killing William. He was the sort of man who frustrates all plans, out of sheer obstinacy. As he did now, lying halfway between life and death and coming back to the world slowly, his grunts and groans at times beginning to sound almost like speech again.

I went several times to the yard, hoping for some gap in reality through which I could see the starlit sky and the pale gravestones in that other world. Had Bairstowe glimpsed them too and perhaps interpreted them as an augury, as an omen of Doom. I did not suppose I would ever know.

I saw nothing.

Thomas Saint's boy came every day to report how many tickets had been sold for the organ. In the usual rush of charity with which the rich placate the gods for their good fortune, there had been a surge of ticket buying by ladies and gentlemen who had no interest in music; nearly two hundred tickets had been sold and Heron told the boy to continue showing the organ until Monday when the draw would be made. Bairstowe would need as much money as possible if he was not to live in destitution. I thought he was receiving a great deal more generosity than he deserved.

Early on Saturday morning, Mary Bairstowe's spirit disembodied and was interviewed. Lawyer Armstrong came into the organ manufactory afterwards to tell us what had happened. It was a strange meeting; Armstrong was surprised to find us all there, frowned at Heron, at Mrs Jerdoun and at Hugh in turn, and was half-distracted throughout by the rants of the drunken nurse upstairs. But he accepted Heron's offer of a glass of claret and sat down with a satisfied sigh. We were in the kitchen; the fire was still unlit and it was as cold as the grave.

"It's quite clear." He eased himself on the hard kitchen chair. "Though how the maid got possession of a pistol, I cannot understand."

"The maid?" I echoed, startled.

Mrs Bairstowe had told a coherent, lucid tale – I should have guessed she would not be a spirit that suffered from the usual initial disorientation. She had said that she'd had trouble with the maid ever since William's seizure; the girl had been reluctant to work, she said, had rebelled at every order. She had always been trouble, Mrs Bairstowe said, but William had disciplined her; once that discipline was removed, she seemed to think she could do what she liked. And nursing a sick man and cleaning his soiled bed was not what she liked. She'd run off and Mrs Bairstowe had discovered she had taken the silver spoons with her. (These were indeed missing, Heron said.) So Mrs Bairstowe had gone after her and found her in the church.

"Though why the girl should have gone into the church I don't know." Armstrong sipped his claret with distinct appreciation. It was one of Heron's and excellent. "If she'd run off to her kin in the chares, she could probably have sold the spoons without anyone being the wiser."

There had been an argument; according to Mary Bairstowe's spirit; the maid had brandished a pistol defiantly. When Mrs Bairstowe had seized the girl to drag her off to the constable, and after that the jail in Newgate, the girl had screamed and fired.

It was all a farrago of nonsense and the only thing that reconciled me to it was the fact that Hugh and Esther and I were left out of it.

Armstrong took me aside as he left, hesitating at the entrance from the yard into the alley. It was a cold day but dry and still, as if the wind had blown itself out. "There's a spirit round here, I think, the oldest in the town," Armstrong mused. "From the siege."

"She dissolved," I said. "The other night. I saw it."

He nodded. "We all come to that, sooner or later." He wedged his tricorne on his head and turned a sombre look on me. "The deed is valid – I have had it thoroughly examined." (I had given it to him the day after Mrs Bairstowe's death and he had promised to let me know the outcome of his study of it.) "Though much good it will do Bairstowe." He glanced up at the window of the house; the nurse's ranting could be heard along with Heron's more moderate remonstrations. "Gale the surgeon tells me he'll live, though in what state I know not."

"He cannot use his left arm or leg."

He sighed. "Well, he will have money enough to buy help if he sells the land. And the proceeds from the organ sale will help, of course." He reached into the pocket of his waistcoat and pulled out a small bag of coins. "Your ten guineas, Patterson, with my thanks. Perhaps we can do business again?"

I grimaced. "I doubt it, sir. I have come to the conclusion that I prefer a quiet life."

He chuckled. "You weren't born for it, sir."

And he bade me good day and walked sombrely down the alley into the street.

I waited until he was out of sight and turned to go towards the church. But I heard a voice behind me and glanced round to see Esther Jerdoun come out of the house. She was dressed particularly finely, I thought, in a pale blue gown with tiny embroidery, and a warm cloak of a darker blue. She studied me for a moment before speaking.

"I haven't yet thanked you, Mr Patterson. For rescuing me."

"Or I you," I said, smiling. "For attempting to do the same."

She gave me the ghost of a smile in return and sighed. "Alas, I was too credulous. I should at the least have gone to your lodgings to see if their claim to have kidnapped you was true."

"And roused my landlady and all the neighbours? It would not have been good for your reputation."

"Oh, yes," she said with some acerbity. "My reputation. Sometimes, I am so impatient with the prohibitions respectable society places on women."

I could have said I had realised this; I kept silent diplomatically.

"So we will meet for my lesson tomorrow at the Assembly Rooms as usual."

"Tomorrow is Sunday," I reminded her.

"Then on Monday?"

I bowed.

She looked at me a moment or two longer. "I do not ask what you will do now, sir. I can guess. You want to talk to Mary Bairstowe – to find out why she gave Armstrong a false tale."

I nodded. She smiled, put a finger to my lips. A warm, feather-light touch. I was astonished.

"Do what you must in this matter, Charles, and I will consider how best to order our affairs elsewhere."

Elsewhere? What in heaven's name did she intend to do?

But she was gone, drawing her cloak closer about her and casting me an impish smile over her shoulder.

The nave floor had been scrubbed but there was still a faint stain on the worn stones as if it had not been possible to remove all the blood. I had hardly come up to the place when the spirit said sourly, "I was expecting ye."

I sat down in the front pew; the lock, I saw, was broken and hung loose on the door. I was thankful for it; it had saved my life and Esther's. The church was dark and chill as always.

"Why throw all the blame on the girl?" I said.

The spirit was a faint gleam on a flagstone scored with writing so ancient it was worn to illegibility.

"She betrayed me. Ran off the moment I was dead. Raided the house for the money and the silver, and ran off to London. That was all she cared for – to get to London by any means she could."

I began to suspect why Mrs Bairstowe had been so lucid in her tales with Armstrong and the others. She must have disembodied earlier than they had expected. "You have already spoken to your brother? He told you what happened?"

"Aye. He didn't betray me. He waited here, day and night he waited, until I came. And he told me what she'd done. But I have her now. She's branded as a murderer." She laughed softly. "You're not going to tell them otherwise, are you?"

I shifted on the hard pew. I could not give the lie to Mrs Bairstowe's story without threatening not only myself, but Hugh and Esther too. The spirit knew it had my silence.

"They'll not do anything about the girl," I said. "Oh, they'll raise the hue and cry, and send a description of her to the London papers, but she'll not be found. Not in London. Plenty of places to lose herself."

"She'll be found," she said, confidently, with chilling malice. "John'll find her."

"Holloway?"

"I've sent him after her," she said. "He'll find her, wherever she is, however long it takes."

I stared at the faint gleam on the front of the pew, astounded by her venom. "But she did not kill you! Your brother killed you – though it was an accident."

"She abandoned me," Mrs Bairstowe said. "And showed her true colours. All those protestations of loyalty, of love. They meant nothing."

A noise at the door. I rose, turned to see Solomon Strolger enter the church, followed by the cat and two toddling children. Strolger had his arms full of music books; the two infants carried one small book each with some pride. Strolger beamed on me.

"You've come to talk to our new spirit, Patterson? We're getting quite crowded in here. Two spirits – very unusual for a church!"

"You'll hear no more of me," Mary Bairstowe said contemptuously. "What have I got worth saying?"

"Two quiet spirits," Strolger said, mischievously. "I'm happy with that. Nothing to spoil my nap during the sermons."

I took some of the books from his arms; he took the psalm books from the children and told them to play for a few minutes then climbed the steps to the Sailors' Gallery ahead of me.

He had neat fussy steps and pattered on ahead without a care in the world.

The clerestory windows lit the gallery rather better than the church; glancing over the gallery railing, I saw the cat sniffing at the pew where Mary Bairstowe's gleam showed. The gleam shifted rapidly out of sight; the cat, bored, yawned and started to wash itself. It was already looking much plumper than before.

I should have trusted that cat. I knew how curious cats are about spirits, sniffing them out as if they are a potentially delicious mouse or bird. I remembered how the cat had come up to the organ loft with us when we found Bairstowe, how it had sniffed around the corner of the organ case. I even remembered seeing some movement and dismissing it as a spider scuttling about.

"You know about the spirit in the organ loft then?" I asked Strolger as we reached the charity children's pews. He edged past towards the organ.

"Heavens yes! But he's no trouble. I thought at the beginning that he might disturb my rest during the sermons but he doesn't. Doesn't talk much at all." Strolger lowered his voice to a whisper. "Sour individual."

I stared at the corner where the cat had sniffed. There was no sign of a spirit there now. Nor anywhere here. But he might hide in the depths of the organ, even inside a pipe, totally unseen.

"How did he die up here?"

"He was trying to steal the organ pipes – for the lead you know. There were three villains." Wheezing, Strolger dropped the books on the organ stool and gestured to me to do likewise. "They had an argument, he says, and a bit of a fight, and he fell over and hit his head on the corner of the soundboard. Dead before he hit the ground. The others fled in panic, which saved the organ pipes, thank goodness."

"I hadn't heard of it."

He considered. "You were in London, I fancy." He started to push the music books on to the shelves beside the organ, musing over their rightful places then making sure the books were straight. "Poor fellow. Quite educated, I'm told, but fallen low because of drink and debt. Got into bad company, you know the sort of thing."

I thought of another man who had done the same thing.

"He's a good singer, mind," Strolger said reflectively. "Knows all the tunes." I remembered the spirit intoning the funeral sentences over Mary Bairstowe's body. "And talking of London," he beamed suddenly with pleasure. "I'm off there myself for a month or two."

"They're shutting up the church then?"

"Until they sort out all the formalities. A week or two, they say."

"But you'll be away longer?"

"No point in going all that way for a few days! My mother hasn't seen the two youngest at all, you know. Must give her a few weeks to get to know them. Two months at least." He winked at me. "Don't tell the churchwardens, though." He poked me in the arm. "Which means I am going to need a deputy."

I stared at him blankly.

"To fill in while I'm away," he pressed, "and to play one or two Sundays after I've got back. Will you consider the position?"

I was so startled by the unexpected offer that I could say nothing.

"Nothing plain, mind," he said, severely. "Good strong tunes and ornaments in your voluntaries, and a nice measure in your psalm tunes. I can't stand all these fellows who insist on just playing a chord or two. What kind of music's that?"

I remembered Strolger's over-elaborate, over-exuberant playing. Not my taste at all. Well, if he wasn't here, he couldn't know what I played. "What salary?" I said.

We haggled over the price and settled finally on less than I would have liked but more than he wanted to give me. I came out of All Hallows a deputy organist, halfway to one of my chief ambitions – and felt no joy in it.

I had one thing left to do.

37

And Justice is the end of all.
[Revd Righteous Graham, Sermon preached on the Sandgate, Newcastle, May 1742]

There are few times when the town is completely silent, so it seemed like fate, or the will of God, when I walked up on to the Tyne Bridge and found all the shops shuttered, the roadway deserted. Lanterns burned above two shops, but beyond the bridge the hill of Gateshead was almost completely dark under a star-flecked sky. Long after midnight, I had walked down the Side from the Fleshmarket, down past St Nicholas's church, down on to the Sandhill. Past the ruined remnants of the town wall and on to the Key. On to the bridge.

My footsteps echoed.

In the darkness, lit only by the waning moon, it was difficult to spot the blue stones that marked the centre of the bridge, or the dark gleam that was Edward Bairstowe. I leant against the bridge parapet and peered over. The water below was dark as Hades in the shadow of the bridge; only a glimmer or two of light, shining from a moored ship on to the gently rippling water, showed that there was anything there at all.

Bairstowe was uneasy. He said: "Who's that? Who's there?"

"Patterson."

"Oh, you," he said, with some obvious relief. "A fine fuss you've been making. I've heard what happened in the church."

Curious to know how good his information was, I encouraged him to talk. "About your sister-in-law's death?"

He was gleeful now. "I must thank you for that, sir."

"Thank Holloway. He shot her."

"So I heard, so I heard."

He must have heard the true story from his spirit friends, for the tale among the living was still that the maid was to blame. I looked out along the river, at the few faint lights in the brothels and taverns on the Keyside, at the glimmer of house lights on the south bank of the river amongst the outliers of Gateshead, and wondered if I could ever look upon it the same way again. There were spirits, a whole world of spirits, out there – I had always known that, but I had thought them the relics of friends and even family, acquaintances with whom I could pass a greeting, friends to linger in conversation with.

But now, could I trust any of them? Would I not always be wondering if allegiances change with death, and the living become the *other*, and the community is with the dead? Or is it merely that Edward Bairstowe and his friends, and the lowest sorts in the town, who have always been the lost, ready to fight the entire world for envy, still feel the same after death and still wage their old battles?

"Odd you should regret Mary Bairstowe's death so little," I said, feeling the cold gritty stone beneath my fingers. "You were thick as thieves once, weren't you?"

He said, in a tone that spat anger, "I loved her. Oh, none of what you're thinking, sir! There was nothing carnal between us. She wasn't a woman to lust after – she was one to talk with and scheme with and plan with. God, what a mind she had on her! And that fool brother of mine never knew what she was really like."

"William is a remarkably unobservant man," I agreed. "He never guessed you were plotting against him, that night on the bridge. He never knew he was in danger until those notes started coming."

"She had to write those," Edward Bairstowe said. "Or get the maid to do it, at any rate. Else there would be no scapegoat when he died. She knew he'd tell someone – she was counting on it. But she thought he'd complain to one of the whores at the brothel. She never thought he'd have the sense to ask you to look into it." His voice thickened. "I can still appreciate her good qualities, sir. She was unique amongst women."

"I agree," I said dryly.

"But I underestimated her," he said almost conversationally. "I thought she and I were plotting against William, but she was plotting against the pair of us. She wanted all the money for herself. Well, I can't blame her. I should have thought of it myself." He laughed softly. "That doesn't mean I forgive her, sir. I forgive no one who crosses me. What's that?"

Something in my pocket had chinked against the bridge parapet.

"You didn't expect me to come so late without protection?" I said. "Not after your recent exploits."

"Ah," he said. "Believe me, sir, I do regret those attacks on you by my dear departed friends."

"No, you don't," I said. "But you will."

"I beg your pardon, sir?"

I eased myself to the ground with my back to the parapet. "You'll forgive me if I light my lantern. It's damnably dark here, not to mention chill." The houses on the other side of the bridge hid the moon which was beginning to sink down the sky; we were in almost total darkness here. "What I cannot conceive, sir," I mused, "is what profit you got out of this business." I dragged the tinderbox from my pocket, struggled to strike the flint. "Mary Bairstowe and the maid were off to London to spend the fruits of their plotting; Holloway would have lingered long enough to sell the land and then followed with the money. But apart from any brief enjoyment of my bumps and bruises, I cannot see what you get from the matter."

"Mary Bairstowe's death," he reminded me.

"Yes, but that was none of your doing. It was a tragic accident." In the light of the lantern, I could see the stone now, the sheen on it, the darkness of the faintly luminescent slime.

"Alas, sir. The habit of plotting is not so eagerly set aside."

"Don't insult me," I said. "I refuse to believe you did it all merely out of mischief. Shall I tell you what I think?"

"Pray do," he said cordially. "I am enjoying this chat, Patterson. I get to talk so little, to the living, at least."

"I think you have been brooding all this while on one hope."

"Revenge," he said, without hesitation. "On William, on Mary, on the entire world. Do you know what it is like to be confined here?"

I almost flinched at the venom in his voice.

"You have already played that tune."

"William thwarted me, that night on the bridge. If he hadn't danced back out of the way of the knife, I'd never have slipped. And it was an accident, not self-destruction!"

I was astonished that he could still maintain that story, in the face of the evidence. "One cannot argue with death," I said. "Death always knows the truth."

"No!" he said vehemently. "No!"

"I should have looked closer at that column in the *Courant* when I first read it," I said. "But I rectified my omission; I went back and looked again. Claudius Heron first told me the story of an elderly woman frightened to death in an attack by spirits. It was a matter of days before your own death, was it not?"

He was silent.

"Heron told me there were bystanders who stood by laughing, not even attempting to help the woman. I thought he could not be right, that he was merely displaying a jaundiced view of human nature. But the paper confirmed his story. In fact, according to the *Courant*, there were those who even gave the spirits a helping hand, by kicking the elderly woman as she lay on the ground. And there were moves to arrest those bystanders and charge them."

He said nothing. I pressed: "Would I be wrong in guessing you were one of those bystanders, sir?"

"Guess what you like," he snapped.

"Mary Bairstowe told you that you had been recognised, did she not? That's why you were so eager to be rid of William that particular night. Such an inhospitable night for any plot of that sort, in the rain and the sleet and the freezing cold. But you feared arrest and were desperate to get away from the town. It was that night or none. What were you going to do? Take what money William had on him and ride off to London, trusting Mary to sell the land and send you your share of the money?"

He swore at me.

"But at the very moment you went to attack your brother," I continued, "what did Mary Bairstowe do? Did she shout out that the constable was on the way, or the mob? And in fear of facing the hangman's noose, you panicked, despaired, took your own escape. You were always a coward, were you not? Attacking a poor woman lying on the ground is hardly the act of a courageous man."

I knew he was never going to admit the truth but I did not particularly care. "And so," I went on, "to the matter of your brother and his seizure."

"The hand of God struck him down," he snapped.

The moon had all but disappeared now. In the thin light of the shielded lantern, the spirit seemed unsettled, sliding from one end of his stone to the other. I felt a stab of hard, vicious pleasure at his unease. After all the pain he had caused other people it was time he suffered a little himself.

"It was my understanding," I said, "that until this business the only spirit in a church in this town was the spirit in the porch of St Nicholas. But Solomon Strolger put me right about the fellow in the organ loft of All Hallows. You have heard of him?"

"One hears of so many people – "

"I asked around after him. One of the whores tells me he was a man called Jem." The spirit was silent, shimmering. "He was often seen with you, I understand. Died four years ago."

"You cannot hold me to blame for that," he said, resentfully. "I was dead a year myself."

"Great friends, I'm told you were. He was a schoolmaster with expensive tastes and few scruples as to what he did to pay for them. He and some friends went out one night to steal the lead organ pipes at All Hallows, but had a falling out. He fell, and died of his injuries."

"I am wrung with pity," he said. He had never so much reminded me of his brother.

I eased my back against the hard stone of the bridge parapet. "He at least does not forget his friends. He sent you a message to say that your brother had come to mend the organ at last, after all those years. And quite apart from wanting to make sure he didn't find the deed, you couldn't resist a last plot for revenge."

"This is vastly entertaining, sir," he said, sounding as if he was trying to stifle a yawn. "I am so glad I asked you to come and keep me company. I wouldn't have missed this for the world." But the spirit was still shifting restlessly across the top of the stone.

"I know only too well how spirits can buffet," I said reflectively, "and you told Jem not to hold back."

"Really, Patterson, such imaginings!"

I shivered. A chill night breeze was finding its way through my clothes. I was ready to finish this business.

"Of course if William had been hale and hearty it would hardly have mattered. He would have had a few uncomfortable moments and another fright like the one he had in the chare a week or two ago. But that first attack was meant only to scare him. This one was much more serious."

He started to protest; I overrode him ruthlessly. "Come, sir, your own father died of a similar attack in the prime of life. Choleric men often suffer from such ailments. And you had the example of that elderly woman in front of you. To put it plainly, sir, you told Jem to attack your brother and to continue until William succumbed and died."

"Prove it!" he snarled.

"And all within reach of that deed, which you had hidden there, thinking he'd never go near the place because of his enmity with Strolger. William even handled the pipe and set it on its soundboard. But he didn't do the job properly – he didn't attempt to tune or voice the pipe or to test it by playing. If he had he would certainly have known something amiss."

"Prove it! Prove it! Prove it!" He sneered. "You can't."

The sheen was almost sparkling now; it was gratifying to know I agitated him so much.

"I can't prove it," I admitted. "But I don't need to."

He clearly sensed me shifting. "What are you doing? Damn it, Patterson!"

I pulled from my pocket a chisel, taken from William Bairstowe's own toolkit – I had thought that a fine thing, a fitting gesture. When I pushed it into the earth around the stone, the ground resisted slightly, then gave way. I worked round the stone, easing the cobble. I had already remarked that it was loose, and it was soon unsteady in its hole.

"Damn it, Patterson. What are you doing?"

"You wanted revenge," I said. "And so do I. For the attacks on me, on my friends, on the woman I love, and yes, even on your brother who is, apart from you, just about the most objectionable man I ever met. But most of all, sir – " The stone came fully loose and I used the chisel to lever it out of the hole. "Most of all, I want justice."

"No!"

The touch of the stone was unpleasant on my hands – I could feel the chill emanating from the spirit. I tried to cup the stone on my palm, to touch only the grimy healthy underside of it, but it was a large cobble and heavy, and my fingers touched grease and slime. I shivered and almost dropped it.

"As I told a friend, it is difficult to have justice on a spirit. One cannot call out the constable to clap it in chains in Newgate."

"I have contacts, sir!" Bairstowe's voice was cracked, hysterical. "I can get you money. As much money as you like."

"Thank you but no." I had already had ten guineas from Armstrong for the deed, and I still had the prospect of William Bairstowe's thirty guineas. Especially when I told him what had happened to his brother. Though perhaps I was being optimistic in expecting Bairstowe to keep his bargain. He would probably say, in his slurred, almost incomprehensible speech, that the maid wrote the notes and I have not apprehended her, so therefore he will not pay.

The cobble was heavy in my hands. I rested it on the parapet of the bridge. Below ran the dark water, untouched by the moonlight, deep and tidal and impenetrable. Once at the bottom of that, Edward Bairstowe would see no one, hear no one, talk to no one, for the rest of his years as a spirit.

"I can get you money!" the spirit said hysterically. "I know where fortunes are buried!"

"No doubt," I said. "But that knowledge will not save you, sir. I told you, I want justice. But most of all, I find myself simply wanting to rid the world of you."

And with that, I opened my hands.

The stone dropped. Leaning over the parapet of the bridge, I heard Bairstowe's despairing cry all the way down, until the splash, and the momentary blossom of white, as the stone crashed into the river.

NEW TITLES FROM CRÈME DE LA CRIME:

A CRACKLING DEBUT FROM KAYE C HILL

DEAD WOMAN'S SHOES

A trip to the seaside suddenly got dangerous…

All she wanted was to get away – and suddenly it's raining cats, dogs and bodies…

Lexy Lomax has run away from her obnoxious husband, taking with her a cool half million of his ill-gotten gains and a homicidal chihuahua called Kinky. Holed up in a decrepit log cabin on the Suffolk coast, Lexy finds herself mistaken for the previous owner of the cabin, a private investigator, now deceased. Before she knows it she's embroiled in a cocktail of marital infidelity (possibly), missing cats (probably) and poison pen letters (definitely).

Oh, yes – and a murder or two…

ISBN: 978-0955-1589-95 **£7.99**

READ ABOUT *the events before Christmas* and
the Caroline Square business
IN

BROKEN HARMONY

THE PREVIOUS ADVENTURES OF

CHARLES PATTERSON,

HARPSICHORDIST, CONCERT ARRANGER
AND ACCIDENTAL INVESTIGATOR

by

ROZ SOUTHEY

available from a bookshop near you

Another taut thriller from Adrian Magson

NO KISS FOR THE DEVIL

Riley Palmer and Frank Palmer are back
– and this time it's personal.

A young woman's body is found dumped in the Essex countryside.

Investigative reporter Riley Gavin recognises her as Helen Bellamy, a former girlfriend of her colleague, PI Frank Palmer.

Ex-military policeman Palmer is accustomed to death, but this is different; this is the brutal murder of someone he was once close to. He knows only one way to deal with it: find the killers.

Meanwhile, Riley's next job is a profile of controversial businessman 'Kim' Al-Bashir. She soon realises that there are sinister forces working against him, and if she doesn't tread carefully she could end up losing her assignment.

And, like Helen, quite probably her life.

ISBN: 978-0955-7078-10 **£7.99**

Praise for previous books by Adrian Magson

...strong echoes of the classic prickly relationship between Modesty Blaise and Willie Garvin... Gritty and fast-paced detecting of the traditional kind, with a welcome injection of realism.

- Maxim Jakubowski, The Guardian

The excitement carries through right to the last page...

- Ron Ellis, Sherlock magazine

You'll no doubt read (it) as I did in an afternoon.

- Sharon Wheeler, Reviewing the Evidence

A tense, fast-paced follow-up from Gordon Ferris

THE UNQUIET HEART

Private eye Danny McRae battles with black marketeers, double agents and assassins in 1940s London and Berlin.

Lovers by night, gang-busters by day...

Danny McRae, struggling private detective. Eve Copeland, crime reporter, looking for new angles to save her career.

The perfect partnership...

Until Eve disappears, a contact dies violently and an old adversary presents Danny with some unpalatable truths.

His desperate search for his lover hurls him into the shattered remains of Berlin, where espionage and assassination foreshadow the rise of political terrorism. The ruined city tangles him into a web of black marketeers and double agents – and Danny begins to lose sight of the thin line between good and evil...

ISBN: 978-0955-7078-03 **£7.99**

Praise for *Truth Dare Kill*, Gordon Ferris's first Danny McRae adventure

... a believable world of desperate people... will keep you turning the pages...

- Catherine Turnbull, Dursley Gazette

...dark atmosphere... a riveting read...

- Gloucestershire Echo Weekend

... populated with a carnival of misfits... an exciting debut

- Crimesquad.com

More Second City mayhem from Maureen Carter

BAD PRESS

Detective Sergeant Bev Morris tangles with the media

Is the reporter breaking the news – or making it?

A killer's targeting Birmingham's paedophiles: a big story, and ace crime reporter Matt Snow's always there first – ahead of the pack and the police.

Detective Sergeant Bev Morriss has crossed words with Snow countless times. Though his hang-'em-and-flog-'em views are notorious, Bev still sees him as journo not psycho.

But a case against the newsman builds. Maybe Snow's sword is mightier than his pen?

Through it all, Bev has an exclusive of her own...a news item she'd rather didn't get round the nick. DS Byford knows, but the guv's on sick leave. As for sharing it with new partner DC Mac Tyler – no, probably best keep mum...

ISBN: 978-0955-7078-34 **£7.99**

Crime writing and crime fighting: Maureen Carter and her creation Bev Morris are the Second City's finest!

- Mark Billingham

Praise for Maureen Carter's earlier Bev Morris books:

Carter writes like a longtime veteran, with snappy patter and stark narrative.

- David Pitt, Booklist (USA)

Many writers would sell their first born for the ability to create such a distinctive voice in a main character.

- Sharon Wheeler, Reviewing the Evidence

British hardboiled crime at its best.

- Deadly Pleasures Year's Best Mysteries (USA)

MORE RIVETING READS FROM CRÈME DE LA CRIME

A KIND OF PURITAN by Penny Deacon **978-0954-7634-11**
A subtle and clever thriller…
- The Daily Mail

A THANKLESS CHILD by Penny Deacon **978-0954-7634-80**
Penny Deacon has created a believable, hi-tech future world… In contrast to the electronic efficiency, interesting relationships(are) portrayed with genuine depth of feeling.
- Shotsmag

WORKING GIRLS by Maureen Carter **978-0954-7634-04**
A hard-hitting debut … fast moving with a well realised character in Detective Sergeant Bev Morriss. I'll look forward to her next appearance.
- Mystery Lovers

DEAD OLD by Maureen Carter **978-0954-7634-66**
Maureen Carter's work has a certain style, something that suggests she isn't just passing through. Complex, chilling and absorbing… – confirms her place among… British crime writers.
- Julia Wallis Martin, author of The Bird Yard and A Likeness in Stone

BABY LOVE by Maureen Carter **978-0955-1589-02**
Carter writes like a longtime veteran, with snappy patter and stark narrative.
- David Pitt, Booklist (USA)

HARD TIME by Maureen Carter **978-0955-1589-64**
Carter… leaves plenty of surprises for the reader to enjoy.
- Publishers Weekly, USA

NO PEACE FOR THE WICKED by Adrian Magson
978-0954-7634-28
A real page turner… a slick, accomplished writer who can plot neatly and keep a story moving…
- Sharon Wheeler, Reviewing the Evidence

NO HELP FOR THE DYING by Adrian Magson
978-0954-7634-73
Gritty and fast-paced detecting of the traditional kind, with a welcome injection of realism.
- Maxim Jakubowski, The Guardian

NO SLEEP FOR THE DEAD by Adrian Magson
978-0955-1589-19
The book is well-paced, the style is readable, and the story… lively.
- Martin Edwards, Tangled Web

NO TEARS FOR THE LOST by Adrian Magson
978-0955-1589-71
The pace… whizzes along, with new surprizes at every turn. An unputdownable mystery, gritty and fast paced.
- Angela Youngman, Monsters and Critics

BEHIND YOU by Linda Regan **978-0955-1589-26**
… readable and believable… extremely well written…
- Jim Kennedy, Encore

PASSION KILLERS by Linda Regan **978-0955-1589-88**
… confidently told and kept me hooked…
- Sharon Wheeler, Reviewing the Evidence

A CERTAIN MALICE by Felicity Young 978-0954-7634-42

a beautifully written book... Felicity draws you into the life in Australia... you may not want to leave.

- Natasha Boyce, bookseller

IF IT BLEEDS by Bernie Crosthwaite 978-0954-7634-35

Longlisted for the Pendleton May First Novel Award

A cracking debut novel... small-town atmosphere is uncannily accurate... the writing's slick, the plotting's tidy and Jude is a refreshingly sparky heroine.

- Sharon Wheeler, Reviewing the Evidence

PERSONAL PROTECTION by Tracey Shellito 978-0954-7634-59

... a book which isn't afraid to go out on a limb. It's a powerful, edgy story... the makings of a dark and challenging series.

- Sharon Wheeler, Reviewing the Evidence

SINS OF THE FATHER by David Harrison 978-0954-7634-97

...an intriguing protagonist... an accomplished debut and hopefully the first of many outings for Nick Randall.

- Karl Brown, Brokers' Monthly

TRUTH DARE KILL by Gordon Ferris 978-0955-1589-40

A gripping, if disturbing, read.

- Historical Novels Review

THE CRIMSON CAVALIER by Mary Andrea Clarke

978-0955-1589-57

... an ingenious plot line leading to a surprizing ending.

- Angela Youngman, Monsters and Critics